THE FINAL FIRE

ALSO BY DENNIS SMITH

Report from Engine Co. 82

SATURDAY REVIEW PRESS / E.P. DUTTON & CO., INC.

NEW YORK

Dennis Smith

THE FINAL FIRE

1157251

Library of Congress Cataloging in Publication Data

Smith, Dennis, 1940-
 The final fire.

 I. Title.
PZ4.S6448Fi   *[PS3569.M523]*   *813'.5'4*   *75-6811*

First Edition

10 9 8 7 6 5 4 3 2 1

*Published simultaneously in Canada by Clarke, Irwin & Company Limited,
Toronto and Vancouver*

ISBN: 0-8415-0385-0
Designed by The Etheredges

For
Mary Smith
and
Bill Smith

PART ONE

1

THE SMOKE ROSE HEAVILY THROUGH the iron grates on West 45th Street and up and over the ancient marquee on the landmark building. Pedestrians watched from across the street, from Broadway, and from Schubert Alley. A soft September wind occasionally pushed the smoke west, making the marquee lettering visible to the crowd: "O'Neill's *Long Day's Journey into Night.* A Revival."

Two floors below street level the firefighters inched toward the heart of the fire, far from the eyes or even the imagination of the onlookers above. The men of Engine Company 20 advanced the hoseline, making frantic, circular motions with the nozzle, hoping that the cascading water would fall or drip or even ricochet into the fire. It was impenetrably dark with smoke, and the firemen could not see either the men working alongside them or the rushing stream in front, but they could hear the water being forced through the small nozzle, rebounding from the walls and ceiling. And they could hear the voices giving them the confidence to crawl deeper into the dark.

"You got it, Charlie. Just a little more now and we'll be home. Keep low, keep low."

"Jesus, hold it, hold it. I just fell into something."

"It's all right. It's stairs, two steps. Easy now, keep low."

"Hose, we need more hose. Hump some more hose in, Pete."

"You got it, you got it."

"Where's Frank? Hey, Frank, can't you vent this goddam smoke?"

"Yeah, sure, all we gotta do is make the subcellar the top floor and then we can break the windows."

"You got it, Charlie, I can feel it. It's just ahead."

The heat, like a wind, crept around their facemasks and over the surfaces of their necks and ears, reddening the skin. The subcellar was like an Egyptian tomb, encased in mortar and recessed deep into the earth. There was no way for the heat to escape. With each minute the temperature rose, and they were running out of minutes. Soon it would be unbearably hot, and the men would be forced to give up their positions. They crawled in the direction of the radiating heat, knowing that they had to find the fire.

Jerry Ritter's flashlight could not penetrate the thick smoke. It was useless to him, and he put it into the pocket of his rubber coat. He would have to make a search on all fours, pushing his ax before him. The initial search had to be made quickly and thoroughly, for he knew that seconds could mean the difference between life and death for someone caught in the heavy smoke. His job was to work above the fire, to look for victims, to ventilate, and he crawled tirelessly and instinctually around the floor of the first cellar. There was a long corridor with rooms off to either side. Dressing rooms, he figured. Moving his arm like a swimmer, he went over every square foot of each room. The smoke and heat

4

curled up from the subcellar, and Jerry sweated and panted in the oppressive air, his breathing barely contained by the mask he wore.

He reached the last room of the corridor and began his groping, his blind man's journey, starting to the right of the room and working his way around to the left. He realized as he went along the right wall that the room was larger than the others, but he felt the same things, recognizing them instantly—chairs, tables, standing lamps, an upright ashtray. Then he felt bookcases and a large desk. He pushed the handle of his ax across the floor underneath the desk and moved on. He came to a large, stuffed chair in the corner of the room and swept the ax handle behind and underneath the chair. Perhaps a cat, or a dog, or even a child was underneath, he thought, remembering a fire and a dead child in a toy box, a frightened child who had gone there seeking the security of her toys. He came next to a couch and swung the ax handle beneath as he felt on the top with his free hand.

The night before, David Allen, owner and manager of the historic Barrymore Theater, had kept an appointment with a young and promising playwright. The writer had had one play produced, a brief performance by an actors' group in a Delancey Street loft, and the meeting with Allen was important to him. To go from off-off-Broadway to Broadway in one jump was no easy thing, and the writer carefully planned the evening, insisting on paying all the bills. Allen, always conscientious about new writers, allowed himself to be taken to all the places he hated and made a life's career of avoiding. The theater might be dying, but Allen would climb mountains and swim oceans to get a new play, or even weather a long night with a fun-seeking playwright. It was after three when the writer finally tired of the restaurants, the bars, and the discotheques. Allen was always careful about waking his wife unnecessarily, and he decided not to go to his Central Park West apartment but took a cab instead to his office.

Jerry first felt David Allen's shoes, and then his leg. Holy God, he thought. What the hell is this guy doing here? With his shoes on. Sleeping on a couch with his shoes on. Air. Gotta get him into the open air.

It would have been easy to throw the victim over his shoulders, for Allen was not a big man, but the air cannister on Jerry's back made a fireman's carry impossible. He would have to carry him another way, but he needed a free hand to feel his way out, because the smoke was becoming even thicker. The temperature was rising fast, he thought. He could feel the heat on his ears. He had to get out fast. He knew that at any moment the fire would come bursting through the walls.

Jerry threw his ax into the middle of the room so he could find it easily later on and pulled the man to the floor. He laid on his side next to the victim. With all his strength he lifted Allen at the waist and threw the lower half of the body across his own legs, so that the small of Allen's back rested firmly on Jerry's raised hip. Then he reached around Allen's chest in a swimmer's carry and started to dig his rubber boots into the floor. He kicked with all his power and inched toward the door, his arm waving, feeling, and pulling in front.

He reached the office door and started the long pull down the narrow corridor. He had carefully closed all the doors of the rooms he searched, but he could see the glow of fire through the crack beneath the first door he came to. The floor was lighting up, and Jerry made a silent prayer for the time and the strength to make it to daylight. The bell of his air pack began to ring, signaling that there were only four hundred pounds of air left in the bottle on his back. In ordinary circumstances that would give him about four minutes, but he was breathing harder and harder as he crawled down the corridor, and he knew that he had increased the rate of air usage so that he had about two minutes left. Two minutes would do it, if the fire did not break out into the hall and if the ceiling or wall did not fall and block his passageway. Jerry kicked faster and faster, the bell ringing loudly through the darkness. Finally he reached the stairs to the street level.

On the stairs four men were pulling a limp and empty hoseline, and an officer was directing them down the long corridor, the one Jerry had just crawled through. Three firemen passed him, one tripping over Jerry's arm and another stepping on Allen's leg. They were moving quickly, doing what they knew had to be done before the whole building was consumed by fire, and they hadn't the time or curiosity to see what they were tripping over. A fourth fireman passed, and Jerry grabbed the bottom of his rubber turnout coat, stopping him short.

Jerry screamed through his facepiece, "Hey, gimme a hand. I gotta get this guy on the street, fast."

The surprised fireman dropped the hose and felt down for the voice. Jerry, more accustomed to the dark than the other man, took his hand and put it on Allen's leg. The fireman understood and grabbed both legs as Jerry lifted from the armpits. They carried David Allen to the excitement of the street.

Hundreds of facts rambled through Jerry's head as he stepped blind and backward up the steel stairs. He knew the body he carried was either dead or about to die, and when they reached the street he would have to lean over and press his lips to the man's mouth. But, Christ, he thought. What was the exact procedure? It had to be exact, not nearly correct or almost right. He had studied it, and practiced it, and he knew it cold. In his mind he could see the instructor's mouth opening and closing. But it was different then. There was no smoke in the classroom, no excitement, no fatigue. He thought of his days as a lifeguard at Orchard Beach. It was easy then. Put the body on the stomach, rest the head on the hands. Press the back, and lift the elbows. It'll come, he told himself as he passed through the stage door to the cool of the day, and to the intense eyes of the crowd.

Jerry's canister bell was still ringing, making his entrance to the street seem like a triumphant return. An uneasy silence, an anxiety, overcame the throng as David Allen was

7

carried beyond the marquee and out of the smoke. Finally the bell stopped, and the intensity of the moment seemed to fade with the last echo of its sound. The crowd breathed easily again.

The two firemen laid the body on the asphalt. Jerry threw his helmet to the ground and ripped his mask from his face, thinking, cardiopulmonary resuscitation, procedure, life systems, checkpoints, breath, chest, pulse. The other fireman ran back to the stage door, to his job and company, as Jerry put his ear over Allen's mouth. Jesus, don't leave me now. . . . It's easier with two men. He looked for a rise in the chest, but there was nothing, the shirt opened, the chest bared, and unmoving. . . . His two fingers were on the carotid artery. "Hey," he yelled, "hey," but the man had disappeared in the rising smoke. Pulse, next to the Adam's apple. . . . It's easier with two. . . . No movement on the neck, no flowing, pumping blood.

Jerry stuck his fingers in the mouth and felt the tongue. He looked down, raised the neck with one hand, and pressed the forehead toward the shoulders with the other. A handsome man, he thought, easy features. He kept the base of his hand on the forehead and pinched the nose. Probably an easygoing guy. He lowered his head and made a solid seal around the mouth. How many breaths? Two? Three? A fat man with dirty shoes was kneeling alongside. Three, yes, three. Jerry heard the camera clicking as he pushed three heavy breaths into Allen's mouth.

He released the head, but it stayed in position, arched between the sidewalk and the shoulders like a strung bow; he felt for the top and the bottom of the rib cage. What was the term, defibrillation? The sternum, he remembered, the left thumb on the sternum, the breastbone. Aim for the thumb.

Jerry raised his fist, clenching it until he thought it would collapse, and the crowd gasped as it crashed down into Allen's chest. The body seemed to jump from the ground, the head falling so that it lay at a normal angle again. Jesus, did the breastbone crack? He once more put his fingers into the neck, thinking, raging, come alive, goddammit, come alive. A cracked sternum is better than a dead sternum. Think, the instructor had said, you are the heart and lungs of the victim. Blood. Circulate and oxygenate. It all came back clear, even the crusty voice of the old fire lieutenant standing at the blackboard. He felt the carotid artery, but there was nothing, the vein like a frozen river.

The dirty shoes were there as he returned to the mouth, and the clicking of the camera. Adult victim, one breath every five seconds, then one cardiac massage every second. A one-man operation, two breaths and fifteen massages. C'mon mister, come alive. You're young, the day is early. Christ, it could be easier. Send me a man, chief, shove the fire. C'mon, you're a young man, take this spit, this hot breath, it works. Take it, goddammit.

He put one hand on top of the other and leaned with all his weight on Allen's chest, counting one-thousand-one, releasing and leaning, one-thousand-two, releasing and leaning, until he reached one-thousand-fifteen.

He could feel the day's growth of beard, lips against lips, and his mouth began to smart. He blew into Allen with full force, like inflating a Navy raft, being sure to watch the rising of the chest and the lowering. Like inflating a raft with a hole cut in it.

Fingers on the carotid. One breath. Two breaths. God save this man, he looks like he's been a good man. He must have been good to you on this earth, God. Save him, please. C'mon, Jesus.

He went to the chest again, and as he began one-thousand-one a man kneeled next to him, edging him away. Jerry looked up and saw Tom Sullivan, twice the size of a normal man, his face serious, understanding. He leaned over one more time and said "One-thousand-two" aloud.

Sullivan fell into the motion, and counted one-thousand-three, one-thousand-four. C'mon, pal, we can do it now. Fingers on the neck again. Sullivan's got the touch of a savior. One breath, long and spirited, camera clicking. We can do it. Like Lazarus, you're gonna rise and love me and Sullivan.

9

One-thousand-five. One breath, hopeful, forced. Nothing. The chest rose and lowered, and the blood thickened. Nothing. David Allen had been dead too long.

They continued, leaning, releasing, forcing breaths, as the sirens screamed the arrival of the second-alarm companies, as the chief in charge yelled his orders into the static of a portable radio, and as firefighters moved about them, pulling hose, exchanging empty air cylinders for full ones, running for special equipment.

Chief Joseph McDermott of Battalion 5 stood in the middle of the street, radio in hand, watching the movement of the firefighters. He had been in the department for thirty years, and the scene before him was not much different from hundreds of fires he had experienced. As he watched, he allowed himself to daydream.

Retirement had been a constant daydream since he reached his twentieth year in firefighting, the minimum service for a pension. But he could never see his way clear to living on half pay, and as he watched the smoke billowing over the marquee he thought to himself, perhaps this will be my last job, the last fire, perhaps I'll put my paper in today and take the bride for that long trip we've been talking about for years—to County Sligo maybe, even though the relatives are all dead and buried now, or maybe Hawaii or Mexico City. They say living is cheap in Mexico. Anywhere, anywhere at all, as long as it's away from this city and this job.

He pressed the button on the side of the radio and spoke into the transmitter, "Battalion 5 to Engine Company 20."

"Engine 20 to Battalion."

"Have you located the fire yet?"

"Yeah, chief, we know where it is, but we haven't reached it yet. There are lots of obstructions, probably stage decorations, and we have to move around them."

"Ten-four," the chief said as he released the button, thinking, this job is not the same job it was during the war, when men had leather lungs and unquestioning spirit, when fires were put out without complaint, when men wouldn't dishonor themselves by seeing a doctor for a small burn on the wrist or neck, when they did their work in the firehouse, keeping the place spit-polish clean, because they knew they would have to answer to the captain if they didn't. It was different when captains had full control over their men, keeping their companies as sharp and disciplined as Prussian soldiers, rewarding and punishing at will, without the need of reports and chain-of-command appeal rights, before the days of collective bargaining and grievance procedures. It's a changed job, all right. I never thought I'd see the day when a fireman could question the authority of a captain. Now even chiefs can be questioned. If the country ran an army like this, we'd never win a thing, the Capitol building would be in Cuba.

He spoke into the radio again, "Are you there yet, Engine 20?"

A moment passed, and the reply came, "Not yet, chief."

It's a sign of the times, he thought, and it's what's wrong with the whole damn city. There is no respect for authority anymore. How can we expect to keep our men in order when we have to kowtow to every group in the city with a complaint and a microphone pushed into their faces? I even saw welfare people, people on home relief, on the dole, for chrissakes, demanding that we give them rights. Rights. They already got all the rights in the world, a fat check every week for doing nothing, a roof over their heads, plenty of beer in the bag, and extra money to play the numbers every day. Christ, I wish I had some of their rights. I give thirty years of my life to this city and I can't afford to retire, but if I was on welfare I wouldn't have to worry about takin' life easy.

It's the mayor, and them snotnoses he's got working for him, who's at fault. If we could only go back to the days of LaGuardia and O'Dwyer. They were fair men, but if people stepped outta line they were out on their asses, and that's the way it should be. People who don't work and demand rights! It's nuts, just nuts. I gotta get away from all these liberals in City Hall who can't appreciate men who work for a living but who kiss the backsides of them that don't.

11

Chief McDermott's thoughts were interrupted by a loud squawk from the radio. "Engine 20 to Battalion 5."

"Battalion 5 responding," the chief said.

"We're on the fire now, chief, and it's darkening down, but you better get a line to the floor above. That would be the first-cellar level, 'cause I can see the fire going up the side walls."

"Ten-four, lieutenant," the chief replied, stressing the word "lieutenant."

The nerve of that lieutenant even suggesting what I'd better do, as if I didn't know my job. Years ago he would have had the sense to know that a chief would have a line above the fire by this time. I'll have to make it a point to drop in on Engine 20 for a quick house inspection.

At first Chief McDermott didn't believe his eyes when he saw the two firemen appear through the smoke, the body bouncing between them.

Holy Christ, he thought. I thought this place was locked up tight. He pressed the transmission button. "Battalion 5 to aide."

"Aide to chief."

"Freddy, get on the radio and transmit a second alarm for this box, and get an ambulance here. We got a possible DOA."

If that guy didn't move coming out of that smoke, he thought, he probably isn't going to move again, poor bastard. Well, now we'll have all the three and four stars around for the investigation. Let them come in droves for all I care. I'm covered. We don't need a second alarm here yet. But a DOA in a Broadway theater is news, and at least they can't say that this chief didn't have sufficient manpower here—all those Monday morning quarterbacking ballbreakers.

He watched the body as it was eased gently to the sidewalk and then saw one of the firemen run back into the fire, disappearing before he could call to him. Stupid, the chief thought, leaving one man here with a body, here in front of this crowd. It don't look good.

"Chief to aide."

"Aide responding, chief."

"Freddy, send the first fireman you see to the front of the building to help with a victim."

"Message received," the aide, monitoring the radio in the chief's car, replied.

Freddy Tullio looked around and saw Tom Sullivan walking up the street, carrying a large portable lamp.

"Hey, Sully," the aide called, "leave the lamp go. The chief wants you to help with a victim in front of the fire building."

"Ten-four," Sullivan yelled in return, setting the lamp on the street.

Jerry felt the tapping on his shoulder and the voice. "It's okay, fireman. I'm a doctor. Let me have a look at him." He turned in the direction of the voice and saw the man in white who had come with the ambulance. Standing behind the doctor were the men from the department's rescue squad, waiting with a mechanical resuscitator and a stokes basket.

Jerry watched the doctor apply a stethoscope to Allen's chest while checking the dilation of the pupils, and he saw the look of dejection on the doctor's face, the look of frustration and futility. The doctor knew, and Jerry knew, that it was all over.

They had worked on Allen for over fifteen minutes, sensing hopelessness yet never giving up hope. Now there came the final nothing as the doctor nodded to the men of the rescue squad. Jerry watched as the body was placed in the thin-wire body-shaped basket, and as Sullivan and the rescue team lifted it and carried it toward the ambulance. He saw the mechanical resuscitator placed over Allen's mouth and smiled ironically, for he understood it was a gesture for the crowd.

The training-school instructor's voice came to his mind again. "Look good, always. Remember that. No matter how screwed up a victim is, no matter how dead, make it look like you're doing something to keep it alive, because Father Knickerbocker pays you to keep people alive, not to bury

13

them. And remember too that what the crowd in the street don't see and don't know will never hurt them, or us."

His work done for the moment, exhausted and forlorn, Jerry sat on the sidewalk, leaning against the theater wall and listening to the murmurs of the crowd.

"That's David Allen."

"He's one of the most important people of the theater, a producer."

"Is he dead?"

The fat man with the dirty shoes walked past, stopping momentarily before Jerry. He said, "Thanks, pal. My editor will give me three days off for this."

Jerry avoided his eyes, looking up at the words on the marquee. Christ, a long day's journey, an endless journey, and for what?

Looking at those words, he felt the need to focus the moment, to engrave it on the stone of his memory. For as long as he could remember, even before he had learned to read, Jerry had loved words, especially the way words sometimes floated together or bounced from one to another, and in his confused and tired mind he began to compose.

The titan stole the gift, he thought, the words flowing through his mind like thick lava.

It is left loose in the world's theater, and the player's die, no, and the player dies, or wonders at the star, or what? Or laughs for three days off . . .

I must remember, Jerry thought, I've got to plant some words in my head and keep them there until I can put them down somewhere. But his mind became clouded and he lost the words; he cursed his incapacity to structure his thoughts and to remember.

Jerry was not sentimental. He never cried at movies or choked up at funerals. He wrote poems to control his feelings, to curb his emotions. He never told anyone.

The day Jerry Ritter graduated from St. Raymond's Grammar School in the Bronx his mother gave him a green leather-covered diary, the kind with lock and key. His mother had wanted to give him an initialed ring, but Jerry told her he preferred the diary. He got what he wanted, for up until then graduation was the most important day of his life.

Jerry was thirteen years old, and he wanted a private book, one that his three older brothers could not pick up and thumb through. It was to be the first private thing Jerry ever had.

His love for words had grown stronger, and he wanted to be a songwriter then. He wrote songs about the girls in his class, simple rock-and-roll verses:

I love you, Peggy
I don't feel blue, Peggy
When I'm with you, Peggy
So please be true, Peggy

Songs like that. He seldom talked to the girls he wrote songs about. And although he thought about little else, he never had enough confidence to ask one of them to a Sunday afternoon movie until he was in his junior year at St. Helena's High School.

Peggy and most of the other students in his class followed Jerry to St. Helena's High School. In the Bronx, going to St. Helena's from St. Raymond's was like going to Harvard from Phillips Exeter, and Jerry wrote songs about them in his diary until his diary was filled. When the last blank page was covered with a song, Jerry stopped writing songs altogether and started dating Peggy.

That was when Jerry started writing poems and reading the poets—Blake, Yeats, Thomas—loving their words, thinking of himself as one of them.

The Ritters lived on the first floor of a gray-sided two-family house on McGuire Avenue in Throgg's Neck, a part of the Bronx known for basketball players and bar fights. For as long as anyone could remember there were always three or four guys from the neighborhood playing or coaching in the pros. Jerry's oldest brother, Mike, was scouted by the Knicks

15

when he played for Iona, and he would have made it, everyone told Jerry, if it wasn't for the accident. Staggering drunk one Friday night, Mike took a swim in the Whitestone Bay and drowned. The following year the next oldest brother, Davey, was shot by an off-duty policeman in a Tremont Avenue bar. The cop had been asked by the bouncer to leave the place because the customers were annoyed with his loud mouth and the spilled drinks; the next thing anyone knew there were bullets flying. Three people were shot, and Davey, sitting alone at the end of the bar, was the only one killed. He was a student at Fordham at the time, on a basketball scholarship.

Both funerals were neighborhood affairs, like St. Raymond's annual bazaar. Everyone knew, and everyone understood, their duty to attend. The first funeral shattered Mrs. Ritter, and the second destroyed her, leaving her semicatatonic, refusing to talk to anyone. Her remaining sons continued to live with her, but she never saw them after Davey's funeral. Her husband cooked the meals, and she sat at the kitchen table across from her sons, but she never saw them. Friends and priests came to visit, and she sat silently on a kitchen chair, staring the whole time at her worn hands. When she was alone, her shoulders shook in quiet, constant sobbing.

Jerry's stomach pained before both funerals, and he vomited, but he persevered through both days without crying, without letting his body break into rage at the senselessness of each loss. He gauged the emptiness he felt and wrote poems about his dead brothers, for he was learning about death and knew of no other way to go about understanding it. He wrote a promise in verse after Davey's funeral:

> *Liquor is a world of sin*
> *That I'll never be a victim in*

And he vowed before God that he would keep his promise. He was seventeen then, and a senior at St. Helena's.

16

There were four rooms in the first-floor apartment. It was too small for the six Ritters, but the old man, Mike Ritter, was a car cleaner for the subways and the family could not afford anything better. No one complained about not having a bigger place, until after Davey's funeral. The apartment then was not big enough to escape the incessant sobbing of their mother, and Jerry and his older brother Tom looked for a way out, for it was an unhappy house.

Tom was a student at Hunter College, a philosophy major, and a part-time attendant and mechanic at a garage. He found his way out by quitting school, marrying the girl he loved through his high school years, and becoming a full-time mechanic. Jerry found his way out by graduating in the middle of his class, kissing his Peggy a final good-by, and signing the bottom line on the Army enlistment form. The apartment on McGuire Avenue would never hear another laugh.

Engine Company 20 and Ladder Company 7 returned to their quarters on East 48th Street shortly after noon. The men had stopped at a Lexington Avenue deli for sandwiches, and Jerry carried the large brown paper bag across the apparatus floor and into the kitchen in the rear of the firehouse. He ripped the bag open, sending the wrapped sandwiches sprawling across the table. He looked through the pile for one marked RB $1.40, found it, and after searching his pockets put a dollar bill and four dimes on the corner of the table. It was a long table, formica-covered, centered in the middle of the kitchen, and Jerry sat at the far end, away from the pile that the hungry men picked through. He opened his roast beef hero as Tom Sullivan sat in the chair next to him.

"Too bad the sonovabitch died, Jerry," Sullivan said. "It would have been a nice rescue, maybe a medal. The mayor would kiss your ass as he pinned it to your chest, if you can picture that."

"The mayor can kiss my ass anyway," Jerry said, indifferently.

"Yeah, but with a medal comes two or three points on

17

the lieutenant's test." Sullivan grinned. "Now tell me you don't care about that."

Jerry didn't answer but looked around at the faces of the men now seated at the table. They were covered with grime, their eyes red and watery, looking as if they were at the end of a three-day drunk.

Jerry threw a quarter to one of the men at the soda machine, saying, "Get me an orange soda, will you?"

None of the men had bothered to wash up before eating, and Jerry noticed the dirt prints on the top of his sandwich. He took a napkin from the holder and wrapped it around the sandwich as a child might wrap paper around an ice cream cone. He felt the grime on his own face, and it gave him a good feeling—a sense of working, a sense of satisfaction and pride that came with the job.

"Well?" Sullivan asked.

"Well, what?" Jerry replied.

"Tell me you don't care about points on the lieutenant's test."

"Oh, I care enough about it, but I care more that we didn't get to that guy in time. You know, I searched six or seven rooms, dressing rooms, I guess, before I got to that office. Maybe if I had gone there first I would've reached him in time."

Jerry put his sandwich on the table. Suddenly he didn't feel like eating, for the image of David Allen jumping from the sidewalk with the force of the blow to the sternum came to him. He remembered Allen's face when the doctor shrugged, and the unalterable realization that the man he had saved was dead.

"Ex post facto," said Dan Fanilli, a man from Engine Company 20.

Jerry looked up the table, and although he knew the meaning he asked, "What does that mean?"

"It means that you're looking at it after the fact. It means that you did everything you were supposed to do, and it doesn't make any sense to look back on something you did right and say that if you had done it another way it would

18

have been more right. Suppose you went to the office first, and the guy ended up being in the first dressing room? Then you would have reason to complain, because then you wouldn't have done the search right. Anyway, it's all in the cards, and the guy was probably long dead by the time we got there."

"Yeah," Tom Sullivan said, "you did the right thing, and maybe some good will come out of it, 'cause that fat guy there taking pictures was from the *Daily News*, and maybe our picture will be on the front page of the *News* tonight."

Vinnie Grant walked into the tall building on 42nd Street, took the elevator to the sixth floor, walked through a long room, and plopped at a desk. There were two things that made Grant stand out in the copy room of the *Daily News*. He was bigger and sloppier than anyone else.

He was six feet tall and weighed two hundred and ninety pounds, a flabby hulk of a man whose pants zipper was never properly closed. It was a problem of strategy to reach over his stomach to pull the zipper up.

He wore the same brown sports jacket in all seasons, dark brown gabardine. Occasionally, he wore brown checkered pants that complimented the jacket, but most of the time the pants were blue or gray. He wore thin ties, slim-jims, that barely covered the pressured buttons of his shirt, and his shoes were never shined.

Vinnie Grant liked the way he dressed, liked the image he felt he conveyed. He was a who-what-where reporter, and nothing mattered to him as long as the information was delivered to the city editor.

The day he graduated from St. Agnes' High School, he walked around the corner to the News Building and marched, still in his cap and gown, down the center aisle of the newsroom. He put his diploma on the city editor's desk and said, "I've wanted to be a reporter since I was ten years old, but I figured I'd better know how to read and write first. Now I know, and I want a job."

The city editor was only slightly amused by the fat kid

standing before him. He said, "You know, there is a story behind every good reporter, an anecdote he can mumble to friends when he feels good about himself. Your entrance makes a good anecdote, but we'll see if you ever feel good about yourself. Go to the fifth floor, personnel, and tell them you're the new copy boy. Come back nine o'clock tomorrow."

Vinnie propped his dirty shoes up on the corner of his desk. He was taking the film out of his camera, waiting for the phone to ring. The city editor would call, because he always called when Grant came into the newsroom and propped his feet up on his desk. The editor knew that Grant had a story they would use. If Grant didn't have a story, he would not be in the newsroom but out in the streets looking. If he had come in with a soft story, he would have gone straight to the city editor's desk, with a con job and a plea for publication in the night's edition. But his feet were on the desk. He had a hard story.

The phone rang.

"Grant here."

"What do you have?"

"A fire. Barrymore Theater. David Allen, theatrical personality, dead. Superheroic rescue attempt. By a fireman. Great pictures. I already stopped at the obit desk. The film is on its way. I have to call the Fire Department for the particulars. The text will be on your desk in an hour."

Vinnie called the stories he wrote "the text." He called the photographs he took "pictures." A story in Vinnie's mind was a combination of the two.

"All right. It'll be on page three tonight."

"The pictures are front-page pictures."

"We'll see."

"Listen, I need three days next week. It's the last week in Saratoga, and I have a girlfriend there. In the fifth on Tuesday."

"Talk to me after we go to bed."

"Talk to ya."

"Jesus," Fanilli said, "they would never print your picture, Sullivan. You're so goddam ugly your picture in the *News* would force all those illiterate bastards who buy it every day to buy the *Times.*"

"Don't bullshit me about being ugly, Fanilli, you without-passport foreigner, 'cause you're the kind of guy who goes to bed at night expecting to wake up in the morning with a tag around his toe."

All the men around the table, except Jerry and Fanilli, laughed loud and long. Fanilli was the senior man of Engine 20, having worked there for seventeen years, and was also the union delegate. He didn't like being the butt of a joke, especially one from a man like Sullivan who had only a few years in the department and who never went to union meetings.

Jerry rolled the remains of his sandwich into a ball and threw it into the garbage can as he left the kitchen. He went upstairs to wash and change clothes, for Ladder 7 was scheduled for field inspection duty at one o'clock.

As he stood washing his face at the bathroom sink, Jerry thought over and over, the titan took the fire . . . the titan stole the fire . . . the titan . . . Prometheus!

It was no good. The words meant nothing unless they were the exact words he thought of when he first knew David Allen was dead.

The hook and ladder truck is never driven through the streets on inspection detail, for the eighty-five-foot ladder is essential for rescues and must remain in the firehouse. So the men of Ladder 7 began to exchange places with the men of Engine 20 for the afternoon. In this way, the two companys could then perform an equitable share of the inspection duty.

As Jerry was taking his gear, his rubber coat, his boots, and his helmet from the hook and ladder, Tom Sullivan was saying, "Talk about an energy crisis and saving gasoline. How many gallons of gas are we going to waste this afternoon, going through the streets, making a pain in the ass of ourselves on inspections?"

Jerry laughed silently to himself. He didn't agree with Sullivan, but it wasn't worth an argument. Many firemen complained about leaving the firehouse, sometimes going to the very end of their district, doing inspection duties that they thought should be done by the building inspectors. But Jerry thought that a good, thorough fire inspection, coupled with a familiarization of the buildings, the exits, the stairs, the particular hazards, was fundamental to the professional image of the firefighter.

"Hey, you guys," Dan Fanilli yelled through the apparatus floor, "let me have your attention for a minute."

The firemen gathered at the front of the apparatus floor, next to the housewatchman's desk. Fanilli, a short, hook-nosed man, the only man in the firehouse with a college degree, had been union delegate for ten of his seventeen years in the department. Many of the men did not like him, for he used big words with calculation, never letting anyone forget that he had gone to college. But he did his job as delegate, keeping the men informed of union matters, and was therefore respected.

"Give me just a minute of your time, fellas," Fanilli said, "for this is important. You all know, I suppose, that, regrettably, we have been working without a contract since June 1, which is over three months. The city negotiators have been recalcitrant and intransigent regarding our demands. They have been screwing us around, and the time has come for us to stand up as a united group and demand our rights. You might have seen a notice on the bulletin board, but if you have not, I tell you now personally that there is a union meeting tonight at seven o'clock, at Union Hall on 34th Street. It is a crucial meeting, and I suggest that we all attend, for we will determine what action we will take to press the city into meaningful negotiations. That's it. Thanks for your attention."

One of the men said, "Okay, Dan, thanks," but there were no questions or replies. The men knew that it was

22

contract time, that it was time to think union. They had been through negotiating periods before, and they knew what was expected of them.

Fanilli looked at the men as they went to the pumper, up the stairs to the bunkroom, or back to the kitchen and thought of a day in the future when he would be president of the local, addressing ten thousand men rather than ten. He had been looking forward to that day for seventeen years.

The pumper pulled into the hydrant space at the corner of Madison Avenue and 58th Street. The lieutenant of Ladder 7, Jack Killane, rolled down the cab window and held out a copy of a violation order paper-clipped to a building card. Jerry reached up for the card.

"This is the Malcolm Lehman School," the lieutenant said, "just up the block. The VO is for a failure to provide red lights at the exits. Make sure the lights are on."

"Okay, Lieutenant, I'll take Sullivan with me," Jerry said as he motioned to Tom Sullivan. The other men sat on the side step of the pumper waiting for the officer's hand to appear at the cab window with another building card.

Jerry and Tom climbed the ten steps of the converted brownstone that was now the Malcolm Lehman School and walked through the vestibule into a large entry foyer. There was a yellow marble stairway on one side of the foyer and two doors on the other. Printed in gold script on one door was the name "Malcolm Lehman"; "School Office" was printed on the other.

"Listen," Sullivan said, "there's got to be a bathroom around here, and if I don't find it soon you're not going to be happy to walk around with me. You can handle this on your own, right?" He didn't wait for Jerry's reply but skipped, two by two, up the marble stairs.

Jerry opened the school office door and saw a woman sitting at a desk, a book propped between her hands. He read the jacket copy and felt a confidence he was not used to. The book jacket read *DYLAN collected THOMAS poems.*

Jerry stood before her as she gazed quickly at his dark

23

blue pants and tie, his light blue shirt with the small Maltese cross insignia at the collar points, his round-topped dark blue cap. She smiled and pointed a finger at him. "You're a fireman, aren't you?"

Jerry looked down at his shirt and pants as if in appraisal of himself and said, "Evidently."

"Isn't that interesting," the woman said. "I was just reading about a fire raid and here you are."

"You mean *after*," Jerry said.

"After?"

"Ceremony After a Fire Raid," Jerry said. "It's a favorite of mine."

Jerry deepened his voice in imitation of the voice on the Thomas records he had listened to so many times, and he recited:

> *Myselves*
> *The grievers*
> *Grieve*
> *Among the street burned to tireless death*

Jerry had intended to go on, but the words forced him to picture the morning's fire and he stopped.

The way the woman's eyes met his made him uncomfortable, for no one had ever studied him so intensely before. "Go on," she said softly.

He relaxed a little and said, "Oh, I know more of it, but I don't think I could get through all three parts. Anyway, I'm here to check the lights by the exit signs. There was a violation order. If you could call the man in charge of maintenance for me . . ."

The woman put the book of poems on the desk and rose from her chair. Her hair was long and full, hanging to her elbows in easy black waves, her face deeply tanned and brisk.

She wore a white silk-like dress, cinched at the waist by a belt of gold coins, and Jerry felt an anxiety by her presence.

"My name is Susan Sachs Goldman and I am in charge of everything, including maintenance." She held out her

24

hand elegantly, yet casually, in the way of a person filled with confidence. Jerry held it briefly, as she continued. "You see, Mr. Lehman and Mr. Bernardo, the assistant headmaster, have not yet returned from lunch. The maintenance man, Mr. Gilbert, is not here today, and Liz, the receptionist who normally sits at this desk, has gone to the dentist. I am a teacher with a free period who has risen, if only for the moment, to the position of supreme power in this institution. So, since I have the time and you have the time, and since the safety of the school seems to be in question, let's go check on—what was it you said, the exit lights?"

Jerry smiled. "Are you always so dependent on dependent clauses?"

"Yes." She laughed as she ushered him out of the office. "Particularly when I am around people who recite Dylan Thomas."

"The violation order says that the exit lights in the gym and the main floor rear are out."

"We'll go to the gym first. It is in the basement."

Jerry walked slightly behind her as they went down the steps, trying to memorize the movement of her hips and the swing of her dress.

"Do you read much poetry?" she asked.

"Some," Jerry said, and then, feeling a great need to impress her, added, "I write as much of it as I read."

She turned at the bottom of the stairs. "Really," she said. "I knew there was something special about you."

"Would you like to come to my place," Jerry winked, "and read my etchings?"

She looked at him intently for a moment, paused, and said, "Yes."

They went to the gym, and Jerry saw beyond the basketball-playing boys that the exit sign was shining red. They went to the rear of the main floor, and that light too was bright.

They returned to the entry foyer, and Jerry could see Sullivan standing on the stoop top. Jerry turned to Susan and said, "How about dinner tonight? You pick the restaurant."

25

She seemed pleased, and he was glad of that. "Let me check," she said, entering the office. She went through her bag, which she had put on the desk. "I can't do anything without looking at my calendar."

She pulled a small red book from her bag and began to turn the pages.

"No," she said, "not tonight, anyway. We have guests coming."

Jerry remembered the union meeting and thought it was just as well.

"Tomorrow night is filled too," she said, disappointedly. "How is the night after for you?"

"Okay. I'll pick you up at seven-thirty. Susan Goldman, right? What's the address?"

"It's 1088 Park Avenue, at 81st Street," she said, writing in her book.

"Park Avenue, huh?" Jerry said. "Maybe you better let me pick the restaurant."

"Fine," Susan said, and understanding his meaning she added, "I am fond of spaghetti."

"Terrific, see you then." Jerry waved as he began to walk from the office.

"Hey, wait a minute," Susan said.

"Yes?" Jerry stopped with the door open.

"What's your name?"

"This is too important a date to be concerned about names." Jerry winked. "But if you must know, it's Ritter— Jerry Ritter. See you."

Jerry said nothing to Sullivan as they walked down the street to the pumper, but he was excited by Susan Goldman of Park Avenue. He had never before known a girl who had to look in a calendar to find out what she was doing from hour to hour.

2

TOM RITTER WAS SCREAMING, "WATCH the floor, watch the floor," as Anne pressed both hands into his shoulder and shook him with all her strength.

"It's okay, Tom, honey, it's okay," she said as he awakened, perspiring from the same nightmare he had been experiencing for over eight years.

Tom Ritter had always wanted to be a fireman.

As a young boy he "buffed" the firehouse on East Tremont Avenue, a few blocks from his home on McGuire Avenue. He would go there after school each day and on Saturdays and stand around quietly, trying to keep out of the firemen's way. The men soon got to know young Tom and they liked him, for he was a modest boy, polite and respectful. The firemen began to send him to the store for sand-

27

wiches or ice cream, always giving him a nickel for his errand. After a time they began to let him help with the hose cleaning and the brass buffing. They also let him read department magazines, department orders, and training bulletins. He was a scholarly child, a prodigious reader, and from the firehouse bookshelves Tom read the histories of the New York Fire Department. When a particular fire interested him, he would go to the public library and read about it in the back issues of the city's newspapers. He seemed always to be in either the firehouse or the library.

Each day he went to the firehouse he would ask a different question about equipment, procedures, or rules and regulations, and the men would answer him when they could and shrug their shoulders and laugh when they couldn't. They told him, "If all the firemen around here had your interest in the job, we'd all be chiefs, and then how would the fires get put out?"

Tom loved going to the firehouse, but his older brothers and his mother and father thought it was a waste of his time. His brothers said that he should be at the schoolyard playing basketball, and his parents thought that his interest in the Fire Department was taking time from his studies at school, even though he always did better at school than any of the other Ritter boys.

Soon Tom stopped going to the firehouse and spent most of his days at the library, for his work at St. Helena's took all his time, but he kept his interest in firefighting alive by reading the fire magazines.

It was during Tom's second year at Hunter College, where his impressive work was the talk of the philosophy department, that his brother Davey was shot. At the funeral mass, the church filled with friends and neighbors, his mother sobbing uncontrollably behind unblinking eyes, Tom decided that his philosophy classes no longer had meaning for him. The next day he sent a letter of withdrawal to the school and began to work full time at the garage with grease valves and socket wrenches. In his spare time he studied for the fireman's test.

28

He married Anne Phillips, his steady girlfriend for four years, the day after he took the examination for Fireman, New York City Fire Department. They moved to a small apartment next to the elevated line on Westchester Avenue and stayed there, hoping with each passing train that the fireman's job would come, giving them the security and salary to move to a better apartment. Five months later Tom was called to report to the probationary firemen's training school on Welfare Island.

Tom had no "hook," no "rabbi," in the Fire Department, and because he knew no one to ask for a choice assignment he was resigned to go to whatever company the department sent him to. On the day he graduated from the training school the department orders were read, and Ritter, Thomas P., was assigned to Engine Company 22 on the Lower West Side of Manhattan. If Tom had had a choice, he would have preferred a more active company, but he was happy with the assignment, for it would give him that much more time to study for promotion.

Life as a fireman went smoothly for the first two years in Engine Company 22. He and Anne moved to an apartment in New Rochelle, a town just above the Bronx, where they hoped to buy a house someday. There Anne had her first child, a boy. A fireman's salary was not the best salary in the world, but it was better than a garage mechanic's, and they bought an English pram for their first born so that the baby could be wheeled around New Rochelle in style. They were a happy family, a couple and child one might read about in a storybook, laughing always and loving.

Tom grew to love his job more and more, and with each day, each firehouse meal, each fire, he grew to love the men he worked with. He had become a part of the firehouse family, the family that had so impressed him as a child. Realizing a buff's dream, he had become part of the excitement, the tradition, the glory of the Fire Department, and he liked himself for that.

Then, one wintry night six years later, Tom Ritter's life was changed.

Joe Mullin had cooked the meal, a lasagna that Tom had called an Irishman's wonder. Four men had shared the meal with Tom in the narrow firehouse kitchen—Mullin, McCafferty, Lieutenant Cohen, and Goss. The conversation centered around the meal.

"Jeez, this is good," McCafferty said as he reached for a piece of garlic bread.

"How the hell would you know?" Mullin said, "You'd eat bird droppings if they were mixed with potatoes and gravy."

The other men were still laughing when Lieutenant Cohen said, "What we need is an Italian in the group, someone who knows the difference between catsup and tomato sauce. I'll speak to the captain about it."

Goss, a black man, and the youngest in the company, said, "You don't need to be Italian to know that this is good."

Goss was shy and sensitive, perhaps because he was the youngest, the "johnny" in the group, perhaps because he was the only black in the company. He spoke so softly that Tom, who was sitting next to him, was the only one to hear.

Tom said, loud enough for all to hear, "What the fuck would you know about it?" No one laughed.

It was a remark the men thought unlike Tom, out of character, motivated by a naive desire to assert his place in the group, to impress them at the cost of the younger man's feelings. It was a remark that Tom never forgot and never stopped regretting, for Goss lowered his eyes to his plate, fixing them there, and said nothing until the alarm sounded a few minutes later.

On the back of the fire engine Tom yelled to Goss above the scream of the siren, "You know I was only kidding, what I said back there."

Goss looked straight at Tom, his eyes showing disbelief and a lifetime of understanding, and said, "Yeah, I know." He then looked straight ahead through the cold night until the pumper pulled to a hydrant at 15th Street and Ninth Avenue. He never spoke to Tom again.

It seemed a simple fire.

The building was an old five-story warehouse being used

30

as a merchandise showroom. The men broke open the front door as Tom pulled the hose, watching the light smoke wisp out into the street.

Tom wrapped one hand around the heavy, water-filled two-and-a-half-inch hose and put his other hand on the bridge of the nozzle handle. Engine Company 22 moved in through the showroom, past counters filled with bolts and draped samples of cotton and linen.

Deep inside the building Lieutenant Cohen ordered Tom to stand by with the line as a search was made for the fire. Cohen, Mullin, McCafferty, and Goss advanced together, their flashlights easily penetrating the thin smoke. Tom felt foolish breathing through a mask in such easy smoke, and he was about to take his facepiece off when he felt the first shudder in the floor.

As he yelled a muffled cry through his facepiece, he saw the four flashlights turn and bob quickly up and down toward him.

"Watch the floor, watch the floor," he yelled, as the bobbing lights appeared closer and closer.

The floor shuddered a second time and seemed to slide beneath Tom's knees. "Hurry, come on," he screamed, as the floor began to split before his eyes.

The showroom was made momentarily bright as if illumined by a thousand flashbulbs, and the fire leaped up in a great surge as the flooring fell into it.

Tom saw McCafferty holding onto Mullin's arm as they slid together, down with the slant of the floor, their eyes wide and raging with fear. As their cries fell deeper and deeper into the fire, Tom saw Goss, only a few yards away, tearing at the asphalt floor tiles for a grip, a chance ridge to save him from sliding. But Goss' gloved hands went over the floor as smoothly as a buffing rag, and he fell from view with agonizing sounds.

Tom saw Lieutenant Cohen clinging to a falling counter display.

Suddenly he realized that the floor beneath him was sinking, and as he turned to escape, conscious for the first time of his own endangerment, the floor gave way.

He grabbed for the hose as his body plunged downward, and he felt his fingers slide over the nozzle and over the four-inch controlling handle. Then his fingers sank between the handle and the body of the chrome nozzle, and he fixed his grip with all his strength.

He hung there for a moment, suspended over the fire, the energy of the heat rising up and around him, and he knew he was going to die. He thought of his mother sitting in a kitchen chair, her body lurching rhythmically with sobs, staring into nothing, and he saw Goss staring into his dinner. He saw Anne in a photograph he had taken of her, her brown hair swept by the wind as she held their son beside the English pram. He felt the pain in his fingers, his knuckles wrapped white around the handle, and he let loose a scream as the hose moved, until he realized that the hose was not moving into the depths of violence but up. He saw the gloved hand reaching for him.

He was only two feet from a steel crossbeam as the floor caved beneath him; the firemen were standing on the buckled edge, pulling the hose, and the man.

There was a slow march up Fifth Avenue, a dirge, a high school band playing "The Death of Ase" over muffled drums. The parade stopped at St. Patrick's Cathedral and the remains of Mullin and McCafferty were carried from a fire engine, damson-colored draperies flying in the chilled breeze. The parade continued to St. Thomas' Episcopal, where the marchers watched as Goss' coffin was carried up the stone steps. It continued again up the avenue to Temple Emanu-El, where after receiving permission for a delayed burial the family of Lieutenant Cohen cried behind his casket.

There were thousands of firemen in the three houses of worship, giving homage to and praying over the bits and pieces of their fallen brothers.

Tom did not go to the funeral parade but stayed at home and wrote a letter to the fire commissioner. He could never

32

again return to Engine Company 22, and he asked for a transfer to a Harlem company, Engine Company 51, where there were more fires than in any other section of the city.

He knew that if he didn't keep active he would have to leave the Fire Department. He would have to go with the action, for he knew that it was from the action that he would learn about living again, as a man, and as a fireman.

"I'm all right, Anne," Tom said. "It's nothing, I'm all right. Go back to sleep now."

Tom propped his pillow against the headboard of the bed and lit a cigarette. He looked at the clock. It was almost five. He would be getting up in an hour. With one arm across his head, Tom settled back against the pillow and reconstructed his dream as he had done so many times before.

Four men, seated around a lace-covered table in a restaurant, were eating a leg of lamb. The lamb was sitting on a serving cart next to the table, and Tom called for the waiter to cut more meat. The waiter approached and Tom looked up and saw the waiter's black face. "Cut it thin and close to the bone," Tom said. The waiter looked at him scornfully, saying, "Yeah, I know," as the cry of "Fire" spread through the restaurant. The four men, in sports jackets and ties, ran from the restaurant to the building across the street, followed by the waiter. Hose had been laid throughout the building, and Tom knelt by a nozzle, pulled a rope from his pocket, and lashed himself to the hose. He noticed beside him two men dressed like executives. One, who wore a small gold badge on his lapel, said, "This floor has been recovered over nine times. You'll have to support it with lolly columns from below, for it's beyond its weight capacity." The other man said, "We'll have to get through the season somehow," and pulled a roll of bills from his pocket. He counted them off into the hands of the man with the small gold badge as the two walked out of the building. Tom tried to move to the others, but he was lashed to the nozzle and hose. The lights were on in the building and there was no smoke, and Tom saw the frozen, fearful faces as he yelled, "Watch the floor."

33

Tom crushed his cigarette in an ashtray and leaned over against his wife, stroking her hair. She was turned away from him, and he put his body full with hers.

"You shouldn't smoke in bed, you know," Anne said, her voice flattened by the pillow she hugged.

"I do know," Tom said, his hand gliding over her waist and hip and thigh until it came to the bottom of her nightdress. "Beds were made for two things," he continued. "One is sleep." His hand under her nightdress, he caressed her stomach, still firm after four children.

Anne turned to him and said, "It's been a long time."

"Even if it was an hour ago," Tom whispered, "it would be too long."

The alarm rang at six o'clock, and Tom shaved and dressed as Anne cooked breakfast. The children began to stir, the two boys wrestling as they did every morning, the two girls down in the kitchen helping their mother with the breakfast cereal.

After bacon and eggs, Tom took his coffee into the living room and browsed through a magazine. Anne came in and sat next to him, laying her arm over the back of the couch so that she could curl her husband's hair.

"Tom," she said, "you've been having that dream for so long. Don't you think you ought to see a doctor about it?"

"No," Tom said curtly, flipping the pages of the magazine.

Anne looked at him with apprehension. "Why do you always put me off?" she asked. "Don't you think it would help if we could talk about it? You know that it scares me."

"I'm not putting you off, Anne," Tom said, throwing the magazine on the coffee table and putting his hand on her knee. "It's only that I know what it is, I understand it, and that's that."

He took a final sip of coffee and rose from the couch, checking his watch.

Anne looked up at him. Her voice rasping with concern, she said, "But a doctor could make them stop."

34

Tom grinned slightly. "Yeah, sure," he said, "and make others begin. Doctors are like television repairmen. They - can't stay in business unless they keep finding things wrong, and you know what it has cost us to keep our TV working."

He leaned over and kissed her full on the mouth. "I gotta go, and remember I'll be home late. There's a union meeting."

"It's a big price we pay for this job," Anne said resignedly.

"But it's worth it," Tom said, waving good-by.

Anne remained on the couch, watching her husband move to the front door. She wished silently that he did not keep every important thought to himself, but she knew it was a futile wish.

"Okay, kids," Tom hollered. The children ran to the front door. He squatted down and kissed them all on the lips.

Tom drove his battered economy car through the streets of New Rochelle thinking of Anne's final statement. It *is* a big price we pay, he thought, looking at the wire coat hanger bent across the fender of the car where an aerial should be and where two aerials had already been replaced, only to be torn off again as inevitably happens when cars are parked in streets, in front of ghetto firehouses.

He drove down the Hutchinson River Parkway to the Bronx, and as he passed the City Island and Orchard Beach exit he wondered what it had been like over three hundred years earlier when Anne Hutchinson first settled the area— before there were estates on the shores of the Long Island Sound, before there was miniature golf on the Pelham marshes, when people worked for their food or died trying, before tenement slums. He remembered the life of Anne Hutchinson, and college lectures. Personal grace, he thought, laughing to himself. Even the Bible must defer to divine knowledge inspired in the individual by God. There is no dogma but that which is developed in one's own mind —an idea that caused grief and turmoil in Boston and Providence so many years ago but that now lives, accepted, and unquestioned. . . . Tom smiled at the irony, wishing it were

35

not so. "Do your own thing" was a phrase that did not work for Tom, although it seemed to engulf him like the unclean air, it was so pervasive.

"O my God, I am heartily sorry," Tom began reciting to himself, sincerely and contritely. Not a day had passed since the 15th Street fire that Tom did not say an Act of Contrition.

He drove down the Bruckner Expressway, past the blackened walls of the burned-out tenements of the South Bronx, the city's Dresden, and concluded the prayer, "to avoid the near occasion of sin. Amen."

He drove over the Willis Avenue Bridge to avoid the toll on the Triborough, although the route was longer and more congested. Bumper to bumper, he made his way west on 125th Street, past the check-cashing offices, the furniture-on-credit stores, the pawn shops, the corner wig stands, the outdoor vegetable stands. He turned down Fifth Avenue and saw the broken hydrant spewing its water full force down the avenue to 123rd Street, where it backed up at a clogged sewer in front of the firehouse.

There was a big puddle of water over twelve inches deep on the street and sidewalk, flowing in small ripples onto the apparatus floor of Engine Company 51. Tom shook his head as if to say "It figures" and thought to himself that this would not happen south of the Mason-Dixon line, the 96th Street borderline that separates the exclusive and rich Fifth Avenue of Manhattan from the Fifth Avenue of Harlem. Sewers, for some reason, never seem to clog south of the Mason-Dixon line.

The water was covered with oil, and tin cans, empty milk containers, and brown paper bags floated freely on it.

Tom double-parked his car on 123rd Street and walked around the perimeter of the water, realizing there was no way to get into the firehouse without getting his feet wet. Dominic Gallo, Tom's closest friend, and one of the biggest men in the department, was standing in front of the firehouse in hip boots, laughing at Tom's problem. Other men came out of the firehouse and joined in the laughter.

"Do you need a boat?" Dom asked.

"I think a raft would do it," Tom replied.

Dom Gallo walked through the water, saying, "How about a piggyback ride?"

"Any port in a storm." Tom smiled, jumping up on Gallo's back. He held Dom's neck tightly, saying, "You know, there is a story in the Bible about this."

"Oh, yeah," Dom said, "and what is that?"

As Tom was about to reply, Gallo lost his footing and began to fall. Tom quickly jumped from his back, landing almost knee deep in the water. He looked at Gallo disgustedly and said, "All I can tell you is that St. Christopher never tripped."

Gallo laughed almost as hard as the onlooking firemen as Tom trudged through the water into the firehouse.

When, three years before, Tom had first walked into these quarters, he had been sure that he would make no strong friendships. The deaths of his friends in the 15th Street fire had taken too much from him, had caused him too much pain. He had loved them too much, and he vowed to be guarded in his affection for other firemen. But Dominic Gallo was standing housewatch that day, and as Tom entered the firehouse Gallo threw his arms around him, called him a sweetheart, and kissed him on both cheeks. Gallo had also lost friends in fires, and a bond of understanding developed naturally between them. Gallo quickly became his tutor, teaching him the ins and outs of firefighting in Harlem, in the tenements that were new to him and in the tall, low-income housing projects that required firefighting procedures different from those in the industrial section of lower Manhattan.

There were three companies housed in the firehouse on 123rd Street. Engine Company 51, Ladder Company 22, and Battalion 10. It was the busiest firehouse in the city when Tom was transferred. But then the companies in the South Bronx and Bedford-Stuyvesant began to get more work and rose to the top of the statistics list. The deterioration of the city can be measured by its fire statistics, and Harlem had simply stopped being the worst ghetto in the town. New

37

York has the distinction of having three major ghettos, and Harlem became a better place to live than the South Bronx or Bedford-Stuyvesant. The firehouse on 123rd Street did not become slower; in fact, it became busier and busier every year, but the firehouses in the Bronx and Brooklyn ghettos became busier still.

The 123rd Street quarters was a firehouse of reputation. Engine 51 had won more unit citations than any other company in the department, and hardly a year went by that one or two firemen from 51 or Ladder 22 did not receive individual citations and medals for heroism.

And the firehouse was famous for its firefighters. Gallo of Ladder 22 was the department's most-decorated fireman. In his twelve years on the job he had been awarded seven medals for saving lives at extreme personal risk and had accumulated over twenty points to be applied toward a promotional exam, although he refused to study for promotion. Ernie Edwards of Engine 51 was president of the Raven Society, the department's social organization of black firefighters, and Pete Dwyer, also of Engine 51, was president of the St. Steven Society, the Catholic organization.

Tom loved the firehouse, the rapidity of responding from one alarm to another, the fires, the action. He was at his happiest when working, but he was still careful in his love for the other men. Gallo had befriended him early, and Tom nurtured that friendship, but he remained aloof from the men in his own company. It was the reciprocation of friendship that was binding, and Tom knew that if he was to love the men he worked with, he would have to love them from afar. Even Dominic's friendship was a risk he took with calculation.

Tom had changed into work clothes after drying his feet and sat in the kitchen, drinking coffee. Dominic Gallo approached him from behind and put his arms around Tom's neck in a loving gesture.

"First chance I ever got to rescue a brother fireman, and I muffed it," Gallo said. "Do you forgive me?"

38

"In spades, Dom," Tom answered.

"You're a sweetheart," Dom said, kissing Tom on the top of the head, "and there's only a few of us left."

Ernie Edwards entered the kitchen, looked at Gallo, and said, "Oh, my God. What did I walk into here, an X-rated kitchen?"

Dom took his arms from around Tom's neck and went over to Ernie, putting his arms around him.

"Here's another sweetheart," Dom said, "one of the few. With all his connections he could be downtown drivin' one of the commissioners, but he fights fires in Harlem with all the other sweethearts."

"That's me," Ernie said, "a sweetheart, sometimes known as a poor girl's muff machine."

Ernie put his arm around Dom and walked him over to the electric coffee pot on the counter next to the sink. "How ya doin', ya gettin' much?"

"Much of what?" Dom asked in return.

"Anything that comes to mind, baby, but let's just think about gettin' some coffee now."

"You're a sweetheart, Ernie, and the coffee's on me."

"Hey," Ernie said, "my kinda guy. A sport. You're like a madam I knew in Korea who charged extra for VD."

"Anything for a friend."

The kitchen began to fill with firemen, some going off duty from the night tour, the rest in for the day tour.

Tom was reading a newspaper, searching for news of the firemen's contract negotiations, when the second alarm banged in. The voice alarm echoed through the firehouse like a racetrack loudspeaker: "A SECOND ALARM IS TRANS-MITTED FOR MANHATTAN BOX 451, 45TH STREET AND BROADWAY."

Tom thought immediately of his brother, Jerry.

A young fireman, Walter Smith, who was sitting across from Tom and Dominic at the kitchen table, said, "It's about time those rubbers down there did some work."

Tom folded his newspaper, saying, "Listen, Smith, tell me what you mean by 'those rubbers down there.' "

39

Smith could see the concern in Tom's face. He did not like Tom, for Tom barely acknowledged him and never went out of his way to say hello. But he did not want to argue with Tom, and he could see by Tom's look that an argument could come easily.

"Let's forget it," Smith said.

"Uh-uh," Tom said, leaning over the table. "I want to know what you mean by 'those rubbers down there.' "

The kitchen had become quiet, the other firemen listening with interest. The focus was on Smith, and Smith realized he would have to assert himself if he were to come out of it a man, and the best defense, he thought, is offense.

"I mean," Smith said, "that those guys don't have their hearts in this job, because if they did they would be up here in Harlem, or in the South Bronx, or in Brownsville, Bedford-Stuyvesant, or anywhere else where there are fires. Those guys go to bed at night, and nine times outta ten they get a full night's sleep, and they wake up fresh to go out and work on the side, and that's where their hearts are, with the side jobs. If they weren't rubbers they'd be up here with the fires."

Tom's face became red with anger, and he made a conscious effort to control himself. He was about to say something when Gallo grabbed his forearm and squeezed until it hurt. Then Gallo rose from his chair, put both hands on the table, and leaned over until he was just a few inches from Smith's face.

"Ordinarily," Gallo said, very slowly, the veins rising in his neck, "I would put a guy like you through the wall, Smith. But I'm going to forget it this time, because there are a lot of things you don't know, and you don't know them because you're a johnny in this job, a puppy, and you're going to learn a lesson now, and the lesson is that you've been saved from being put through a wall because of what you don't know. From now on you keep your opinions inside you, or you change your opinions."

Smith felt the fear tremble through his body. He knew there was no way he could come out of it a man. Not only was

40

Gallo the biggest guy in the firehouse, he was also the most respected. The thought occurred to Smith to take a swing at Gallo, and he would have if Gallo were just another big man, but his reputation as a fireman was even more formidable than his size, and it commanded respect.

"All right, all right," Smith said, backing his chair away from Dom. "Let's forget it, okay?"

The confrontation was interrupted by the harsh, reverberating sound of the voice alarm: "ENGINE 51, LADDER 22, BATTALION 10. RESPOND TO BOX 1257, 120TH STREET AND MADISON AVENUE."

The working firemen hustled out of the kitchen and onto the apparatus floor. Those who had worked the previous tour remained, unperturbed, drinking coffee. Tom and Walter Smith stopped behind the pumper of Engine 51 and stepped into their boots. Dominic stopped beside Smith and put his hand on his arm, saying, "Okay, Smith, let's forget it, huh?"

"Sure, Dominic," Smith said, stepping up onto the rear of the fire engine and avoiding the gaze of Tom, who had stepped up next to him.

The rest of the crew joined them in grabbing the rear crossbar above the back step, and the pumper moved out and down Fifth Avenue, followed by Ladder 22 and the chief's car, the sirens and air horns announcing the small caravan through the garbage-strewn streets. They turned left at 120th Street.

A small crowd stood in front of a slate-stone tenement stoop on the corner of Madison Avenue and 120th. Tom saw the thin, white smoke curling into the air from a window above their heads. He grabbed the nozzle and shoved his arm through three folds of the carefully pleated hose. He pulled the hose to the street, followed by Walter Smith, who had also taken three folds. With the two fifty-foot lengths of hose taken off the pumper, the lieutenant of Engine 51 yelled "Take off" to the driver of the apparatus, and the fire engine drove up Madison Avenue to a fire hydrant, the connected hose flipping off its rear bed.

The smoke was coming from an apartment at the front

41

of the second floor. The door of the apartment was locked, and Dominic began working on it with a haligan tool, a piece of equipment similar to a crowbar. In a few moments Tom arrived, boots drawn up, collar closed, ready for the advance.

Dominic placed the forked end of the haligan tool in the area of the lock, between the door and the door jamb. He pushed on it, then pulled with his full weight. The lock was forced, its screws splintering out of the wood of the jamb, and the door popped open. The smoke rushed out into the hall-way.

A fireman appeared next to Tom, wearing an air mask. Tom turned casually to him in the smoke, saying, "I don't think we'll need the mask. It smells like a mattress."

The fireman lifted his facepiece and smelled the smoke. "Yeah," he said, sampling the smoke as a gourmet might distinguish a sauce, "a mattress." He grabbed for his heavy air pack, which hung from his back like a scuba tank, and swung it to the floor.

Tom followed Gallo, nozzle in hand, into the apartment. A man carrying a pressurized water can pushed past him, saying, " 'Scuse me, beg pardon." Tom chuckled at the po-liteness.

They reached a front bedroom, and Dominic opened the windows and pulled down the curtains as the other fireman aimed the small hose and pressed the handle of the extin-guisher. The thin stream of water burst upon the flaming mattress, and the smoke became denser and darker.

A voice called through the apartment, "Do you want to start water?"

Tom laid the empty, limp hose on the floor and called back, "No, it's only a mattress."

The fireman emptied the can of water, and the flames died.

"Let's get it out the window, Charlie," Gallo said, "but be careful it don't light up."

The two men struggled to bend the smoldering mattress so that it would fit through the window opening. Their faces

42

became coated with smoke, and slime ran from their noses.

Tom joined in the struggle, and the three men carried the mattress to the window. As they shoved it forward the street air met the dying embers, and the mattress flared wildly with fire. The three firemen jumped back, but not before the flame had reached up and over Tom's left ear. "Sonovabitch," Tom shrieked, as he lifted his foot and kicked the remainder of the mattress out the window.

To the crowd on the street, it looked as if the sun was falling from the second-floor window. Chief Gelman of Battalion 10 was approaching the building, holding his radio in one hand and a portable lamp in the other. His aide was a few paces behind. As he saw the fiery mattress falling, the aide screamed, "Watch it, chief, above ya." But it was too late. The chief had just tucked his chin down into his chest when the corner of the mattress hit his back. The chief was pushed to the sidewalk by the impact, and his helmet was knocked from his head.

He got up quickly, holding the back of his neck, and looked up to the window and through the still-thick smoke at Dominic. He could see the mistake in Dominic's face.

Dominic turned from the chief's view, saying, "Jesus S. Christ, we just glanced Gelman with the mattress."

Tom sat on the bed frame, holding his ear. The other fireman picked up the extinguisher and said, "See ya later, Dom. You're the senior man. You handle it."

Gallo looked at Tom, who still held his hand to his ear. The lieutenant of Engine 51 entered the room and ordered the hose to be taken up. Smith and the other enginemen carried the hose to the street, and the lieutenant of Ladder 22 looked carefully about the room to make sure that the fire was confined to the mattress. Gallo sat next to Tom on the bed frame.

"What's up, pal?" Gallo asked.

"Nothing much," Tom answered. "I think it got me in the ear."

Gallo took Tom's hand from his ear and saw that it had

43

been burned around the edges, from the lobe to the top curl.

"It's already blistered," Gallo said. "You better go sick and get a couple of days off."

"Yeah, it should get looked at anyway," Tom replied. He rose from the bed and was about to follow his company to the street when the chief arrived.

Chief Gelman stood at the doorway of the bedroom, holding his helmet in his hand, and glared for a moment at Gallo.

Just one year before, Morris Gelman had stood on the red carpet of the chief of department's office, holding his gold-braided cap in his hand.

The chief of department was holding a manila folder in his hands. He looked up from his desk and said, "I don't know who you know, chief, but I can see from your records that you know somebody. You were a fireman in Staten Island, a lieutenant in Staten Island, and a captain in Staten Island. You are now a battalion chief in Staten Island, and last night you were in command of a fire in Staten Island. Now there aren't that many fires in the borough of Richmond that we shouldn't always be in full control of them."

As Chief of Department Eugene Golden talked, Gelman was thinking of Irv Shapiro, a fireman who worked in the personnel division. Irv had worked in that office, shuffling papers from one side of his desk to the other, for over ten years, ever since Bernie Feldman had retired and Irv had been elected as the new president of the Shophar Society, the department's cultural organization for Jewish firemen. Like the St. Steven Society for Catholics, the St. George Society for Protestants, the Raven Society for blacks, the Verrazzano Society for Italians, and the Emerald Society for the Irish, the Shophar Society had little to do with culture. They were organizations of political influence peddling, each group looking out for its own, and it happened that some years earlier Irv Shapiro of the Shophar Society had fortuitously married a girl named Sara Bernstein, who was a sister-in-law of a man who was a cousin of Mrs. Morris Gelman.

44

The day Shapiro was elected he received a call from Fireman Gelman, who was then working in a Brooklyn firehouse, requesting a company anywhere in the farmlands of Staten Island, the borough of Richmond.

"Yours last night was a fourth alarm," the chief of department continued, "when it should have been at most a second alarm. Six frame houses were lost instead of one, which we could have lived with, and God knows how many people don't have a place to sleep because of you. The deputy chief on the scene told me that the exposures on either side of the building were not covered . . ."

"But, chief, I ordered two lines into the front entrance and another line into the rear. I had no more manpower until the second-alarm companies arrived."

"Don't interrupt me. There are many of the two hundred and fifty battalion chiefs in this job who deserve a Staten Island battalion, and one of them is now going to get lucky. I am sending you to a battalion in Harlem where you will get the needed experience to act effectively as a battalion chief. That's all."

Morris Gelman gave the chief of department a half-hearted salute, turned, and walked out of the office, saying to himself, "Goddammed anti-Semite."

"Listen, chief, I'm sorry," Gallo said.

"Don't tell me you're sorry," Chief Gelman said, "after I've been knocked to the ground and burned on the neck. I could've been killed because of your stupidity. That's right. It was a stupid thing to do, and you of all people should know better than to throw something to the street without first checking to see if it's clear. My goddam neck is burned, and I have to overlook it because chiefs can't explain getting their necks burned because stupid firemen throw things out of windows. The idea would make me the laughingstock of the medical office. I'm going to see that you get three late watches for this, Gallo."

Gallo stood in front of the chief, put his hands in the pockets of his rubber turnout coat, and spoke softly and dis-

45

tinctly. "Chief, you can do whatever you want to do. I said that I was sorry, that I made a mistake. I don't make many, but that's why pencils have erasers. You have my apology, and that's as much as I can do as a man."

Tom grabbed the sleeve of the chief's coat, saying, "It was really me who kicked the thing out the window, chief. It lit up, and I figured it would be best to get it out of the room fast. No one had time to check the street first. I'm sorry."

Chief Gelman glared first at Tom and then at Gallo, the anger coming through his eyes. He then turned and left the apartment.

"You're a sweetheart," Gallo said to Tom.

"Yeah," Tom said, smiling, "I always do the right thing. If you have three late watches coming, I have too."

"Hell." Gallo laughed. "I'd ask him to formalize a complaint before I'd take three late watches, and you know he's not about to do that. The word would get out that Gelman was having trouble with his battalion, and that's the last thing he wants. It's all chickenshit. But he ain't a bad guy for all of this. After all, we did almost cream 'im."

It was funny, but not so funny that they both did not think of the seriousness of the incident.

Gallo picked up his ax and haligan tool and put his arm around Tom's back. They walked out of the bedroom, down a narrow corridor, and into the hallway.

"Let's go see about that ear," Gallo said.

"You're kiddin' me," Tom said. "If the chief can't go sick with a burned neck, I'm not about to report to him with a burned ear."

"Yeah, I guess you can manage without dying."

"Like a piece of cake."

The two men walked arm in arm down the worn marble steps to the street.

The hose was already repacked when Tom arrived at the fire engine. He took off his turnout coat and threw it over the rear crossbar, for the cool September morning had become a hot day.

46

The company chauffeur made several blasts on the air horn, and the lieutenant had his finger in the air, waving it in circles. An alarm was dispatched by radio, and the firemen responded to the lieutenant's signal by grasping the rubber covering of the rear crossbar. The pumper, followed by Ladder 22 and the chief's car, cried through the city streets until it came to the corner of 126th Street and Fifth Avenue.

The firemen walked a short distance up 126th Street and up and down Fifth Avenue, passing old men standing in doorways, old women carrying grocery bags, young girls caring for their babies, small groups of teenagers hanging out. The neighborhood was at once busy with activity and labored with idleness.

It was a false alarm, and the lieutenant of Engine 51 gestured a thumbs-down signal to the chief, who would report a signal ten-nine-two, a malicious false alarm, over the radio.

Tom was about to step up onto the back of the pumper when a woman came out of a laundrymat at the corner.

"Firemans, hey, firemans," she called.

Tom went to her while the others watched from the back and side steps of the ladder truck, and from the chief's car.

"It's a terrible shame," the woman said with the singsong accent of the South, "the way these childrens pull false alarms." She pointed to a group of three boys sitting on a stoop across the street. "It was that boy there, him in the orange sweater. I watched him with my own eyes, and he be no good if you don't do somefin. He ought to be in school anyway."

The three boys stared at the pointing woman.

"Thank you, miss," Tom said, and he walked across the street to the stoop. The boy in the orange sweater met his eyes defiantly.

"The woman across the street," Tom said, "says she saw you pull the false alarm."

"Man," the boy said, shaking his head, "that ain't nothin' but an old shithead woman. I didn't pull no false alarm."

47

Tom reached down and grabbed the boy's arm gently, as if to lead him, and said, "Why don't we just go over and talk about it?"

The boy pulled his arm back sharply, saying, "ain't goin' nowheres, man." He swung his fist up in a right cross, connecting solidly into Tom's left ear.

The impact of the blow, coupled with the sting of the burn, sent a surge of pain through Tom's head. He staggered backward. The doors of the chief's car opened, and the other firemen jumped from the apparatus.

The boy stood up as Tom recovered, and as his two friends stepped away he threw another right. This time Tom caught the moving arm by the wrist and in one jerking, twisting motion pulled it high behind the boy's back. The boy's voice convulsed with pain. "Okay, man, okay. Easy, please."

The firemen stood around Tom and the boy.

Walter Smith, forgetting that Ernie Edwards was standing behind him, grabbed the boy's other arm and said, "Smart-assed nigger."

Smith twisted the arm as high as he could, hoping that the bone would break. Then he noticed Ernie Edwards standing next to him.

"Leave him go, Smith," Tom said, annoyed at the interference.

Smith released his grip, conscious of Edwards' sour scrutiny.

One of the men said, "The lieutenant called for police assistance."

Tom noticed that a crowd of people had gathered around the stoop, looking over the shoulders of the firemen. Crowds in Harlem mean incidents, and Tom did not want to make this incident any bigger. "Let's move across the street," he said to the boy, "and don't give me any trouble or I'll break your arm."

"I'm not gonna give ya any trouble, mista," the still-shaking boy said. "I didn't do nothin'."

"We'll see," Tom said, crossing the street, still encircled by the firemen.

Chief Gelman approached with a questioning look.

"Where'd that woman go?" Tom asked, looking about. "She'll have to be a witness."

He walked the boy to the entrance of the laundrymat and looked inside. The store was empty. He looked up and down the street. The woman was gone.

"Wait until the cops come," Chief Gelman said, "and we'll have him arrested for assault."

The boy, his hand still high behind his back, turned to Tom, saying, "I'm sorry I took a swing, man. I really am. I'm sorry."

Tom was surprised he said that.

Tom looked at the chief and said, "Is it up to me?"

The chief nodded his head in the affirmative and walked away.

Tom let go of the boy's wrist but continued to hold him by the shoulder. He whispered, just loud enough for the boy to hear, "I want you to know that it's only because of me that you aren't going to spend the night in jail. Now, don't break the firemen's balls with false alarms no more, understand?"

The boy held his head down dejectedly and said, "Yeah."

The firemen made room as he walked through them, his eyes focused on his shoe tips.

In the firehouse Dominic Gallo quietly asked Tom why he had let the boy go, home free. Tom replied, "He was only proving something to his friends, and I didn't think he should be locked up for that. We do it ourselves, sometimes."

Dominic was puzzled, but before he could ask what Tom meant the voice alarm sounded: "ENGINE 51, LADDER 22, BATTALION 10. RESPOND TO BOX 1299, LENOX AVENUE AND 119TH STREET."

It was another false alarm, and Dominic forgot the question.

Later there were two more false alarms, a fire in an abandoned car, and two fires in backyards where the garbage was piled three and four feet deep, in the alleyways the firemen called the Flying Missile Sanitation Service.

The smudge-faced men sat around the kitchen table, waiting for the next false alarm that they felt was sure to come when the schools let out at three o'clock.

Gallo was saying, "We ought to have a big turnout at the union meeting tonight. All you married guys better call home to see if your old ladies will let you out for a few hours."

He was thirty-four years old, and although his mother, with whom he lived in a North Bronx apartment, was constantly chiding him and thought he was a failure for not taking any one girl seriously, Dominic was a chest beater about being single. He loved the life of a bachelor, the life of a bachelor fireman, and often teased the other men about being chained to a wife, a house, a family. "Life is too short," he would say, "to give this sweetheart up to just one woman."

"Now don't be bitter, Dominic," Tom said, "just because there is not a woman in the world who would marry you and because you never get kissed more than once a month."

"Once a month," Dominic shouted, acting astounded. "You'd be sick with jealousy if you only knew, and I'd never get married even if I had a woman who shit fifty-pound gold bars. Not me, I'm not a sucker, I'm a sweetheart."

The laughter that filled the kitchen was stopped suddenly by the announcement over the voice alarm of a second-alarm fire on 105th Street and Second Avenue.

Tom said, "We probably go on the third alarm," and then the voice alarm screeched: "LADDER 22, YOU ARE BEING SPECIAL-CALLED TO FILL OUT THE ASSIGNMENT."

The housewatchman's voice filled the firehouse. "Get out, 22. Ladder 22 goes."

Tom sat and listened to Ladder 22's siren fade down Fifth Avenue, silently hoping for the third alarm, which would take Engine 51 to the fire. His hope was cut short as the loudspeaker boomed: "ENGINE 51, BATTALION 10. RESPOND TO A FIRE AT 22 EAST 124TH STREET, ON THE FOURTH FLOOR."

The pumper raced up Fifth Avenue against the traffic

50

and turned east on 124th Street. As Tom looked up at the horror of the burning building in the middle of the block, he made a quick prayer that a ladder company would come in fast. Christ, he thought, if only they hadn't special-called 22 to the second alarm.

The fire was on the fourth floor of a five-story building. There was smoke pouring from the window frame at the fire escape and from the window beyond the fire escape to the right. At the third window to the right were a man and a woman and three children screaming frantically.

As the pumper stopped in front of the building, Tom saw the fire crash through the fire escape window and the window to the right, rolling in great waves up the side of the building. As the fire heightened the day sky above was made night with smoke.

Tom pulled the heavy, two-hundred-and-fifty-foot roof rope from a side compartment as the lieutenant ordered a hoseline stretched.

"I need one man," Tom yelled, "with a safety belt and a hose roller."

Walter Smith ran to another compartment and grabbed the safety belt and hose roller.

"Do the best you can," the lieutenant said to Tom. The men ran in different directions, the lieutenant into the fire building and Tom and Smith into the adjoining building to the left.

Tom ran the five flights of stairs two by two, and Smith was close behind. On the roof they crossed over to the fire building and to the front parapet.

Tom looked over the wall of the tile-covered parapet and called to the trapped family two floors below, "Just hold on. We're going to get you, but you have to kick the windows and the window frame out."

Smith put the hose roller over the parapet and secured the attached rope to a vent pipe sticking through the roof, as Tom unrolled a hundred feet of the roof rope, made a bowline on a bight knot at the rope's end, and stepped into the two thigh-sized circles of rope. Smith then buckled the

51

safety belt around his waist. Tom made a large half hitch and put the circle of rope under his arms and around his back and chest, making his rescue harness secure.

Tom heard the window below being broken and felt relieved.

Smith took the loose rope and made three turns around the heavy steel clip connected to the safety belt, pulling in the slack until there were four feet of rope between the steel clip at his waist and the knot at Tom's chest.

Tom straddled the parapet and prepared to go over the side, the rope between him and Smith snug in the confines of the hose roller. He looked at the hose roller for a split second, thinking that the rope would slide easily over its roller pin, that there would be no friction to wear the rope. Then he realized that once his weight was on the rope, the rope would be inextricably bound to the roller. Smith would not be able to lift it off.

He quickly took the rope in his hand and kicked the hose roller from the parapet, saying to Smith, "We need more room to work. Maybe I can take them to the floor below, one by one, and then climb back up the rope. Just maybe. Listen to me carefully, because you have to control the rope perfectly. There may not be time to get more than one or two."

Tom laid the rope on the smooth surface of the parapet tile and swung his body over the side of the building. The fire was climbing at his left, reaching almost to the rooftop. Walter Smith pressed the steel clip against the parapet wall and drew in the slack.

"Okay," Tom said loudly.

Because of his rigid position against the parapet wall, Smith could not look down at Tom. He yelled at the fingers clutching the edge, "Okay, I got it." The fingers slid off the parapet, and Smith felt the pressure of Tom's weight on the rope.

"Lower easily," Tom yelled up, and Smith loosened his grip on the rope, carefully judging the slide and controlling the speed by hand pressure. Tom began the descent in jerks, slowly, and as Smith got the feel of it Tom went down in one

52

easy motion, kicking his way out from the window ledge on the fifth floor.

"Okay, okay," Tom screamed as he reached the fourth floor window and the huddled family choking in the smoke. Tears were flowing from their red eyes, and their bodies were shaking from fright. The rope stopped perfectly as Tom's footing became solid on the window sill.

"Thank God. Oh, thank God," the man cried. His wife and children were clutching at him as at a raft in a storm-swept sea.

"Just be calm," Tom said, seeing the ember glow of the interior bedroom door and realizing that the fire would break through at any moment. "Give me one of the children," Tom said. The children cried and cowered behind their father. The father picked the smallest one up in his arms, a girl, but the child screamed and kicked furiously.

"Give me the mother," Tom said, trying to win the confidence of the children. The father pushed the mother forward, and she climbed up onto the window sill, her face frozen and streaked with her tears.

Tom yelled again up at the roof, "Hey, Smith, can you hear me?"

"Yeah," came Smith's voice clearly.

"We can't go down; there isn't enough time. I'm going to try to swing over to the fire escape. It's about eight feet. Do you understand?"

"Yeah," came the reply, "toward the fire escape."

"Let out some slack, and move over about four feet to give me a pendulum point."

Smith moved four feet and again pressed the steel clip against the parapet wall, pulling up the slack.

The angle of the rope from Tom to Smith was now dangerously close to the fire, which was lapping out of the window between Tom and the fire escape.

"We don't have much time," Tom said to the woman. "Hold my neck tightly, and put your feet around me. If we miss the fire escape on the first try, we'll make it on the second. Just don't let go. Do you understand that?"

53

The woman nodded and hugged Tom's neck. "That's it," Tom said, "now jump up and hold me with your legs."

The woman jumped up, and Tom almost lost his grip on the window casing as her body smashed against his. He looked at the fire coming from the window he had to pass, and from the fire escape window. The wind was in his favor, blowing the fire against the building and up, but he knew that if it changed course the fire could reach out and engulf him.

He put one arm around the woman, studying the fencing of the fire escape as he said "Jesus, Mary, and Joseph," and kicked off the sill with all the power of his legs. He felt a blast of heat as he passed the first burning room, and his concentration was interrupted for a brief moment. Then suddenly he was at the fire escape, and his foot went through the fence opening. He put his hand out and grabbed for the top rail as his other foot hit the landing of the fire escape. They hit the fire escape hard with the momentum of the swing, but they were there.

Tom held fast to the fire escape as the woman climbed over the rail and started down the iron steps. He turned to push off again and realized that the angle of his position on the fire escape had put the rope directly above the fire. The rope had been singed. He swung out, thinking, Christ, don't let it burn through.

He landed on the window sill, grabbing the father's arm for balance, and looked up at the rope. It was blackened but not yet burning.

"Give me one of the children," Tom said, louder than he had wanted.

The father pushed the oldest boy forward, but the boy said, "No, take her first, my sister."

The small girl did not scream this time but held tightly to Tom's neck. Her feet swung wildly in the air as they sailed to the fire escape, but Tom held her against his chest with all his strength. He lifted her over the railing and looked up at the rope.

It was burning.

He pushed off again and returned with the second child, a boy younger than the oldest child.

He swung back to the window sill and said to the oldest boy, "I want to take your father first. You're lighter, and I want you last. Okay?"

The smoke was very thick, and the boy was coughing. Tom didn't wait for an answer but helped the father to the sill. As he kicked off, he looked up at the burning rope, half expecting it to sever.

He left the father at the fire escape rail and swung for the boy. "Quickly, quickly," he said as he pushed off with the oldest son. In midair he said to himself, God help us.

Tom grabbed the railing and stood on the outside of the fire escape with the boy in his arm. He made no movement but held the railing as hard as he could. He closed his eyes and opened them only when the boy said, "Put me down, mister, please."

He lifted the boy over the railing and then felt a tug from beneath him. He looked down and saw the rope end, still burning, dangling in the air two floors below. He looked up at the roof and made contact with Smith's anxious eyes. They both smiled.

As he climbed down the fire escape he saw the ladder truck below. The aerial ladder was being raised to the fire, and he heard the water hitting the walls inside the burning apartment.

The firemen from the specially called ladder company were on the fire escape, helping the children down the drop ladder to the street. Tom looked and saw the fire darken, the flames turning to smoke as the men of his company pushed into the rooms with the streaming hose.

As Tom reached the street he saw the woman's legs buckle, but a fireman grabbed her before she fell to the ground in a faint and placed her gently on the sidewalk. Her children ran to her, crying fearfully, "Momma, Momma."

The husband, a middle-aged man, walked to Tom and

grabbed his hand, saying, "I don't know what to say to you. I guess nothin' can be said. But I thank you, mister, I thank you."

Tom looked into the man's large, red-veined eyes and watched as his grainy black face broke into a wide smile. He shook the man's callous-hard hand, replying, "It's all right, thank God."

Walter Smith came out of the adjoining building, carrying the rescue equipment. He walked to the pumper, where he dropped the rope and hose roller, and sat on the back step of the rig.

Tom walked to him and gave him a small slap on the side of the arm. "Nice job," he said, "terrific." And whatever differences they might have had were forgotten, for the fire had swept them clean.

Late that afternoon the department phone rang. The housewatchman picked it up, listened for a moment, and then called through the firehouse, "Hey, Ritter, it's for you."

"Fireman Ritter speaking, sir," Tom said into the crud-covered mouthpiece.

"Fireman Ritter, my ass," the voice came through. "This is Fireman Ritter at this end."

Tom smiled, saying, "How you doing, Jerry?"

"Fine, Tom," his brother said. "I had a hell of a day. I'll tell you about it when I see you. You're going to the union meeting tonight, right?"

"I was going to, but I'm tired, really beat."

"C'mon, being tired is the price you pay for a reckless life. I'll meet you at the diner next to Union Hall at six-thirty. Right?"

"Right, six-thirty," Tom said.

He put down the phone and laughed to himself, thinking, yeah, the price.

3

ON ONE SIDE OF UNION HALL ON WEST 34th Street was a diner, and on the other side was a bar called McMahon's. At six-thirty Jerry Ritter was in the diner finishing a hamburger when his brother entered with Dominic. Dominic spoke first.

"Are ya finished?"

"Just about," Jerry answered.

"Good," Dom said. "Let's go next door for a drink before the meeting."

Jerry called for the waitress, who was standing with nothing to do, the place being more than half empty. He asked for the check.

McMahon's was crowded three deep at the bar, all firemen waiting for the Union Hall doors to open at seven o'clock. The firemen were clustered by boroughs along the bar—on the near end the men from Brooklyn, in the middle the men from Manhattan, and on the far end the men from the Bronx, Queens, and Staten Island.

"Hey, there's Dom Gallo," a man yelled as Dom and the Ritter brothers pushed their way to the center of the bar.

"Is that Dom Gallo, the hero fireman from Harlem?" another asked laughingly.

"That's him," came an answer.

"Well you hold him while I bite him on the ass."

Dominic turned to Jerry, saying, "I'm always surrounded by ballbreakers. The whole world is filled with ballbreakers." The crowd of firemen continued in their laughter.

Dominic held a ten-dollar bill across the bar, yelling above the noise to the bartender, "Give us three beers, will you?"

Jerry put his hand on Dom's shoulder and said, "I'll just have a coke, on the rocks."

"You're kidding me," Dom said. He turned to Tom. "Hey, Tom, I thought this brother of yours was a sweetheart, but he comes into a joint and orders a coke. He can't be your brother."

"Buy the man a coke, Dominic," Tom said, "and stop acting like the rest of the ballbreakers around here."

"One coke and two beers," Dom said to the bartender, adding, with a wink of the eye, "The coke's for the kid here. He's a veteran, got shot between the legs in Vietnam, and his pisser don't work good anymore." As the bartender made the drinks Dominic asked Jerry, "Did you ever get shot at over there?"

"It's a boring story, Dominic, and a long time ago. But I never got hit."

"Thank Christ for that. Did you hear what that brother of yours did today?"

Jerry looked at Tom and smiled. "No, I didn't hear."

"You didn't hear? I thought the whole job knew about it, but I guess they don't talk much about Harlem downtown. Anyway, he got five people out on a roof rope, on the outside of the building, swinging like a monkey from the window sill

58

to the fire escape, back and forth, five times, like a goddam monkey. It'll be in the papers tonight probably."

Jerry thought of his own rescue attempt at the theater. If David Allen had been alive, it would have certainly been a class-three rescue, made at significant personal risk, or even a class-two at great personal risk, depending on the opinions of the chiefs assigned to study the facts and make the award. Roof rope rescues were rare enough when even one person was involved. But five!

Jerry grabbed for Tom's hand and shook it. "Terrific," he said. "Congratulations. Man, five people on a roof rope. That's gotta be a class-one rescue. Did they write you up?"

"Did they write him up?" Dominic interrupted. "They're still up there writing, the report is so big."

"Beautiful."

They talked for a while about the Harlem fire. Then Jerry told them about the producer sleeping in the basement of the theater. It was too bad, they agreed, that the man was dead, for it too would have been a good rescue.

At seven o'clock the bar began to empty. Dominic had met a friend he had not seen in several years and was sitting in a booth talking about old times.

Tom and Jerry walked to the booth, and Tom said, "Let's go, Dominic, the meeting is gonna start."

"Listen, this is the guy who broke me in up in Harlem. I want you to meet him. Pete Flanagan, this is Jerry and Tom Ritter."

They talked for a few minutes, and then Jerry said, "Well, it's getting late. Let's go."

"I think Pete and I will just stay here and wait for you guys," Dom said. "If you've been to one union meeting you've been to 'em all, and it's all a lot of bullshit and hollerin' anyway."

"Okay," Tom said, "we'll meet you here after the meeting."

As they walked out of the bar, Tom said to Jerry, "If it's a long meeting, we'll have to carry him outta here."

The sergeant-at-arms was at the door of Union Hall, saying, "Badges, badges, let's see your badges."

"Ah, dammit," Tom said, "I left my badge in my locker."

"I guess I'll have to vouch for you," Jerry said.

The sergeant-at-arms stopped Tom, saying, "I gotta see your badge, pal."

Jerry shoved his own badge out and said, "Listen, I know this man personally. He's a firefighter."

"All right." The sergeant-at-arms shrugged. "As long as he's not from the newspapers."

"He's not heavy, father," Jerry said, smiling. "He's my brother."

Tom put his arm around his brother, and they walked down the center aisle looking for two vacant seats.

They sat in the first two empty seats they came to, just off the center aisle and next to a floor microphone placed for the use of the speakers.

Jerry looked around. On the walls on either side of the hall were frescoes, allegorical images painted in the heavy, muscled style of the 1930s. Jerry studied one, trying to discern its meaning. It showed a black man encumbered by broken chains, carrying on his shoulders a white man who was holding high a steel girder. Lettered across the bottom were the words "FOR THE FURTHERANCE OF INDUSTRY, RELIGION, AND THE ENJOYMENT OF LEISURE." That was America in a nutshell, Jerry thought, an America of long ago. It's for leisure now.

Around him, sitting and standing, were men of different styles, brought together by the badge. There were men in plaid flannel shirts and khaki pants, in cotton turtlenecks and suede bellbottoms, in dungarees. There was one in a pink sports jacket. Before him were heads, rows of long straight hair, crewcuts, Afros, heavy curls, and tonsures. And there were bald heads, clean and reflective.

On the stage in front were three rows of faded red velvet curtains, soaked with the cigarette and cigar smoke of thousands of meetings, a long table for the executive board, and a podium for the local president. On the side was an American flag standing upright.

It was a dingy hall, unpainted and uncared for, except for a swept floor. It cost the local eight hundred dollars in rental for the night.

Jerry looked to the rear of the hall. Above him were two balcony tiers, packed with working men from Flatbush, Bensonhurst, Castle Hill, Hunt's Point, Astoria, Woodside, Hell's Kitchen, the Bowery. The greatness, strength, pride, ambiguity, frustration, and anger of the city could be found in the balcony faces. There were a few scrawled placards waving about. One of them said "SCREW THE MAYOR." Jerry heard the snap of beer can tops as the men began drinking. He listened to their words.

"I had the double goin' in but the old bitch broke on the turn."

"Hey, Joey, you see Pruzzoto?"

"I'm gonna meet her again tonight. I told the old lady I was stayin' at your house."

"I sent him down for a utility rope and the dope brings back a roof rope, all hundred and fifty feet of it."

"At least he's outta intensive care, but he won't be back on the job for a while."

"Jesus, wouldn't it be a lot of laughs if the balcony collapsed."

Men were greeting one another, men who had been neighborhood friends, or probationary school classmates, or long-separated co-workers. They were genuinely pleased and happy for the reunion.

Suddenly there was loud, sustained booing, a small symphony of Bronx cheers. The executive board of the local appeared on the stage.

Nine men walked to the seats behind the long table and sat down. The union attorney, a small, rotund, pimply faced man, sat on the side of the long table. The president of the local, Angelo Sorvino, went to the podium and nervously adjusted the microphone, shaking his head in disgust at the boos and catcalls from his membership.

"All right," the president yelled above the jeering, "let's settle down. We got a lot of business to go over, and let's try

61

to get it over with as soon as possible." The crowd still roared above the amplified voice.

A man from the audience called out, "The hell with settlin' down; let's settle the goddam contract."

Sorvino ignored the remark, but he noticed that it came from one of the younger men. A man would not have spoken to him with such disrespect eight years before, when he first became president of the local. The men were different then. They understood the power and the importance of a union leader, that the president was their only representative, that they had to trust and support him in all things. He was the only representative they had to stand up to the mayor and to the fire commissioner.

The local president yelled into the microphone, "Please stand for the Pledge of Allegiance."

The hall became instantly quiet, and the men recited the Pledge, facing the flag on the stage, their hands over their hearts.

Angelo Sorvino recalled the night, nine years earlier, when he first made his bid for power in the United Firefighters of New York. Patrick O'Halloran, who was then the president of the local, was screaming above the incessant chant of the firemen who sat before him in Union Hall. The words vibrated through the hall in perfect unison, much as the cry of "Hold that line" shakes a football stadium. "Shove it up the mayor's ass. Shove it up the . . ." The words were like a heavy sweat being poured over O'Halloran in the clouded hall. He was shaken, but he knew that he could hold his men, convince them that the contract in question was in their best interest. It would be a long meeting, hot and angry, but he would talk them into it as he had done in years past.

O'Halloran choked the microphone with one hand and hammered the gavel with the other while he yelled with all his strength. "This is a record-making contract with decent money and benefits, and after negotiating and renegotiating we, your executive board, know that this is the absolute best we can do. You must accept this contract that we have labored for. All the men on the executive board, all the men who you voted in office to represent you, know that this is the best contract we have ever been offered. This executive board is unanimous in urging you to accept . . ."

Sorvino, a first-term borough representative from Manhattan, a hardly known newcomer to the union ranks, saw an opportunity that he knew would come only once in his lifetime. He jumped across the long table, screaming, "No, no, no."

The firemen stopped their chant as they saw Sorvino grab for the microphone in front of O'Halloran. O'Halloran was a big man and easily shoved Sorvino aside, but the smaller man was persistent and tried again and again for the microphone. The men started yelling, "Let him speak. Let the man have his say." But O'Halloran knew that he would lose control, or at least the opportunity for control, if he yielded the microphone. Sorvino came at him full force with his shoulder, but O'Halloran turned from the microphone and grabbed Sorvino by his collar, saying, "You little Guinea worm," and brought his fist hard into Sorvino's mouth.

Sorvino fell to the floor and saw the men in the front rows run to the stage, some trying to climb up to the platform as the rest of the executive board pushed them back down. His front tooth was knocked out and he tasted the blood inside his mouth, but his cheeks widened into a small smile.

The local president walked to the side of the stage, being calmed by the attorney, and Sorvino got up and took the microphone in his hand. He was trembling, but he was the master of his moment.

It was a moment Sorvino had worked hard for, one he truly believed he deserved. When he first entered the Fire Department, he studied hard for the promotional examination for lieutenant. He joined a study group in his East 14th Street firehouse, made study flashcards, plowed through the regulations and the reams of building codes, department circulars, guides for procedure, hydrolic and chemical textbooks, training and safety bulletins. He went to study meetings twice a week, convinced that he would work himself up

63

through the ranks so that he would one day be the chief of department. He was like many small-statured men; he wanted to get to the top, wanted to be the boss. But there was one complication in Sorvino's plan: he could not remember anything he read. The facts seemed unrelated to him, isolated, and there were thousands of them. Even the other firemen in his study group told him he had little chance of passing the examination. He realized his failure one evening in the cellar of the firehouse when one of the men said, "Why don't you pack it in, Angelo?" His flashcards seemed trivial, irrelevant, and he did not know the answers to any of the other flashcards in the study group. Another man said, "You're not helping the group any, Angelo," and Sorvino left the cellar, throwing the flashcards he had worked so hard on in the furnace on the way out. As he was leaving the firehouse, he noticed on the bulletin board a union meeting notice for later that night, and although he rarely thought about the union he decided to go, for he needed something to take his mind from the envy he began feeling toward the men in the study group.

The meeting was held in a banquet room of a midtown hotel. It was a regular monthly meeting attended by only the most active of unionist firemen, and there were no more than two hundred in the room. Sorvino sat in one of the back rows of folding chairs and watched Patrick O'Halloran run the meeting. It was then that his future exploded before him, like an idea enclosed in a bubble in a cartoon. What difference was there, he asked himself, between me and the union president? There was a great difference between him and the chief of department—namely, the ranks of lieutenant, captain, battalion chief, deputy chief, deputy assistant chief, and assistant chief. But the president of the union was a fireman, and except for the fact of his election, there was no difference between them. What could he know that I don't? Sorvino asked himself. He's a high school graduate; so am I. He never went to college to be a union president. Never even broke his balls in a study group. All he knows is how to talk, and for that he gets a fireman's salary without having to go to any firehouse, another salary equal to a fireman's from the union, and an expense account. Twice the money I make, and an expense account, all for knowing how to talk. Jesus, I know how to talk.

From that time on Sorvino never missed a union meeting, and he was seen at each meeting, pad and pencil in hand, standing at the microphone, spewing abuses across the floor to the union president. After each meeting he went to the firehouses in Manhattan, talking to the men in the kitchens, convincing them that the union was not doing all it should, offering suggestions, forcing them to remember his name and his face. He worked untiringly, using all his free time to talk to the firemen, sacrificing a normal family life, going to all the dinners of the department's cultural societies, to the lunches, to the awards ceremonies. He worked hard, and now the moment was his.

"Brothers, please, we must have order," he said directly to the few firemen who had made their way to the stage, and who were pushing and arguing with the executive board. The men took notice and jumped from the stage, and the hall was quiet, waiting to hear from the challenger.

"Brothers," Sorvino said, the blood now spilling over his chin and onto his shirt, "that is a punch I will gladly take for the good of this membership, and more importantly for the good of the wives and children of this membership who aren't getting out of life what is justly theirs."

The men went wild with cheering and approval, clapping, whistling, shouting. Sorvino let them go for a minute, and then held his arms high so that the hall quieted again.

"I only have one thing to say, and that is that Angelo Sorvino does not think that this contract should be accepted." The crowd again started to yell, but Sorvino raised his arms once more. "In good conscience, we must do better than this for the firefighters of this city who suffer more and give more than anyone else."

Sorvino returned to his seat at the long table, glowing in the cheers of the membership.

O'Halloran was defeated, he understood that, and he

65

walked to the podium wondering if he should tell his men that just hours before Angelo Sorvino had not objected to the contract in executive session. The cheers, Sorvino's cheers, turned to curses as O'Halloran stood before the microphone, and he knew that the membership would not believe anything he said. Not then, anyway.

"We must take one vote," the local president said, "and then the meeting will be adjourned. All those in favor of acceptance of the contract before us say 'aye.' "

Perhaps fifty voices or even a hundred voices responded. It made no difference to O'Halloran.

"All those opposed signify by saying 'nay.' "

The membership returned a resounding "nay," and the cheering burst again through the hall.

O'Halloran hit the gavel once, ritualistically, saying, "So be it, motion defeated. The meeting is adjourned."

Most of the men left the hall quickly, but fifty or so rushed for the stage to congratulate Angelo Sorvino.

After two weeks another contract was proposed. It offered the same total value as the contract that had been defeated, but the fringe benefits were diminished and the money taken from that allocation was switched to the base salary increase, so that there was more money up front and less behind.

Sorvino spoke in favor of the contract, and it was accepted by the membership.

Nine months later Sorvino was elected president of the local.

After the Pledge, the hall again became loud with cursing and jeering. Jerry Ritter was on his feet, cursing, while his brother Tom remained seated, watching pensively the routine that he had been through so many times before. It seemed somehow different to Tom this night.

Sorvino stood before the podium, his arms in the air, but the noise would not diminish. He grasped the microphone with one hand and reached below him to the volume control, which had recently been installed at the request of some

66

other union. He turned the control as high as it would go so that there was a deafening squeal. He lowered it a little, so that the squeal was minimized, and spoke into the microphone. His voice was thunderous and carried above the combined voices of the members.

"If we don't do this in an orderly way we'll get nothing done, and we might just as well adjourn and go home. So quiet down now, and let's get to business."

The hall became still, except for a few calls from the balcony.

Sorvino turned down the amplifier to a normal level and went right into union business.

"This is the regular monthly meeting for the month of September. The executive board members present are the borough representatives from Manhattan, Brooklyn, the Bronx, Queens, and Staten Island, the sergeant-at-arms, the treasurer, the financial and recording secretary, and the president. The vice-president is in Albany talking to members of the legislature about the lung bill we have pending there."

"You mean in Albany getting drunk," someone shouted.

Sorvino ignored the remark. "The attorney is present and the union secretary. Let the record show that a roll call of the officers has been taken.

"I would like now a motion to suspend the reading of the minutes of last month's meeting, and I do this so that we can get right into the president's report."

"I make a motion," a man from the floor said.

"Is the motion seconded?"

"I second the motion," said another.

"All in favor?"

There was a conditioned, almost bored response by the membership. "Aye."

"Opposed?"

A few "nays" were heard, mostly from men who responded negatively to everything.

"The motion is passed. I call now for any amendments to the constitution to be submitted."

A man sitting across from the Ritters ran down the aisle and handed a piece of paper to Sorvino, who then handed it to the recording secretary. It was an amendment that would be read at two future meetings and voted on at a third. The man returned to his seat, and Jerry leaned into the aisle, saying, "Hey, pal, what's the amendment?"

The man looked over at Jerry, pleased that someone had taken notice of him. "It's a no-strike clause," he said. "I want a no-strike clause in the constitution."

"I see," Jerry said, leaning back into his seat. He became momentarily troubled, for he had not thought about a strike before, at least not in such a hostile setting. There had been talk of a strike at the last two contract meetings, but nothing had come of it. Union negotiations were long and drawn out, but they always got settled eventually.

Jerry's thoughts were broken by a sustained booing as the local president said, "We move now to the president's report."

Sorvino waited until the booing subsided and said, "I would appreciate it if I could get through this without interruptions. It's important, and our futures depend on it."

"You mean yours and the executive board's," a man cried out, and the hall filled with clapping and whistling.

Sorvino turned up the amplifier again, saying, "I know exactly what you men want, and I want it too." His face became tense, and the veins in his neck rose as he said, "And I'm gonna get it for us."

The membership cheered him, and Sorvino smiled to himself, knowing that he had said the right thing. "Now let's get down to business. The city has not been negotiating with us in good faith." Realizing the sound was almost deafening, he reached down and lowered the amplifier again.

"We have been trying to get a meeting with Edward Jefferson, the mayor's administrative aide, for the last month, but he won't meet with us. Instead, he sends over a few flunkies from the Bureau of the Budget who tell us that our demands are too much, and that we are negotiating not just for the firefighters of this city but for the civil service force

68

of three hundred and fifty thousand people, because every city worker in town is looking to see what the firefighters get. Well, I don't care about what the other workers get. I just care about the eleven thousand, three hundred men of the United Firefighters of New York." The men rose to their feet in applause, and Sorvino relaxed, satisfied that he was in control again.

"The mayor and Edward Jefferson know what we want. They have our demands in front of them, demands that are fundamentally not out of line, calling for an increase of wages to catch up with the inflation of the last two years, an adjustment in our retirement system so that we can retire at half pay in eighteen years instead of twenty, and an increase in our benefits system so that we can get a better medical plan. While I'm at it, I might tell you that not long ago my wife took my son to the doctor—nothing serious; he had a chest cold. We paid the bill, which was fifteen dollars, and just today we got payment from the group hospital plan—a lousy check for five dollars. They are paying at rates of fifteen years ago, and you, the men who know what it is to earn a dollar in this city, deserve better than that." Sorvino smiled as the men applauded. It was a nice touch, he thought, bringing his wife and son into it. The men can relate to that.

"We are also calling for a reduction in the work week to thirty-two hours, hazard pay of twenty percent above base pay, premium pay for weekends, an annuity fund of three dollars a day, and longevity awards of five hundred dollars at five, ten, fifteen, and twenty years of service. Now, you all oughta know the full list of our demands—the individual company delegates have a list of them—and you oughta know what the contract negotiations process is. We are not reaching for the stars in our demands, but we know that we will have to bargain some demands away and take a strong position on others. That is up to us in negotiations, but we can't negotiate a contract with flunkies from the Bureau of the Budget. We have to meet with Edward Jefferson, because he is the only one who can act in the mayor's behalf. And he *is* going to meet with us soon. I promise you that."

Jerry was on his feet cheering with the rest of the membership, but Tom was impassive, remaining in his seat.

"It seems," Sorvino continued, "that the administration of this city reacts only to crisis. The poverty groups have proved that for us. When there's a threat that they might be done out of funds, all they gotta do is get a group of people marching around City Hall and talk about the explosiveness of the ghettos. They get front page in the newspapers, ten minutes on the television news, and a meeting with Edward Jefferson, who gives them everything but his jockstrap."

Sorvino started to pound the podium with his fist, saying, *"It is time now that the firefighters of this city create a crisis."*

The members heard what they wanted to hear and roared their approval. Sorvino held up his arms for quiet, and the men responded. "We have been without a contract for over three months now," Sorvino said as the men returned to their seats, "and if we don't progress, and by that I mean if we don't meet with Edward Jefferson and come to some agreement, in good faith, in three weeks by Monday, October 1, then we will have the biggest job action this department has ever seen."

Sorvino began to shout, bringing the men to their feet again. "There will be no work done by firefighters except actual fire duty. There will be no cleaning of firehouses, no maintenance of equipment, no clerical work, no inspection duty, no housewatch duty, no abiding by the book of rules and regulations, no company drills, no respect for the traditions of this department. We will not wear our uniforms. We will throw our dedication out the goddam window, because it evidently doesn't work for us. We will now put the city on notice that if we don't have meaningful negotiations by Monday, October 1, they will have the most undedicated group of workers they have ever seen." Sorvino sipped a glass of water, then said, "The president's report is now concluded. The floor is open on the question of the president's report."

Men rushed from all directions to the floor microphone in the aisle next to Jerry Ritter.

"Wait a minute," Sorvino yelled. "Every man has a right

to speak and will be heard, but there will be no lineup at the microphone. Each man will be heard after being recognized by the chair. Just raise your hands."

The sergeant-at-arms stood by the floor microphone and waved the men back to their seats.

Sorvino pointed to a man in the front row, saying, "This man here is recognized. State your name and company please."

The man ran up the center aisle, stepped in front of the microphone, and said, "Fireman Segal, Engine Company 287, and I have only one thing to say regarding the president's report. That is that it sounds like a report from a paper tiger. You know as well as we all do that this city doesn't care if we don't wash the windows or shine the poles in the firehouses, or any of that stuff. No one cares if we salute the officers, wear uniforms, or go on inspections. The city cares about one thing and one thing only, and that is about fires, and whether they're being put out or not. On the one hand you talk about our dedication working against us, and on the other you give us a job action that includes stopping everything but the dedication we have to going to work and putting the fires out. This ain't showing the city we mean business."

The firemen rose to their feet amid whistling and cheering, and the noise of the crowd forced the man to pause for a few moments.

Sorvino grew anxious, realizing the man before him had to be stopped before he turned the membership against the job action. He turned the volume knob up so that his voice bounced through the auditorium.

"Listen, brother," Sorvino said, "you are out of order. You've been making statements and not asking questions, and if you got a question we'll answer it. Otherwise we go to the next speaker."

"I am not out of order, Mr. Chairman," the man quickly returned, "and it says nowhere in Atwood's *Book of Parliamentary Procedure* that a question has to be asked. I'm speaking on the president's report. That's all I have to stay

71

with. But if you want a question, I'll ask one."

Sorvino turned down the volume, saying, "Ask your question, brother."

"The question is this. Why don't you call for a decent job action that takes the men outta work, so that the fires don't get put out so quick? Why don't we have a sickout? A sickout is the only thing that will shake this city up."

Tom sat back in his seat, watching his brother and the others applaud.

Sorvino took another sip of water and said, "This executive board will call a sickout when and if we think it is in the best interests of the membership."

The men began to boo, but Sorvino quickly recognized another speaker from the floor, the man sitting next to the microphone, across from Jerry.

"Fireman John Henderson of Ladder 33," the man said. He waited for the booing to subside. Sorvino hammered the podium for attention.

"I want to get away from this talk of a sickout, or even a job action," the man said.

The men started to jeer him.

"Get off the floor."

"Put your paper in an' get outta the job."

"Are you with us or against us?"

"You're a hardon."

Sorvino pounded the podium with his palm, saying, "Wait a minute. This man has the right to be heard. Now give him a chance."

"I don't understand," the man continued, "why we are planning something that will make the people of the city turn against us at the very time that we need their support. The problem is that the people don't know who we are and what we do. We have lousy PR."

"You're right on that," Jerry Ritter yelled to him, the membership approving.

"Why don't we do something smart for a change, like taking full-page ads in the *News,* the *Post* and the *Times,*

72

telling the people who we are and what we want? The cops took an ad last week, an open letter to the people of New York from the president of the Police Brotherhood Association, saying that the cops have a more difficult job than the firemen and sanitation workers—can you imagine that crook lumping us in with the garbagemen? If the cops lose three men a year in the line of duty they're lucky, and that's in a force of over thirty thousand men, while we lose eight or ten men a year in a force of eleven thousand. And they got a more difficult job, right? Well, the people of this city think they do. The cops say they deserve more than us because they have to use psychology in dealing with people on the street. What a crock of crap that is. I'd rather talk a fire out every time if I could. There is no comparison to be made in the two jobs, they're so different. Their problems are not like ours, except maybe in a riot situation, and even then we get the brown end of the stick. Well, let's get smart and take ads like the cops did, telling the people what we do in a fire, and how many serious building fires we have each day in this city. About 150 every single day. Get the people behind us. Ask the people to pressure City Hall into meeting with us."

Sorvino smiled, saying, "That's a good idea, brother. The executive board will certainly take that into consideration. I might tell you also that the Central Labor Committee of New York City has called the president of the Police Brotherhood Association on the carpet because of that advertisement. Labor has got to stick together, and it was very wrong of him to demean any other group of workers—even garbagemen."

"That's all well and good," the man said, "but I don't want you to just take it into consideration. I want to do it. I would like to make a motion to that effect."

"A motion is not in order at this time," Sorvino said. "The president's report is before the membership. You'll have to wait until we get to new business."

The man walked away from the microphone dejected; then he came back and leaned into it, saying, "I've been

73

coming to union meetings for four years now, and I never seen you get to new business yet."

Sorvino dismissed the remark and pointed to another raised hand.

A small man stepped up to the microphone, and the sergeant-at-arms turned the adjusting screw to lower it for him.

"I am George Benedict, delegate of Ladder 16, and I'm for a job action, 'cause anything we can do to shove it to these scumbags we should do, and fuck 'em."

The man walked back to his seat to the applause of the men.

"That language is out of order at these meetings," Sorvino said. He paused a moment. "But thank you, brother," he added, and then pointed to another waving hand.

The parade of speakers continued for close to two hours. Those in favor of a job action were cheered, and those against were booed.

During that time Jerry Ritter jumped up and down from his seat, yelling with the consensus of the men. Tom did not yell or move, but sat quietly, transfixed by the anger around him.

A man concluded a statement in support of the job action, and the members cheered him, although only half-heartedly, for they had tired of clapping and yelling. The meeting was growing tired. The night was growing tired.

Sorvino looked across the auditorium to recognize another speaker. It was after ten o'clock, and he knew from all past meetings that the men would soon be bored with the proceedings and vote to adjourn the meeting. They would still have time to stop for a few beers and make a night of it.

Sorvino too was tired. Without searching faces, he recognized a man waving a folded newspaper in the back of the hall. Sorvino regretted the recognition as the man walked down the aisle, for it was Dan Fanilli, the delegate from Engine 20—a constant critic of the executive board in general and Sorvino in particular.

Sorvino would not have been concerned if it were a

74

regular monthly meeting, with two hundred or so in atten-
dance. But it was contract time, and there were over four
thousand men before him, angry, and as ready to be influenced and molded as clay.

But, Sorvino thought, I'm still in control here.

Dan Fanilli took time to adjust the microphone to speaking level. Jerry Ritter leaned into the aisle and tapped him
on the leg, saying, "Atta boy, Dan."

"How're you doing, Jerry?" Fanilli said. "It's good to see
you here."

He turned to the microphone and, as an afterthought,
bent over to Jerry, saying, "Listen, Jerry, if I make a motion,
will you second it right away?"

"Sure thing," Jerry replied.

Tom whispered to Jerry, "You should tell him it depends
on what the motion is."

"Aw." Jerry shrugged. "He's all right, and anyway we
can always depend on the guys here to vote on the good of
it."

"Don't be too sure," Tom answered quietly, but Jerry
did not hear.

Sorvino spoke. "State your name and company,
brother." Of course, he knew Fanilli's name.

"Dan Fanilli, company delegate, Engine 20." He spoke
clearly, and directly to Sorvino, making eye contact.

This was Fanilli's chance to perform for the membership, to speak, to represent the floor, the fundamental act of
a sought-after union career. He wanted a confrontation with
Sorvino. That was all that mattered to him.

"I would like to reiterate something that one of the previous speakers said." That's it, bring the previous speakers
into it, make them feel they all said something important. "A
man stood here two hours ago and said that this projected job
action is the work of a paper tiger, and that's exactly what it
is." The men cheered, but again half-heartedly. Fanilli
paused for a moment. He wanted to impress the men with
his vocabulary, but he also wanted to avoid alienating them
by using words that were too difficult. He continued.

75

"The very idea of this projected job action is fatuous, and that is a word meaning stupid, which I use for the benefit of our attorney, whom you pay with our money to advise you in legal matters. I don't understand how he consented to this."

The attorney, who was daydreaming, looked up.

"The Taylor Law of the state of New York defines any work stoppage or, pay attention now, *partial* work stoppage as a strike. Now, there is no benefit whatever in making this membership liable to prosecution under the Taylor Law, particularly when the projected job action has about as much power as a line with a burst length." Good. A good metaphor, for every firefighter has experienced the futility of a burst length in a hoseline. Fanilli was pleased, and the men cheered with their earlier enthusiasm.

His eyes were still focused on Sorvino's.

"This job action will not create the crisis that you say you want to create, because you know, and I know, that the mayor of this city is not going to consider any union contract until after the City Council elections in November. That's two months away, and in the meantime the mayor would not care if we tore the firehouses apart as long as the men and the apparatus continued to respond to alarms."

The firemen liked Fanilli's style, the way he pronounced his words, the way his voice carried. They liked what he was saying, and they stood to applaud him.

Sorvino hit the podium with his fist. He said, "That's only your opinion, brother. That's just an opinion."

Fanilli let the president's response go by and continued. "I have a few questions. The first is about your demands. I want to know if the reduction in hours, in work week, is a negotiable demand."

"All demands are negotiable, brother," Sorvino said, with acerbity.

"That's certainly true of the last couple of contracts you negotiated for us," Fanilli said sarcastically. "And the demands seem to be negotiated downward all the time. However, I am out of order." Good, said it before he did. "I just

76

want you to take one goal, just one, and stick with it for once. We are the only workers in this city who are working a forty-hour week. The cops and all the other workers get an hour a day for lunch or dinner. Do we? The cops get two twenty-minute personal rest periods each tour of duty. Do we? Add that up and you'll find that cops work over eight hours a week less than we do. People might think that we are in the firehouses anyway, doing nothing, so we can eat our lunch or dinner, but you ask any man working in the South Bronx, or Harlem, or Brownsville, or Corona, or Bedford-Stuyvesant how many times he gets to eat a meal through without going to an alarm. Damn few, that's how many. I'm not trying to jerk any tears here, but only suggesting a route you can take in bargaining. We must stick fast to the demand of a thirty-two-hour week."

The applause was great, greater than any other of the night.

Fanilli waited until the cheering subsided.

"I have one other question," he continued, staring now at Sorvino. "Have you seen the contract that the Yonkers firefighters just settled with the city of Yonkers?"

"I have heard about it," Sorvino replied, dejectedly, knowing what was to follow.

"Well, I have seen it, and I have read it, and I suggest you make yourself conversant with it, for it is the most important piece of information you can have at this time. The firefighters of Yonkers just got a thirty-five-hour work week. And that is in a city where the average fire company responds about eleven hundred times a year, and where the busiest company responds about nineteen hundred times a year. In New York City the average company responds over three thousand times a year, and our busiest company responds over nine thousand times a year. Nine thousand. Now, you tell me why the Yonkers firefighters need a shorter work week than we do. No, don't tell me. I know. Because with eleven hundred calls a year they still have a tough job." Fanilli meant this last statement to be ironic, perhaps even a little humorous, but the words were delivered with bitterness.

"Goddam right," someone in the auditorium called out. "So what do we got for a job, a walk in the park?"

"No, brother," Fanilli answered. "Our job is not a walk in the park, as every man in this hall knows. But the real reason the Yonkers firefighters now work only thirty-five hours a week is because they have a good union leadership, a smart union leadership, a union leadership that cares about the men they represent, which is a good deal more than we can say here."

Sorvino pounded the podium. "You are out of order, brother." He glared at Fanilli.

"I am still on the president's report, Mr. Chairman, and I only made an observation. I'm still in order." Fanilli glared back.

"Then would you finish?" Sorvino said. "There are other men who want to speak."

"I have one final statement, about the job action. It has no bite, it has no power, it's not smart. Let us now do something that will work for us, something intelligent, something that all the members here on the floor want." Fanilli's voice became unreasonable as he yelled into the microphone, "I now make a motion to conduct a strike vote!"

Jerry Ritter rose and grabbed the microphone, saying, "I second that." The sergeant-at-arms grabbed him by the arm and said, "When you're recognized, brother, you can talk."

Jerry returned to his seat. Next to him, Tom held his hands together as if in prayer, his fingertips to his lips. The rest of the men on the floor were on their feet, screaming through the stale auditorium.

Sorvino turned up the volume of the speakers, saying, "A motion is out of order, brother. We are on the president's report. Furthermore, this executive board will conduct a strike vote when and if we think it is in the best interests of the membership."

"Tell me this, then," Fanilli said. "Do you think that the strike is the only effective weapon in labor's arsenal, or better yet do you think that the firefighters of New York have the right to strike?" It was now a person-to-person confrontation,

78

and the thousands of men in Union Hall faded before the clash between the two men.

Sorvino took another sip of water. He was shaking with anger.

"Of course we have the right to strike," he said, almost indignantly, "but we have other considerations to think of."

"What considerations?" Fanilli asked.

"That this city has the highest fireload in the world, and that people would certainly die if we had a strike." Sorvino was saying what he believed. He continued, "We have a moral responsibility that other labor unions don't have. Our product is life." Sorvino didn't think to turn down the volume, and the sound pounded the eardrums of the men.

"Don't talk to me of moral responsibilities," Fanilli said. "That's a two-way street, that street of moral responsibility. Don't forget that the Germans killed the Poles, they killed the Norwegians, they killed the Belgians, they killed almost all the Jews, they killed the Dutch and the French, and then the Americans went to Europe to kill the Germans. The Americans did to the German people what the Germans did to other people. They had to. It was a two-way street. It's a two-way street in New York too, and this city is killing firefighters. If we firefighters are different from all other unions, if we have a moral responsibility because our job is fundamentally a life-and-death job, then the city has a moral responsibility to deal with us differently than they do with other workers. But the city does not think we are any different from file clerks at City Hall. We can meet our moral responsibility when the city meets theirs, and we know that they never will. So there is only one course of action for us to take, and that is to prove once and for all that we *are* different. I hope I never see the day that this union goes on strike, but unless we show a sign of unity behind a strike vote, unless we show them that we are willing to take that route, then maybe we deserve to be treated like City Hall file clerks. We need a strike vote. We want a strike vote. *A strike vote has power, like a full stream of water.*"

The words were ringing through Sorvino's head, but he

still did not think to turn the volume down.

The hall was wild with yelling, whistling, stamping, clapping. Men in the balconies began to chant, "Strike, strike, strike."

Sorvino had lost control of the meeting, he knew that, and he hoped he could get through it without damage, without motions to force him into something he did not want.

There were still men with waving hands, seeking recognition.

"This man here," Sorvino said, pointing to a man in front.

"I still have the floor," Fanilli said.

"There are other men who want to be heard," Sorvino yelled. "The sergeant-at-arms will insure that this man I recognized will speak at the microphone."

The sergeant-at-arms pulled Fanilli away from the microphone, saying, "That's all brother. Give another man a chance."

Fanilli was not going to be overpowered, not now, not when he had the full support of the membership. He had dreamed of this moment. The sergeant-at-arms fell back with the force of Fanilli's shove. He came back at Fanilli, saying, "Don't give me a bad time, brother. Another man has been recognized. You know the rules."

Fanilli closed his fist, ready to punch the sergeant-at-arms, but the man who had been recognized grabbed him by the wrist, saying, "Don't worry, Fanilli, you still have it."

The man turned to the microphone, saying very quickly, "McHanrahan, Ladder 66, and I yield the floor to brother Fanilli."

"Thanks, brother," Fanilli said. The man returned to his seat, dissatisfied that he had not been able to offer his opinion but satisfied that he hadn't been used to prevent another fireman from talking.

Fanilli stood in front of the microphone. "I want . . ."

"State your name and company, brother," Sorvino interrupted. It was a failed attempt to assert his authority.

"Fanilli, Engine 20. I realize I can't make a motion during the president's report, so let's get to the matter at hand. I'll call for the question, go to new business, and make the motion for a strike vote."

Blood rushed into the veins at Sorvino's temples.

"I call for the question on the president's report," Fanilli said. There was a chorus of seconds from the floor.

"I think there are a great many men here who have not had a chance to speak on the president's report, and to call for the question at this time is premature and unfair to those men." Sorvino was red-faced, incensed at what was happening, and his voice quivered with the strain of his rage.

Fanilli stood firm. "The question has been called for," he said. "It has been seconded, and you have no choice but to . . ."

He was cut off. Sorvino had reached down and turned off the microphone. The men were on their feet booing, stamping their feet, and catcalling.

"Let him speak."

"Turn it on, you rubber."

"Scumbag."

Sorvino walked to the end of the long table on the stage. He spoke to the local attorney for a few seconds. The attorney shook his head, grimacing.

Fanilli walked up and down the center aisle, his hands raised, pleading for quiet. "We don't need the mike," he said again and again.

The call for silence spread quickly through the auditorium, reaching even the upper balcony, and the hall was suddenly quiet.

Fanilli stood behind the microphone, grabbing it, tilting it to the side, and yelled through the heat and the clouds of smoke to the stage. His voice barely carried, yet it was loud enough for all to hear. "The question has been called for," he said again, "and seconded. You must take a vote according to Atwood's *Book of Parliamentary Procedure.*"

Sorvino returned to the podium. He would have to call for a vote or lay himself open to union charges and possibly impeachment and recall. If it were a regular monthly meet-

81

ing—but four thousand men. He couldn't risk adjourning the meeting. He was defeated. There was no choice.

"The question has been . . ." Sorvino started, but he realized the microphone was cut off. He turned the volume up.

"The question has been called for to accept the president's report," Sorvino said dejectedly. "All in favor signify by saying 'aye.' "

A universal "aye" rose through the auditorium.

"Opposed?"

There was silence, except for a single, muffled, inconsequential "nay" from the man sitting across from Jerry.

"The president's report has been accepted," Sorvino said.

"I make a motion now," Fanilli snapped, biting into his words, "to suspend the regular order of business and go into new business." He was now in the position he had hoped to be in since the day he became a fireman. He was directing the destiny of the union.

There was another chorus of seconds to his motion.

Sorvino, disconsolate, almost as indifferent to the proceedings as an ancient general must have been in giving up his sword, said, "A motion has been made to go to new business. All in favor so signify by saying 'aye.' "

Union Hall shuddered in response. His sword had been taken.

"Opposed?"

The man opposite Jerry stood on his feet and yelled a powerful, if lonely "nay."

The membership chuckled, looking for a laugh.

Fanilli said, "I asked to be recognized on new business." He hesitated a moment, and then added with a slight laugh in his voice, "My name is Fanilli, delegate of Engine 20." That will keep the edge, he thought.

"Have your say, brother."

"I make a motion that we engage the Integrity Balloting Company to conduct a referendum of this membership to

82

determine if we should or should not strike for our just demands, and that if the membership so decides, and if the city does not come to terms with us, we will strike this city on the morning of Monday, October 1."

The two balconies resumed the chant "Strike, strike, strike." It was taken up by the rest of the hall.

Sorvino pounded the podium without effect and then turned up the microphone. His voice boomed, "The motion has been made. The floor is open on the question."

The chanting stopped, but the hall was still loud with anger.

"You're through, Sorvino."

"You'll be outta office in a couple of months."

Sorvino heard these words filter through the hundreds of curses being yelled up to him, and he became tense with rage, gripping the sides of the podium with his full strength. He then walked away from his microphone.

The men were repaying Sorvino for the three contracts he had negotiated for them over the nine years he had been in office. He had done the best, in his mind, he could have done for the firefighters, but with each contract the firemen gained only a little while all the other city workers gained a lot. The city screwed him, Sorvino thought. Mayor Gravane screwed him. With each contract signed by the United Firefighters of New York the other unions had something to fight for, and the mayor was bought or conned into acceptance of me-tooism. The firemen became no different in salary or prestige from other civil servants. But that was in the past, and Gravane was gone now, defeated by Kevin Keneally. Mayor Keneally did not believe in parity for all workers, or so he said during his campaign, and the firefighters had a chance with a new contract to be the number-one job again.

The microphone was still at a high level, and it squealed as Fanilli spoke into it. "I don't think we need to talk on the motion, for it is evident what the men here feel. I call for the question, Mr. Chairman, and if you would come back to your position at the podium we can vote on it."

Sorvino was talking to the union attorney, who was gesturing frantically.

"The question is called for and seconded, brother Sorvino," Fanilli said with feigned frustration.

Sorvino walked back to the podium.

"If you'll quiet . . ." Sorvino lowered the volume. "If you'll be still for a minute, we can conclude this business."

He paused for a moment until the clatter subsided. "I want to say first that the executive board and myself are opposed to this motion, but if this is what you are determined to do, we'll do it. We ask only that you don't tie our hands in negotiations with a cutoff date. Give your elected leadership a chance to work out the problems of this union, give us the option, the responsibility, to call a strike on whatever day we figure is in the best interests of this membership. We will conduct a strike vote, and we ask you to vote your conscience. It won't be an easy thing to do. If you vote strike, then it's strike, but don't cripple us with a cutoff date. We are your elected leaders. We are for you, not against you, and we will do as you say. Let me then offer you, brother Fanilli, this motion in place of yours. I move that the Integrity Balloting Company be engaged to conduct a strike vote of this membership, and if so voted a strike will be conducted by this membership on a date to be determined by the executive board of the United Firefighters of New York. Is there an objection to that?"

Fanilli was momentarily torn between changing his motion and doing what was best for the union. The strike vote was the important thing, and he had won that, so why bind them to a date? Still, this was his moment, and he knew the men would back him on whatever position he took. He could press Sorvino to the first motion, but was it right? If he were the president, he thought, would he be able to negotiate successfully with a strike date zooming in? He grabbed the microphone with both hands.

"The strike vote is what is important here," he said, "and your motion is acceptable. This is an historic event in our union, and I am quite sure none of the brothers here will forget it. I again call for the question."

"All in favor?" Sorvino asked.

Few men said "aye." Instead, they whistled, clapped, yelled, and knocked over chairs on the way to the exits. The meeting was over for them. An issue was raised, a vote was taken, and they won. It was at least something. A movement ahead.

"Opposed?" Sorvino asked, speaking to the backs of the members.

"Opposed, opposed," the man sitting across from Jerry yelled over and over.

Tom Ritter sat in his chair, his hands folded, staring at the empty chairs before him.

"A motion to adjourn," a man called out.

"Seconded," another said.

"A motion to adjourn," Sorvino said. "All in favor?"

It didn't much matter.

"Opposed?"

4

MCMAHON'S BAR WAS AGAIN PACKED with firemen. Jerry and Tom pushed their way back to the booth where they had left Dominic Gallo over three hours before.

Dominic was drunk.

"I heard already," Dominic said as the Ritters approached. "That's all these hooples around here are sayin'. 'Strike, strike, strike.' That's why I don't care if I go to union meetings or not. It just makes the goddam blood boil, don't put a goddam cent in your pocket."

The Ritters sat in the booth. Jerry looked at Dom's red and watery eyes and said, "You don't look any worse for wear since we left you, Dominic."

"Goddam right," Dom said, his mouth remaining open between phrases and sentences as he continued to talk. He nudged the man sitting next to him. "Me an' old Pete here, we been bullshittin' about old times." He grabbed Pete by the wrist, saying, "This here is Pete Flanagan, the guy who broke me in up in Harlem. Pete, I want you to meet . . ."

"We already met," Jerry interjected, laughing slightly.

"You did? That's good," Dom said, continuing to hold Pete's wrist. "This here man is a good fireman, one o' the top-shelf good firemen. You know what I mean when I say good fireman? He pulled me through forty-two rooms o' fire one night with nothin' but an inch-and-a-half line. Did I ever tell ya about that, Tom?"

"Forty-two rooms?" Jerry questioned, disbelieving.

"Goddam right," Dom said, becoming suddenly aggressive. "Ya don't believe forty-two rooms, then goddam say so. Don't look at me and just say forty-two rooms like a kid watchin' a fuckin' magician."

Jerry laughed, for he was used to being the lone sober man in a crowd of drunks. He said, "I believe you. That's just a lot of rooms, that's all."

"Goddam right," Dom returned.

"I need a drink," Tom said, handing a five-dollar bill to Jerry. "Do us a service and get us a round, huh?"

"No sweat," Jerry said. He took the bill and walked to the bar.

When he was out of earshot, Tom leaned over the table, saying with dead seriousness, "Listen, Dom, we're friends, right? But that's my brother, and I don't like you coming down hard on him."

"You call that hard?" Dominic asked, surprised by the intensity of Tom's voice. "That's not hard, Tom. You never seen me come down hard. But forget it. Your brother's a sweetheart, and I love 'im."

Tom lowered his eyes to the table, saying quietly, "As long as we understand each other."

Jerry came with the drinks—a coke, three beers, and two shot glasses of whiskey. Pete Flanagan and Dominic gulped the whiskey and sipped the beer. Jerry looked around the bar. The air was hot with cigarette and cigar smoke and loud with the curses of the crowded firemen. There was not a woman in the place, not even one of the many old beggar women carrying shopping bags and old newspapers who roam the streets of New York's midtown and who pass much of their time in the cheap-shot Irish bars.

"There's a lot of action here," Jerry said, "if you can make it with a fireman."

"Any towel will do when you're wet," Pete Flanagan said laughingly.

"We ought to go over to Paddy Muldoon's," Jerry said, "for a little music, maybe a little action."

"Not me," Flanagan said, rising. "If I don't get home soon, my old lady'll give me cabbage for breakfast."

"Siddown, for chrissakes," Dom said. "It's about time you let that bitch know who's who around here."

"Listen, when you're married to the same woman for twenty-three years, ya don't play a young man's game anymore. I'm goin' home. Keep the fires burnin' till I see you again."

Flanagan shook hands with the three men and left.

"Paddy Muldoon's then?" Jerry asked, and the men nodded and drank what was left in their glasses.

Tom double-parked his car on Second Avenue, in front of Muldoon's. It was one of the few places in New York where double-parked cars were not ticketed and towed, for Paddy Muldoon fronted the bar for his father, Michael, who was captain of the 17th Precinct. The 17th Precinct house was around the corner from Paddy Muldoon's, and the cops assigned there knew that it was in their interest to pretend that Paddy Muldoon's did not exist, except when they went there after duty to spend their money.

Beyond the crowded bar an accordianist and a guitarist played Irish music—reels, jigs, and an occasional slow ballad. Before the small bandstand were vinyl-covered booths against a wall and a few small tables. The booths were occupied by women, mostly in groups of three or four, secretaries and clerical workers trying to come down from a day of deadly routine at the office before returning to the studio

88

apartments they shared with too many others. Between the band sets one or two of the men at the bar would walk over to the booths and talk to the women.

Muldoon's was not like most East Side singles bars where the hustling between sexes was constant. It was a cops' bar, owned and patronized by cops, and a place that most men on the prowl for action would stay out of, for arguments develop naturally over available women, and a challenge to a cop's sex is a challenge to his gun. Fortunately, Captain Muldoon was always nearby whenever a gun was exposed in his bar, and he managed to cool the situation by taking the cop into the kitchen and having the other party thrown out. The reputation of Muldoon's suffered among singles, but the business was brisk with cops and women who did not care about the fact that ninety-five percent of the New York Police Department was married.

Dominic and the Ritters stood for a few moments watching the musicians and the booths.

A young woman left the booth nearest them and walked to the rest room alcove at the rear. She was wearing a short plaid kilt, bright and colorful, cinched tightly around her small waist. The three men followed her movements until she disappeared behind the rest room door.

"Did you ever see legs like that?" Dominic said. The girl's legs were muscled at the calves, like a dancer's, and tapered down to smooth, thin ankles.

"I have got to talk to that girl," Jerry replied.

"Let's get us a drink first," Dominic said, "and then I'll fix it up for you."

They pushed into the bar sideways, and Jerry placed a ten-dollar bill on the varnished wood, saying, "I got this one."

The bartender came, and Jerry ordered a beer for his brother, a whiskey and beer for Dominic, and a ginger ale for himself.

Dominic gulped the whiskey down and banged the shot glass on the bar, saying to Jerry, "Have the man fill it up, 'cause you don't get off so easy when I'm around." His mouth remained open after talking.

"You're worth a kicker anytime, Dom," Jerry said, motioning to the bartender for a refill.

The three walked back to stand against the wall, where it was less crowded and where they had a better view of the musicians. Dominic staggered a little before leaning heavily into the wall and then began to talk about a fire he had been at some years ago. It was in a Harlem nightclub, crowded as Muldoon's, but there was no rear exit from the place and a few people were killed. Jerry was interested in the story, as indeed he was interested in any fire story, but Tom had heard it all before and interrupted. The seriousness of his face showed there was something hard on his mind.

"You know, Dominic," he said, "I don't know about this strike vote thing. Do you think they'll go through with it?"

"The brothers all seemed to be for it," Jerry replied.

"Is your name Dominic?" Dominic asked Jerry, speaking with levity, before breaking into a smile.

"I'll tell ya what I think," Dominic said, emphasizing the *I*. "It's all bullshit, 'cause brothers or no brothers Sorvino is gonna do what he wants t' do. He's been around a long time and he's a sly bastid, an' he'll do whatever he thinks is best for Sorvino. He's like any politician, 'cause the next election is the only game in the ballpark."

"Yeah," Tom said, "but what happens if the men vote for a strike and Sorvino calls it? What happens then?"

Dominic replied, "What happens is that we gotta go along with what the brothers want. That's the way it's always been in this job."

"How are you going to vote?"

"Agains' it," Dominic said after thinking a moment, drinking the remaining whiskey in the shot glass, and sipping his beer. "I been in this job too long, always in the fires, ya know, and I know it too good t' go any other way. But it's about time we began to act lika union."

"What about you, Jerry?" Tom asked his brother.

"I don't know yet. I got to think about it a lot. I've learned to love this job as much as you, Tom, but I think we all have to realize someday that we always get short-ended

90

by the city, and the only way I can see that changed is if we put the city to the wall. Look at what the teachers get when they strike. They all get paid a lot better than we do. They work five hours a day, get weekends off, Christmas, Easter, the Jewish holidays, the full fuckin' summer off, a twenty-year pension, and what really burns my ass is they get three dollars a day annuity to our one. And what's the difference between them and us? They have four years of college, and for that they can live safe and clean. The firemen have to stop being their own enemies and get together for once and show the city just how important they are. This might be the time for that."

Dominic continued to sip his beer.

"You mean you'd strike to do that?" Tom asked.

"If we were forced into it," Jerry said, "and if the brothers wanted it."

"You mean if you were picketing in front of a firehouse and you saw a job in a building across the street, you'd just march around with a placard in your hands?"

"No," Jerry answered, "I'd probably do something, 'cause it would be my natural instinct to do something, but you gotta remember too that this is a job, not a fuckin' gift from heaven, and we're laboring men, part of labor and the labor movement, and we get killed at a higher rate than anyone else in the labor movement. The teachers are in the labor movement too, and they don't get killed, yet they're recognized as a special group of workers because they got a college degree. Our degree is that we kill ourselves doing what we do, and that we got a shorter life expectancy than any other group of workers in the country. That's what makes us a special group. On the one hand I might follow my instincts, but on the other hand I'd come right back and pick up the placard and continue to picket."

"Well what about a fire that wasn't across the street from a firehouse? What if it was three blocks from the firehouse and you didn't see it? The alarm would come in, and what would your instincts have you do then?"

"Jesus, Tom," Jerry said, "give me a break. I said I wasn't

91

sure yet. If we strike, we got to go all the way, that's all I know. Anyway, if we ever did strike, you can be sure that it wouldn't last long. Every little mattress fire would take a building, and then a block, and we have hundreds of mattress fires each day in this city. If we did it, the city management would have to give in."

Dominic grabbed Jerry by the arm, saying, "Look-it, here she is again."

Jerry turned and watched the kilted woman move past the musicians, walking very straight, her pocketbook hanging motionless at her side. Her eyes met Jerry's for a moment, but she quickly averted them and turned into the booth, joining two other women there.

"That is a beautiful future sitting in that booth," Jerry said.

"But what if someone died in the meantime?" Tom said, just as the musicians began to play a loud reel, and as Dominic walked to the bar for another round.

"Excuse me a minute," Jerry said. "I just want to make myself known."

He sat at the edge of the booth, slightly startling the three young women.

He smiled for a moment, a broad and handsome smile, before speaking. It was a disarming smile, and the women relaxed.

He looked at the young woman in the plaid kilt and said, "I saw you walking to the back, and then I watched you return, and I realized that I would invent a new language if I had to so that I could sit and talk with you. My name is Jerry."

His attention focused on the one, the other two women became disinterested, looking toward the bar.

"Jerry?"

"Yes, Jerry Ritter. Will you tell me your name?"

"Olivia Scannel."

Tom Ritter joined Dominic at the bar. The bartender came, and Dominic ordered another beer for Tom. As the bartender turned to draft the beer he heard his name being called out, and he put the empty stein down and walked to the end of the bar. Sitting there was a red-faced, white-haired man dressed in a gray sharkskin suit.

Dominic watched as the man pointed to an empty glass before him. The bartender took the glass, washed it, filled it with ice, poured bourbon over the ice, and then returned it to the bar in front of the white-haired man.

Dominic yelled loud enough so that the chatter at the bar diminished to a murmur, "Hey!"

The bartender turned quickly, and a tall, muscular man who had been standing by the door started to move down the bar.

Dominic's mouth was open, his eyes glassy. The bartender stood before him with his hands on the bar, as the bouncer positioned himself behind.

"Whatsa bushit?" Dominic slurred. "I ask ya for a beer, and then a guy calls you and you go t' him. That's not polite, 'cause you know I assed you first, an' I think thatsa lot bushit."

The bartender turned, filled the empty stein with beer, placed it in front of Tom, took the change from the bar, leaned over, and said to Dominic, "I can tell you two things, and I don't want you to think I'm impolite. The first is that the man sitting in the corner is named Muldoon, and this place is named Muldoon's, so I give the man anything he asks for when he asks for it. The second thing is that there are another hundred bars within walking distance of this one."

The bartender smiled in a friendly way and added, "No hard feelings, right?"

Dominic looked at Michael Muldoon, who was studying the exchange, trying to determine if Dominic was a cop. Tom held Dominic's elbow, saying, "Let's just have a drink together, Dom."

Dominic closed his mouth in a smile and said, "No hard feelin'."

The bouncer walked back to the door, and Dominic and Tom, drinks in hands, walked back to lean against the wall. Tom then told Dominic that Muldoon not only owned the place but was also the neighborhood precinct captain.

93

"No, I'm not a secretary," Olivia said in response to Jerry's question. "I'm art director for Ralph Burton, the advertising firm."

"Is that a big company?" Jerry asked.

"There's only one bigger."

"And you're the art director," Jerry said, obviously impressed.

She fingered the small plastic stirrer casually, saying, "Now that *would* make me interesting, wouldn't it? But I'm not *the* art director. There are about twenty of us, and in our business it's not good for the ego to say *an* art director for so-and-so. We say simply art director, so that there's an inference toward *the* art director."

"You could've fooled me if you wanted to."

"What's the point?" she asked, cracking the stirrer in two and dropping it on the table. She shrugged her shoulders, looking at him. It was a rhetorical question.

"So you're an artist."

"No, graphics mostly, design and layout. I studied fine arts at college, but I just never got good enough to make it as a painter."

"And these girls," Jerry said, indicating the others at the table, "are they your roommates?"

"No. Friends. I live with my boyfriend." Jerry was disappointed.

Olivia introduced her friends, Katherine and Vera, the first tall and heavy but shapely, the second slender and petite. They were cordial, and after shaking their hands Jerry ordered another round of drinks.

The musicians began to play "The Irish Soldier Boy" to a waltz rhythm, the guitarist singing the words.

"Where's Jerry?" Dominic asked.

Tom pointed to the booth where his brother and the three girls sat.

"Ain't bad," Dominic said, pulling Tom by the arm. "Let's go see. Maybe we get our hats blocked tonight."

94

Dominic pushed into the booth next to Katherine, and Tom pulled a chair from another table, placing it at the end of the booth seat.

Jerry introduced them to the girls, who seemed pleased that the men joined them.

"This ain't my kinda music," Dominic said to Katherine, "but I know we can make a pretty good couple." He grabbed her hand and began to tow her from the booth.

"But there's no one else dancing," Katherine protested.

"There's no room for anyone else," Dominic replied as he pulled her to the small space in front of the musicians.

Tom sat into the booth, saying as he slid next to Vera, "Do you come here much?"

"No," she said. "Never. We had dinner at Le Madrigal on 53rd Street and decided to just stop somewhere, anywhere, for a drink. We've been here a few hours now, just listening to the music."

"We just came from a union meeting and figured we'd stop here for a drink before we went home. This is my first time here, but my brother comes here occasionally." He looked toward Jerry.

Vera also looked at Jerry, saying, "Yeah, he does look like you a little. What kind of union do you belong to?"

"The firemen's union. We're all firemen."

"Where do you live?"

"Just above the city, in Westchester County. I have a wife and children there. As I said, we just stopped to have a drink too, before going home."

"Oh."

"Does it bother you that I'm married?"

"Men are men in New York, married or not," Vera said resignedly. "I've lived here a long time."

This last statement, Tom thought, was a deliberate opening, and with it came a clear image of he and Anne sitting on the pullout bed in their Westchester Avenue apartment. He was talking above the screeching of the train that was going by, telling her of the bachelor party he had been to the night before. It was in a basement of a friend's house in Throgg's

Neck, and a few girls had been called late in the evening. They came, and one had singled him out, throwing her arms about him and moistening his ear with her tongue. He was laughing as he told his wife the story until he noticed the tears welling in her eyes. He then kissed her wet eyes and told her that he would never let himself be taken from her. His hands wandered over her body, and Anne giggled a little and asked him to wash his ears first.

Tom was staring, his eyes fixed on Vera's small, erect breasts.

"Is there something wrong?" she asked.

Tom heard only the words of angry men, piercing, final sounds falling from the balcony, "Strike, strike, strike." He pictured the crowd in his mind, thinking, I can see the orgone in Union Hall, a blue Reichian glow, but it's not blue at all, it's a nightshade, dark as poison.

He turned from these thoughts as he heard Dominic's scream, and as his brother jumped from the booth.

"Bushit!"

Dominic and the bouncer were toe to toe. The bouncer stood firm and talked low. He said, "No dancing allowed pal. That's it."

"Bushit!" Dominic screamed again, and the bouncer moved to grab him by the arm. Dominic pushed him hard away, and the bouncer went uncontrollably backward a few steps, nearly falling.

Michael Muldoon moved quickly from his barstool, and Katherine ran back to the booth, passing first Jerry and then Tom.

After recovering his balance, the bouncer began to move in on Dominic, who was now braced for a fight, his fists clenched, his mouth closed, and his lips pressing hard against his teeth.

"Hold it, Richie," Muldoon yelled after seeing that Dominic was holding his ground.

"Let 'im come," Dominic said. "This goddam place oughta be ruined anyhow."

He looked at Muldoon, as his glassy and drunken eyes

96

filled with pent-up rage, and said, "The precinct captain owns the goddam place and I get a lotta bushit about no dancing."

He bent over slightly as in a boxer's stance, returning his gaze to the bouncer, and continued, "C'mon, hardon, how tough are ya?"

The bouncer lost whatever self-control or consideration of his job he had and sprang toward Dominic, his right arm level with his shoulder. He threw the punch out with the force of his weight. Dominic, seeing only a blurred movement, took one step aside and connected with a full fist to the bouncer's nose. A bone cracked, and the bouncer reeled around, falling across a table, cups, glasses, and ashtrays breaking on the floor. Some of the patrons ran out to Second Avenue, and the musicians carried their instruments protectively from the bandstand.

Jerry saw a group of men coming from the bar, and his hand reached automatically to his back pocket. He pulled out his badge, the silver Maltese cross of the New York Fire Department, and flashed it to Muldoon, saying quickly, "Listen, we're all firemen. Let's end it now, huh?"

Muldoon cracked the side of his mouth open, saying, "Shove it, son."

Four men were on Dominic, and others were still coming from the bar. Two men held his right arm, another held his left, and Dominic struggled to free himself, but even the added power of drunken fury failed him. The fourth man began banging into his stomach, coming up close to him so that Dominic could not kick his legs out.

Tom wrapped his arms about the man's neck, choking and pulling, and the man loosened his grasp of Dominic's left arm, leaving it free. Jerry's fist sank heavily into the face of the man who was pummeling Dominic, and Dominic swung his free arm around and punched wildly at the two men still holding him. The floor was suddenly filled with men and curses. Tom felt a blow on the back of his neck. A hand wrapped around Jerry's face, pulling him backward, and a knee went far into the small of his back. Three men were

97

again on Dominic, three on Jerry, and three on Tom, and free hands were punching at their bodies.

Michael Muldoon had his hands in his pockets, carefully watching the struggling men, and when he was confident they were controlled, subdued, he cracked through the side of his mouth, "Get them out of here."

While being hustled to the door, Jerry noticed that the booth where they had been sitting was empty, the women gone.

On Second Avenue, Dominic took the bloodied handkerchief from his face, and Tom studied the gash on his upper lip. "It doesn't look too bad, Dom," Tom said, "but maybe it needs a stich or two."

"Naw, fuck it, it's just one o' those things," Dominic said, holding the handkerchief to his mouth. "Let's go." He began to walk, staggering toward the double-parked car. He stepped from the curb, and the weight of his body moving forward caused him to stumble. He fell against the grille of a parked car and then to the ground.

Jerry and Tom helped him up, and Tom said, "I think I'll take you home with me tonight, Dominic."

Dominic looked blankly ahead, not answering. The Ritters ushered him into the car. Jerry shook his brother's hand, saying, "Talk to ya soon. I'll find my own way home."

Dominic put his head out of the car window and said, "Jerry, ya know it wasn't fair, not fair."

Tom shook his head, smiling ironically, and said, "What a man. He starts a brawl and then says it wasn't fair." Dominic didn't seem to hear.

Tom got into the car, and Jerry waved from the curb as they drove away.

It was one o'clock in the morning, and the midtown streets were still ablaze with blinking neon signs and noisy with traffic. Jerry walked up the avenue toward the newsstand on 53rd Street, passing singing drunks, couples necking on street corners, a few gays holding hands. He stopped in front of a picture window to look at himself in the reflection.

He tucked his loose shirt into his pants and combed his hair. He felt the pain in his lower back as he lifted the comb to his head.

Bar fights, he thought, and he remembered his dead brother and the couplet he had written after the funeral. I'm getting too old to fight in bars. I feel like a kid in Throgg's Neck. If it was anyone but Dominic I would have left him there. Tom's friend, my brother's friend. Stupid. Could have been killed, arms broken. God, Dominic hit that bouncer hard. I heard the bone crack. Stupid. Guy was only doing his job. Could have been worked over good. Did we get off easy because of the badge? I wonder?

He turned from the picture window and began to walk toward the corner, but quickly stopped as if he had run into a glass wall. There, in the street, looking impatiently up the avenue for an empty cab, stood Olivia Scannel.

Jerry approached her, saying, "Hello again."

"Oh," she said.

"What happened to your friends?"

"They live downtown and got a cab. I live up, and I'm searching."

"Listen, I'm sorry about what happened back there."

"Forget it," she said.

"Could we have a cup of coffee or something and talk for a while?" The anxiety was evident in his voice. Either she would say yes or he would never see her again. That is the way chance meetings in New York are. Now or never.

Olivia looked up the avenue again, and seeing no taxi she shrugged her shoulders and said, "Why not?" Then she smiled.

"There's a diner right up the block, on First," Jerry said, and they crossed the avenue to the newsstand on 53rd. The newsman, biting on a stump of a cigar, muttered as they passed, *"News?"*

Jerry stopped, nodded, and placed two dimes in the man's calloused hands. The man folded the paper so that the back page, the sports page, was up. The headline said that the Yankees had lost and that they were out of the pennant race.

99

They were so close, Jerry thought dejectedly.

They walked to First Avenue as Jerry apologized again for the fight, explaining that Dominic was really a good person, just drunk, and guys get like that sometimes, although he never got drunk himself.

The diner was empty, except for two men sitting at the counter, the waiter, who was mopping the floor, and the cook, who sat staring out of the window. They sat in a booth, and as Jerry put the newspaper down it unfolded, and he and Olivia saw his picture filling the front page of the *Daily News*. The caption read:

A DEATH IN THE THEATER. *Fireman Gerald Ritter applies cardiac massage to famed Broadway producer David Allen, who succumbed in fire at the Barrymore Theater. The producer, thirty-eight, was asleep in the theater office when fire broke out in the basement and died of smoke inhalation. Story on page four.*

The picture above the caption showed Jerry, his face in full view, pressing into the victim's chest.

Jerry turned the pages quickly, looking for the story of the Harlem fire and Tom Ritter's name. Not seeing it, he began to turn the pages again, more deliberately, passing on page four another picture of himself with his lips sunk into the lips of David Allen, famed producer. As he reached the last page, he realized that the story of the Harlem fire was not covered.

Disappointed, Jerry turned to page four and read the story. It was more an obituary than a story about the fire, and he folded the newspaper again.

Olivia picked the newspaper up and turned it to the front page, saying, "This is you, isn't it?"

"Yes." Jerry smiled self-consciously. "It's just about a fire I was at this morning." He took the newspaper and folded it again.

"Isn't it strange, meeting you one minute," she said,

"and then seeing your picture on the front page of a newspaper the next?"

Wanting to change the subject, he said, "I don't blame you at all for splitting. I'm really sorry about that."

"Oh, stop apologizing. Forget it. I don't like violence."

"With a name like Scannel?"

"What do you mean?"

"It's a joke. You're Irish, aren't you?"

"Am I Irish?" She laughed, holding a paper napkin to her lips. "Only in New York would a person ask that question. I'm from San Francisco, where questions like that have no meaning, but I suppose my name is Irish, although I never think of it as such."

"Well, I'm from Throgg's Neck, which is in the Bronx, where most people have Irish names and where most people fight a lot. That's what I meant by the joke, small as it was."

"And your friend, back at Muldirk's or whatever it was, is he Irish?"

"No. Dom's an Italian. An exception to the rule."

"That's why names make no difference anywhere else. There are so many exceptions to the rule." Olivia cast her eyes down to the table, saying, "But New York is different. About all one can reasonably say about New York is that it's different. In California we might have our fetishes, but we care about each other there. Here only the ego matters. You take care of mine, I'll take care of yours. This is the world's capital of egos. I hate it."

"Why do you live here then?"

"Where else?" she asked, shrugging her shoulders. She then nervously moved the newspaper three or four inches to the side of the table, saying, "New York is the only place where you can make it all happen if you're good at anything. That's why New York is different. It's the top of everything. Even politicians who look to Washington have to look to New York first, to the money here, and to the power that comes with the money. It's the place to be. Being art director here is more congenial to the ego than being *the* art director in

San Francisco. I'm art director for Ralph Burton, the advertising firm, remember?"

"Seems to me," Jerry said, "that what keeps you in New York is the very thing you hate about it. The top of anything has to do with ego first."

Olivia smiled and said, "But at least I recognize it, and that's the first step in curing an illness."

The waiter came, and Jerry ordered two cups of coffee.

"You're very beautiful," Jerry said matter of factly.

"Now that," Olivia said with a laugh, "is congenial to my ego. Thanks."

"Simply a subjective esthetic opinion," Jerry bantered, as the waiter placed the coffee on the table. He sipped the coffee and continued. "Nothing to do with 'You take care of mine, I'll take care of yours.' " They laughed together as the waiter dropped the bill onto the table.

"Do the women you were with, Vera and Katherine, work with you?"

"Used to. They're old friends, and we've been trying for months to get together for dinner. Now, with David gone, tonight was a good night to do it."

"David?"

"The man I live with. He had to go to Cleveland. Till tomorrow."

Jerry changed the subject again, talking about growing up in Throgg's Neck, and Olivia talked about San Francisco. He told her a little about the Fire Department, and she told him a little about the Ralph Burton agency.

Finally Jerry finished his coffee and, after looking at the check, put three quarters on the table. She had finished long before.

"Where do you live, Olivia?"

"On 88th and York."

"I live on 73rd, between York and the river. Shall we share a cab?"

"You can't be too dangerous," Olivia said lightly, "considering your picture is on the front page of the newspaper."

In the street, Jerry looked down First Avenue and waved his arm to stop a passing taxi.

"Perhaps," Jerry said as they sat in the cab, "you'll invite me up for coffee."

"Where ya goin', pal?" the driver said.

"To 88th and York."

"But you just had coffee," she uttered demurely.

"It is a ruse, the coffee, and as you said I can't be too dangerous."

"You're the first fireman I've ever met," she replied as the taxi banged down over an Edison manhole cover.

The driver turned into the semicircular driveway of the luxury high rise and stopped. Jerry bent forward to get out of the cab and felt a quick rush of pain in his lower back.

"Holy God," he muttered, standing alongside the cab and holding his hand on the pain.

"What is it?" Olivia asked, getting out of the taxi.

"A black and blue badge of courage," he said, feigning a small laugh. "Part of that violence you hate. I don't care for it so much myself."

The doorman offered Jerry an arm to lean on, but Jerry brushed him away, saying, "It's only superficial."

Olivia was still grinning in the elevator.

"I have just the thing for you. I use it for my beaten tennis muscles."

The living room was bright, the furniture made of suede and leather, and brass and chrome. "Be with you in a minute," she said, leaving him to read the titles on the bookshelves.

"What's your address?" she called from the bedroom.

"It's 520 East 73rd. Why?"

"I'm writing it down. The phone?"

Jerry yelled the number to her while indifferently flipping the pages of an art book. He replaced the book on the shelf and picked up a piece of rectangular glass. In the middle was a figure of a whale etched in gold. It seemed expensive to him.

"Someone must be making it around here," he yelled, putting the glass back on the shelf.

"Meaning what?" she answered.

"The furniture, the things, the view." He could see the Chrysler and Empire State buildings from where he stood.

Olivia appeared, holding a large beach towel and a tall plastic bottle. "He's an accountant, believe it or not, and I'm good at what I do, and we make ends meet."

"She threw the towel across the length of a wide suede sofa, saying, "Now, take your shirt off and lie down on this. There is magic in this bottle, not medicine. Your T-shirt too. It's an oilcream that doesn't dry or curdle but glides across the body like a skier on ice. That's what the guy at the tennis club said, as he explained that there are no smooth metaphors in tennis except a backhand swing. Just loosen the top of your pants and lie down."

"Just loosen?" Jerry asked.

"Just loosen," she repeated affirmatively.

Jerry lay on the couch, his head resting on his folded arms. She poured the cream on his back, and he flinched at the sudden coldness.

"It's just a little red," she said, leaning over his back and spreading the cream. The kilted skirt rose up her thigh.

"I wonder if I'll survive?" Jerry said, more to himself than to Olivia.

"It's a good back," she said, "a strong back."

Olivia's hands glided up and down his spine, across his shoulders, and around the rib sides, in parallel, rhythmic strokes. She leaned on the small of his back, gently at first and then harder, and the pressure seemed to Jerry a curious mixture of pleasure and discomfort. The kilted skirt rose higher still as Olivia slipped her fingers under and her thumbs over his pants waist, pushing his pants down nearly to his thighs. She poured more oilcream onto his back and worked her slippery fingers over the mounds of flesh and down deep into the crevice of his buttocks.

"What if there's an unexpected return?" Jerry asked.

"People," Olivia said in a whisper, her hands still moving

104

gently over him, "sometimes return unexpectedly from Europe or from the coast, but never from Cleveland."

Dominic was sleeping as Tom drove north on the Bruckner Expressway. To his left Tom saw a red haze in the sky, and above it a mushrooming mass of smoke.

"Hey, Dominic," he yelled. "Wake up."

Tom turned the radio down and reached over to shake his friend.

"Hey, Dominic," he yelled again, shaking Dominic's arm.

"Yeah, yeah," Dominic muttered, his eyes opening halfway.

"You want to go buff a job?"

"Yeah, tomorrow," Dominic replied, closing his eyes once more.

"Just look at it a minute, okay? It's a big glow. Probably a second or third alarm."

"I been there already," Dominic said, not bothering to open his eyes.

"Yeah, I know," Tom said, flipping the radio on so that the music filled the car.

Dominic reached for the volume control and switched the radio off. His lip was swollen and blood was caked where it was split. His eyes were veined from alcohol. His mouth was open as he looked a moment at Tom.

"Whadja mean before, that I start a brawl?" He turned and looked across Hunt's Point. "I didn't start nothin'."

Tom looked at him briefly, laughing aloud. "C'mon, Dom. We're old friends, right?"

"So wha'?"

"So you started the brawl. The man says no dancing, as simple as that, and you react as if he spit in your face. You were wrong, Dom. It was nothing and should have stayed nothing."

"You tellin' me I was wrong?"

"If I can't tell you that, Dom, who can?"

Dominic did not answer. He put his elbow on the sill of

the car door, rested his head on his arm, and slept. Tom turned off at the Hutchinson River Parkway and drove silently to New Rochelle.

"Let's go, Dom," Tom said. "We're here. Anne is probably still awake, and she'll make us some coffee."

Dominic awakened at the sound of Tom's voice. Tom got out of the car and moved around to open Dominic's door. With the door open, Dominic placed one foot on the driveway but then sat back on the car seat as if in deep thought. He looked at Tom and said, "Well, if I was wrong, how come ya got into it?"

"You were there, Dom. What else could I do?"

Dominic extended his hand and Tom pulled him from the car. As they walked to the front door, Dominic put his arm around Tom's shoulder and said, "Ya know, Tom, you're more 'n a sweetheart. You're the finest guy that ever shit a potato."

5

EDWARD JEFFERSON LOOKED AT THE clock as he picked up the phone receiver. It was six in the morning. He had slept just three hours, but it seemed like three minutes.

"Whatever it is this early in the morning, it better be good."

Then, after listening for a few moments, he said, "Wait a minute." He took a pad and a pencil from the night table.

"Give me that again. Captain who? . . . What precinct? . . . The address? . . . How many stories? . . . Are you certain it's fourteen? It's unbelievable. . . . How many dead? . . . Well, that's one less than two anyway. . . . Injured? . . . Okay. Tell the press that the mayor is shocked and dismayed by this great tragedy, and that he is rushing to the scene."

Edward Jefferson, the first special assistant to the mayor

of New York, slammed the phone on the cradle. He lay back on the bed and spoke aloud, as if to the ceiling, "The city really is falling apart."

He then jumped from the bed, shedding his pajamas on the way to the bathroom. Standing naked in front of the medicine cabinet mirror, he said it again, this time with feigned drama, as if speaking to the widow of a cop at a wake, "It really is falling apart, and it's not our fault."

He washed his face and neck and underarms, and as he was brushing his teeth he dialed the bathroom wall phone and ordered the mayor's limousine. He called his secretary and told him it would be an early day, and to make the proper notifications. He gargled with a mouthwash and made a face as if he had swallowed poison. He then dialed Gracie Mansion as the electric shaver glided across his face.

Kevin Keneally was sleeping with his arm wrapped around his wife's neck in the way he had slept with a teddy bear as a child or with a pillow when he was in the Army. His wife's nose was pressed against his chest, and strands of her hair were sticking to the roof of his mouth. The buzzer rang, first in short, polite bursts and then in long, impatient blasts.

Kevin Keneally, mayor of the city of New York, considered himself lucky, like the winner of a state lottery or the Irish sweepstakes. Every time the barrel turned, his ticket seemed to come out on top.

His father was a construction worker, his mother a part-time domestic, and he was born on the Lower East Side of the city during the great depression. "I know the problems of the poor," he was fond of telling the minorities, "for I was born in a tenement in Al Smith's old neighborhood during the worst of times. My father was out of work for the first six years of my life, and what little food came into our house came from the church or the Al Smith Democratic Club. The Republicans gave us sympathy. That's all the Republicans ever give the poor. They know what it is to be hungry for votes, but they don't know what it is to be hungry for food." His mother was also a precinct captain for the 4th Ward

Democrats, and to disdain the Republicans in the Keneally family was as natural as going to mass on Sunday.

He attended St. James' Grammar School, and he was the only boy in his class to pass the examination for Stuyvesant High School, long the highest-rated of the city's public schools. He won a scholarship to Yale to study history. In summers and between semesters he worked as a steamfitter. He never let his union card expire. After graduation, and three months before the agreement at Panmunjon, he went to Korea as an enlisted man. There he was shot in the shoulder while trying to encircle a nested machine gun and was awarded the Purple Heart and the Silver Star.

The barrel kept turning and his ticket remained on top. Without planning, Kevin Keneally was building the ideal past of a politician.

After Korea, he took the law record examination, scoring in the top tenth percentile. He was accepted at Harvard but chose to go to Fordham because he could live at home on the small allowance from the GI Bill.

While at Fordham, two events occurred that gave focus to his future: his mother died, and he met Sheila Donnelly.

His mother died without warning at the Monday night novena at St. James' Church. The priest was leading the scattered women in the beatitudes when Mrs. Keneally fell from the pew onto the kneeler. She had rosary beads in one hand and a missal in the other when her heart stopped.

As with most Irish wakes, there were always more friends of the deceased at the bar next to the funeral home than were sitting around the coffin. Kevin was drinking beer when his father came into the bar, followed by a man he quickly recognized but had never met. The man, who had been Manhattan's borough president for as long as Kevin could remember, offered his respects as he sat on a barstool.

"I want to tell you something," Salvatore Dursi said. "Sixteen years ago I was an assemblyman running for the office of borough president. I came down here to a ward meeting, but the people here liked another man from the Liberal party, a bigshot in the garment workers' union. I

109

remember that your mother, God rest her soul, spoke up for me. Not so much for me and what I stood for, but for the things she didn't like about the Liberal party. Anyway, they endorsed this other guy from the union, but after the meeting your mother came to me and said that she would work in her precinct for my name. And, you know, I won that election by three hundred votes. Your mother, God rest her, brought in over six hundred, and that's in a precinct without an endorsement. So after I'm elected I wait for the phone calls, but I don't hear from your mother at all, so I call her to ask if anyone down there needs help from my office or anything like that. And she said to me, that lovely woman, that she was surprised to hear from me, and that there was one thing that maybe I could help her with. There was a cop in the neighborhood who was looking for a transfer. Can you imagine that, a cop looking for a transfer? I would have given her anything, because I'm sure I would be in the plumbing business today if she had gone with the rest of them and the Liberal party. Your mother, God rest her soul, was a Democrat."

Before leaving, the borough president told Kevin to call him if ever he needed something. That happened during his second year at Fordham.

At the beginning of his final year, Sheila Donnelly sat next to Kevin in a class on constitutional law. She was as beautiful as she was intelligent, and Kevin began dating her the third week of the semester. She was also the daughter of Bill Donnelly, the man *The New York Times* referred to as the "boss of the Bronx."

Bill Donnelly held no elected political office, but he was the president of the Bronx County Democratic Club. He controlled the borough, and no decision, from the appointment of judges to the transfer of a Parks Department litterman, was made without his approval.

Kevin and Sheila married after graduation. Since they were married by a cardinal, their picture was in all the city newspapers. They worked together a short while for Bill Donnelly's law firm, until Sheila had the first of seven chil-

110

dren. When the child was born, Kevin was running for state assemblyman in the 4th Ward. He had Salvatore Dursi's machine and his father-in-law's money behind him.

Kevin Keneally spent six years in the state assembly and then two years in the state senate. He ran for Congress when he was thirty-three, but only after Bill Donnelly and Salvatore Dursi talked him out of the mayoralty race. Kevin wanted to be the youngest mayor in the history of New York but amended his ambition to be the youngest mayor of New York since John Purroy Mitchel, who was thirty-four when elected in 1913. There was time enough left for him.

Bill Donnelly's influence got Kevin an appointment to the prestigious House Committee on Foreign Relations. Kevin was on a fact-finding trip to Israel when a bus carrying the congressional delegation was strafed in the Sinai peninsula, shattering the windows. A piece of flying glass cut Kevin's cheek, leaving a prominent two-inch scar. It was a scar worth two million votes in New York City. His ticket was again on top.

Whenever Kevin Keneally spoke to the working class, which in New York was mostly Catholic, he talked of his past poverty, his experiences at St. James' School, the labor card he still carried, and his Korean medals. When he spoke to the middle class, which in New York was largely Jewish, he spoke of his experiences at Stuyvesant High School, the scar on his cheek, and his Korean medals. When he talked to the Park Avenue and Fifth Avenue rich, he talked of his experiences at Yale and his Korean medals. Sheila once suggested to him that they adopt a Chinese and a black child, for they were the only two groups in the city that could not strongly identify with him. It was a suggestion made facetiously. Kevin gave it hard consideration nonetheless.

After two successful, highly exposed terms in Washington, Kevin Keneally ran for mayor of New York and won easily over an unattractive, rough-speaking Republican who had once been sanitation commissioner. Keneally was only thirty-seven years old and going places in politics.

111

The mayor turned, his wife's hair pulling from his mouth, and sat on the edge of the high fourposter bed. He rubbed his face, searching with his middle fingers in the corners of his eyes for the night's residue. He had slept well, and long.

He lifted the phone receiver, and the incessant buzzing stopped.

"Good morning, your honor," Jefferson said, "although it's not good at all. There has been a serious explosion on East 38th Street. One person is known dead, thirty injured. We should be there. Police, fire, and the press are on the scene."

The long black Continental pulled into the 88th Street entrance to Carl Schurz Park. The patrolman at the gate shack waved it on, and the limousine went slowly, gracefully, up the driveway of Gracie Mansion and around to the gray wooden steps of the front porch.

Ed Jefferson held the door open as the mayor walked down the hollow steps.

"It will be a long day, sir," he said as the mayor entered the car.

"The longer the day, the more accomplished." The mayor smiled.

The two men had known each other for five years, ever since Salvatore Dursi had recommended the bright young researcher from the Rand Corporation's think tank to be the legislative assistant to the bright young congressman from New York. Yet they were not friends, and although they talked casually to one another, they were rarely informal.

The mayor sat back into the plush seat, stretching his long legs before him, and picked up one of the city's three daily newspapers which lay on the seat beside him. He held the *Times* in his hands but put it down when he saw the picture on the front page of the *News*.

"David Allen was a friend and a supporter. We'll miss him."

Jefferson picked up the newspaper and studied the pic-

112

ture of the fireman and the producer. "It is a terrible tragedy," he said.

"See to it," the mayor said, "that the fireman there gets a commendation for his efforts. It will be reassuring to the widow to know that we did everything possible to save him."

"Yes, sir."

"Where on 38th Street is this explosion?" the mayor asked while scanning the front-page headlines.

"On the northeast corner of Second Avenue. It is a thirty-story multiple dwelling. The explosion occurred at five-thirty-five this morning, and the exterior wall on the south side of the building fell off from the first to the fourteenth stories."

The mayor turned to the front page of the second section of the *Times*, glancing at the index of the news. He looked briefly down the international listings and then at the metropolitan list.

"There was a boys' club on that corner," he said, "where I played basketball when I was a kid. Kips Bay Boys' Club. It's in the South Bronx now—there is no need for a boys' club in midtown anymore. How the city changes."

Jefferson was always impressed by the mayor's knowledge of the city. Having been born and raised in the Midwest, the mayor's assistant knew little of the old New York, except for what he had read in history books.

The mayor's eyes stopped on the listing that said "CITY FIREMEN TO TAKE STRIKE VOTE, page sixty-eight."

"What is this about a firemen's strike vote?" the mayor said, turning to the story. "It seems to me I heard reference to a possible job action, but I heard nothing about a strike."

"I just read that myself, Mr. Mayor. I don't think there's much to it. Sorvino has always controlled his men, and there is no indication that he won't continue. As you know, it's been our policy to hold off all unions until after the election in November. We need two seats on the City Council for a majority. Sorvino knows that, and there will be no giveaways until those seats are insured."

113

"It says here," the mayor said, "that a mailing ballot will be sent to the firemen within a week. I don't like it at all, not even the thought of it. They had a hell of a problem with the firemen in Montreal, just a few months ago. The striking firemen just watched as block after block of the city burned away. I think fifteen or twenty percent of the city was destroyed, a loss of millions."

The mayor searched his memory, trying to recall clearly a *New York Times* article about the Montreal strike he had read back in June, three months before. "Yes," he said, "I remember. It was fifteen percent of the city that was destroyed."

He dropped the newspaper to the floor, saying, "Have the fire commissioner send me a report on all this and on whatever contingency plans he has worked out."

Jefferson took a leather notebook from his jacket pocket and wrote in it.

"While you're at it, Ed, make a note to call Hamilton Stein at the Office of Labor Relations. Have him call Sorvino and assure him that we don't like the noise that's being made."

"Yes, sir," Jefferson said, still writing in the notebook.

Four policemen were standing in the middle of Second Avenue, directing the traffic to either First or Third avenues. One waved the limousine through their ranks, saluting it as it rolled past. The car stopped in front of a parked fire engine, and the mayor and his assistant stepped from it.

The fire commissioner, Herbert Thomas, was talking to one of the five or six fire chiefs on the scene when he saw the mayor's car arrive. Dressed in a specially made white canvas coat and a small-brimmed white hardhat with the words "FIRE COMMISSIONER" written across it, the commissioner was the most visible official on the street, and the chiefs, the press, and the police officials crowded about him. But now Kevin Keneally stood in the street, his gray and brown curls being blown by the mild wind. The men and women of the press quickly moved to the mayor, television shoulder cameras from the six local channels bobbing up and down in the

114

air. The questions came as the mayor took his own small-brimmed white hardhat from the trunk of the limousine.

"What caused this, Mr. Mayor?"

"Who is responsible for this?"

"When was the last time this building was inspected?"

"How many other buildings in the city are in danger of falling apart?"

Ed Jefferson caught the fire commissioner's eye and waved him to the limousine.

Mayor Keneally held his hands up to the press and said, "Ladies and gentlemen, as you can see, I've only just arrived. If you will give me just a minute or two to talk to the fire commissioner I will get back to you."

The mayor and the fire commissioner walked to the 38th Street side of the building, the television cameras following behind. "Preliminary investigation shows," the fire commissioner said, "that a hoseline on an air compressor in the basement blew, the force of which in turn weakened a gas pipe above it. The gas then seeped throughout the basement and was ignited, probably by a spark from a thermostat, but we're not sure of the pacific cause of the ignition."

The mayor was about to say "specific" but restrained himself. Instead, he looked up at the side of the building and said, "Good God."

The building reminded him of a huge doll house. The first fourteen stories were a skeleton. The mayor looked at the interior of the apartments, the different decorating schemes, reflections of the differing personalities of the occupants. Hanging from the edge of one of the floors, threatening to fall, was a fourposter bed, large and ornate. It seemed to the mayor to have been placed there by a careless child.

"It is truly amazing that only one was killed here," the mayor said.

"Yes, sir," the commissioner replied. "It was a passerby, a white male, about fifty. Hit by the falling wall. We had a hell of a time digging him out. Lucky, though, that it didn't happen two hours later. We would have had forty or fifty bodies under that pile of stone if it had happened at rush hour."

115

The mayor looked at the mountain of stone and debris before him and shook his head. He looked toward Third Avenue, beyond the barricades and the army of onlookers, and saw hundreds of people on their way to work. The mayor shook his head again.

A group of people, some in nightclothes and bathrobes, were standing behind the police barricade on the south side of the street. The mayor walked to them, the cameramen still immediately behind him, and assured the dispossessed and tried to comfort the angry. One man in pajamas who was holding a valise yelled, "This wasn't an act of God. This was an act of a building inspector getting rich." The mayor put his hand on the man's shoulder, promising a full investigation.

The press crowded around the mayor and the fire commissioner, snapping stills and asking questions. Behind the reporters and photographers the fire commissioner saw a group of firemen rimmed around a small-statured man in a wrinkled brown suit. The fire commissioner glared, wondering to himself, what the hell is that little cement bag doing here? He hoped that the mayor would get through the interview without seeing him. It was Angelo Sorvino.

The limousine was held up in the early morning traffic, and the mayor spent the idle time thumbing through a thick leather-bound report which Jefferson had asked him to look at.

Jefferson said, "It's going to be difficult under the best of circumstances, but if we lock up those two seats on the council we'll be able to push it through."

"I think," the mayor replied, "that we better insist on an environmental study first. I'm not so sure the city needs another sports and entertainment center, particularly one that reaches out over the waterside only ten blocks from Madison Square Garden. This complex would displace fifteen thousand people, all white and working class, and I wonder where we will put them if they are less than enthusiastic about moving to Brooklyn. They will, no doubt, take whatever relocation money is given them and buy a monthly

116

commutation ticket on the Long Island Railroad. That's not good for the future of this city."

Jefferson pulled a folder of correspondence from his briefcase and handed it to the mayor. "I do not want to sound flippant, your honor, but Madison Square Garden has a virtual monopoly on sports and entertainment in New York. If they ever instituted a series of classical music concerts we would have to shut down Lincoln Center, and the only reason they don't do that is because the Garden acoustics are so bad. We ought also to consider that the Garden people have never been supporters of the Honorable Kevin Keneally, or any Democrat for that matter. If you will look through this correspondence you will see how enthusiastic the city's business, labor, and political leaders are about this project. There is a letter there from Salvatore Dursi, and as you know it's rare that the borough president of Manhattan gets enthusiastic about anything."

The mayor flipped through the correspondence until he came to the borough president's letterhead, and he quickly read the letter. He put it back into the folder, handed the folder to Jefferson, and closed his eyes. A hundred pictures of Salvatore Dursi came to his mind, and in each one Dursi was shaking hands with Kevin Keneally the politician. On the platform after each election, the balloons falling, the band playing, the campaign workers cheering, stood Salvatore Dursi shaking his hand. At all the fund-raising drives, club dinners, and quiet restaurant strategy meetings, there was Dursi shaking his hand.

Then Kevin Keneally realized that Dursi was not shaking his hand. It was he who was shaking Dursi's hand. He owed Salvatore Dursi something.

He lifted the leather-bound report from his lap, gave it to Jefferson, and said, "There is no point in discussing it until after the election. Let's get a majority first, okay?"

"Yes, sir," Jefferson replied.

The limousine pulled into City Hall Park and into the shadow of the statue of Lady Justice, which stands on top of the City Hall dome. A police captain opened the door of the

117

limousine, and the mayor got out of the car, followed by Jefferson.

Jefferson looked at the police captain, as he did every working morning, and was forced to smile, knowing that the captain was the highest-paid doorman in the world.

The mayor bounded up the eleven whitestone steps, past the high Corinthian pillars, the four saluting policemen on duty, and through the crusty, cream-colored doors of City Hall.

Instead of turning left at the double center stairway, as he normally did each morning, he turned right and walked to the long, narrow press room. Jefferson was surprised by this but dutifully followed. The mayor stuck his head into the room and looked around at the fifteen desks, topped with fifteen old, high Underwoods. There were only two reporters in the room, which disappointed the mayor, but he realized it was early in the day and winked at the two reporters, who were trying to remember the last time a mayor had come to the press room. He told them, "I'll have a press conference at eleven o'clock."

The stunned reporters automatically picked up the telephones on their desks, and the equally stunned Jefferson, catching up with the mayor as he again passed the center stairs, said, "Well, your honor, you evidently made the decision."

The mayor smiled as the police guard pressed the buzzer to release the lock on the entry gate to the mayor's chambers. "Yes, Ed, I have made the decision."

The mayor stepped into the office of his press secretary, Vincent Bell, and found Bell hunched over his desk, writing on a yellow pad. The mayor did not speak, and as Bell looked up he saw only the mayor's hand waving as he left the office. The press secretary followed him.

The mayor walked to the marred and aging desk facing out from the corner of his office and sat in the high, red leather chair. Jefferson and Bell sat on a long couch beneath Seurat and Matisse paintings that were on loan from the Metropolitan Museum. The mayor leaned back in the chair

118

and studied the dark, foreboding Dickenson portrait of Fiorello LaGuardia on the wall before him. The greatest mayor in the history of New York, Kevin Keneally thought, even though he was a fusion mayor. Yet the painting showed an intense, burdened, unhappy man, one perhaps given to failure.

Mayor Keneally pointed to the portrait and said to the men sitting across from him, "I had this painting brought down from the Museum of the City of New York to remind me of the gloomy business of this office. History may show that this is the last stop on a one-way journey in politics, but I've tried not to let the past influence my future, our futures. And unlike the portrait before you I have kept smiling even through the worst of crises. I am sure you need not be reminded of the hard days we shared in the nearly three years of my administration, the strikes, the race riots, the reaction to school integration in the Bronx. Criticism always overwhelms accolades in this city, but it has not overwhelmed me, and we have managed to survive it all with an image of progress intact."

The mayor rose and walked to the picture of LaGuardia, staring into its unhappy eyes. In a low tone barely audible to the two men, he said, "This office will not be the last stop on a one-way journey from now on."

He then turned to the two men and continued in his natural, self-confident voice, "The results of the informal polls came in yesterday, and I met with Bill Donnelly last night. The polls show I have a shot at it upstate, and my father-in-law assures me that the regulars in Yonkers, Syracuse, Albany, Rochester, and Nassau and Suffolk counties will support us. The primary is ours unless the world collapses. There will be a press conference at eleven o'clock, and at that time I will be officially running for the office of governor of the state of New York."

One block east of City Hall, on the fourth floor of the Municipal Building, Fire Commissioner Herbert Thomas slammed the receiver on the telephone cradle. It was noon.

There was mustard on the side of his mouth, and a half-eaten salami sandwich lay on his desk.

"Goddam Ivy League bastard," he said aloud to himself, "doesn't have a title yet gives orders like a deputy mayor."

He pressed the lever on the intercom next to the salami sandwich and yelled into it, "Have Chief Golden respond to my office."

Down the hall on the fourth floor Eugene Golden, the chief of the New York City Fire Department, listened for a moment and then spoke into the phone. "What's he want?"

He listened a moment longer and said, "Tell him I'll be right there." The chief slammed the receiver on the cradle. The tall, chesty, silver-haired Golden would sooner let a fire burn out of control than respond quickly to an order from the fire commissioner. He lingered at his desk awhile, thinking of the day Kevin Keneally took over the office of mayor. He thought surely that he, Eugene Golden, up from the rank of fireman, the most respected authority on firemanics in the country, would be named the next fire commissioner. There was no one in the city better qualified, and even the new mayor's aides had told him that. Golden never forgot the sadness, the bitterness, he felt that afternoon when Keneally appointed Herbert Thomas, a retired battalion chief, from the lowest of the chief's ranks, a name out of the blue. Still later that afternoon he found out that Thomas shared a season ticket to the Knicks games with an old neighborhood friend named Bill Donnelly.

The chief entered the commissioner's office and sat on a squat, tufted leather chair in front of the desk. He slouched in the chair, crossing his foot casually over his knee. He was in shirtsleeves and his tie was loosened, yet the golden circles of five stars on either side of his collar and his relaxed demeanor gave evidence to his authority.

The commissioner was irritated at his tardiness, but he was used to it and said nothing. He leaned on his desk and clamped his hands together.

"Gene," the commissioner said, "I just had a call—about ten minutes ago—from that Jefferson over at City Hall. He says the mayor is very concerned about this strike vote the union is pulling on us. I told him not to worry, that there's no precedent for it, and that my men are not the kind of men who will walk away from their responsibilities. Nevertheless, he wants to know our preparedness in the event of a strike, and he wants a contingency plan on his desk in two days."

The commissioner took a bite from the salami sandwich and, with the food jammed in his mouth, continued. "Sorvino really shoved it to us this time, and I've got a good mind to order him to duty in a firehouse in the ass end of Staten Island."

"I don't think he had much to do with it," Golden said.

"What do you mean? He's their president, isn't he?"

"According to the report I received this morning, Sorvino didn't want the strike vote and he talked against it. The men forced it on him."

"Did you write me a memo on it?"

"It should be in there," Chief Golden said, pointing to a stack of papers on the commissioner's desk.

"I'll read it later, but for now just tell me what it says."

The chief rose, walked to the window, and looked out at City Hall across the street and at the statue of Lady Justice on top of it. If the roles were reversed here, he thought to himself, I would not have to rely on anyone's memo for information about my department.

Golden took a cigar from his shirt pocket and held it in front of him, rolling it, studying it. He turned to the commissioner and said, "There are two things to be asked. The first is this. Will the firemen vote to strike? I don't think so. There were about four thousand men at the meeting last night who evidently approved a strike referendum. They are mad and frustrated, yes, but at things that are beyond our control. For instance, the inflation rate is twelve percent and their last raise was six percent. The sanitationmen are now making commensurate wages, and the policemen get more time off during the year. Firemen will not strike over such issues. Anyway, there is a significant difference between calling for a strike vote at a union meeting and marking a ballot. When the men are alone in their homes they will investigate their true feelings about this job, and they will vote against it."

The chief struck a match, lit the cigar, and threw the still-burning match into the commissioner's ashtray. He sat again in the leather chair and continued. "The second question has to do with the possibility that I'm wrong on the first. Say they do vote to strike. The question is, how many of the eleven thousand firemen will actually walk off the job? I don't think more than thirty percent would go out. Again, there is a significant difference between the frustration that might motivate a vote to strike and the frustration that would force a responsible man to turn his back on such a responsible job. But, for safety's sake, let's say that seventy percent walk, which is extremely improbable. That leaves us thirty percent, or thirty-three hundred men, in the firehouses. Add to that the two thousand in the officers' ranks, which gives us a minimum force of fifty-three hundred men. The fact is that I can protect this city indefinitely with a force of only forty-five hundred men, using skeleton crews.

"So you're not overly concerned?"

"I'm not overly concerned," the chief said, flicking his ash into the commissioner's ashtray.

The tall Central Labor Building on the west side of Broadway cast a late afternoon shadow over City Hall Park. On the seventh floor Angelo Sorvino was looking out of the window in his large, red-carpeted office. The view before him was a panorama of Lady Justice holding her precariously balanced scales on top of the City Hall dome, the Municipal Building just beyond the statue, and in the background the Brooklyn Bridge and the haze-covered borough of Brooklyn.

It was four o'clock, and he stood with one foot up on the window sill, trying to organize his thoughts for the executive board meeting he had scheduled for four-fifteen.

For the first time in his eight-year tenure as president of the United Firefighters of New York, Sorvino was worried about his future. The smoke from his cigarette drifted aimlessly up and into his eyes, causing them to tear. He had been through rough periods before, but he always had the support of the majority of his men and the majority of his executive board. He knew from the meeting at Union Hall that he had lost the support of his men, and the cries of the membership came back to him.

"You're through, Sorvino."

"Up yours."

"Wait till the next election."

Even if he supported a strike vote, a strike even, it would now be said of him that he was forced, pressured into it. He sat in his large, cushioned wooden chair, thinking of his strategy. He would send a letter out to every fireman, signed by all the members of the executive board, saying that the power they might gain by a positive strike vote would only cloud their demand to sit down in a bargaining session with the city negotiators. In fact, it might even work against them, for the city negotiators could easily refuse to meet with them under such threatening circumstances, and the union would be left with a strike vote but without an issue to strike over. Of course. Why didn't he think of that at the meeting? There was no such thing as a no-contract, no-work clause in the contracts of municipal employees, so there was no way the firemen could justify a strike simply to bring the negotiators to the table. No. The press and the public would not tolerate a strike without an issue. It was in the best interests of the membership, he would say in the letter, to vote against a strike and to support the executive board's recommendation for a harassing job action against the Fire Department.

The question was, how many of the nine members of his board would support him and sign the letter? These were men, he thought, who were influenced solely by their political instincts and by which side of a question the votes were to be found.

One thing Sorvino knew for sure. He was against any possibility of a strike by firemen, for he was sure in his mind that when it came to unions, the press and the public would tolerate anything. God, he thought to himself, it would be devastating.

At four-fifteen Sorvino walked down the hall to a small office that served as a board room and took his seat at the head of a Formica-covered table that ran nearly the length of the room. One by one the members of the executive board entered the room, taking assigned seats according to their importance. The vice-president, returned from the state capital, took a seat one down on the right of Sorvino and opened his briefcase on the table. The Bronx trustee, the newest of the five borough trustees, placed a yellow pad in front of him at the far end of the table on Sorvino's left.

The financial and recording secretary sat one seat down to the left of the president, and the treasurer sat next to him. The sergeant-at-arms sat next to the vice-president, and the four remaining borough trustees filled the empty chairs.

Sorvino greeted each one of them from his position at the head of the table, calling each by name. Then he said, "The meeting is called to order. All members of the executive board are present."

The financial and recording secretary began writing the minutes of the meeting.

"There are one or two items," Sorvino said, "that we ought to talk about before we get to the matter at hand. The first thing is that we'll take a report from the vice-president on legislation pending in Albany."

The vice-president, a rotund, blood-cheeked man, twirled a pencil about in his fingers and said, "I talked with the majority and minority leadership of both houses, and we are assured that the lung bill will be extended another year. As always, it will be assumed that any lung disease suffered by our members is job-related and will entitle the man to a disability pension. I might add, though, that the majority leader of the assembly asked me why we didn't submit a permanent lung bill and have done with it. I told him that we thought a year-to-year bill had a better chance of passage. You'd think a guy who's been around politics as long as he has would know that givin' the same present year after year is better than givin' it only once."

"What about our improved pension bill?" the treasurer asked.

"No one up there knows where the money is gonna come from to pay for the present pensions, and they laugh in your face when you talk to them about better pensions. One guy even said to me, 'Listen, ole buddy, you could pick up my complete campaign tab and I still couldn't touch your bill.' That's how bad things are up there."

"Well," Sorvino said, "it was worth a try anyway. We'll do as much as we can for the governor's reelection next year, and then maybe he'll push it through for us."

Looking up from his writing, the financial and recording secretary said, "That is, if any of us are around next year." It was his idea of a joke, but there was no laughter, there were no smiles.

"The second thing is," Sorvino continued, "this problem about haircuts in Brooklyn. The commissioner has suspended three men because their hair is too long and they refuse to cut it. I got a petition here, signed by a couple of hundred men from the 11th Division, saying that if we don't take this thing to court they're gonna resign from the organization. Now, personally, I don't think we ought to give this to our attorneys. They tell me it might run to two or three thousand dollars, and I'd rather send these three guys the price of a haircut. But it seems that they are well-liked guys out there in the ghetto of Brooklyn, and they have enough signatures on this petition so that it has become an issue."

Sorvino looked down the table at the trustee from the borough of Brooklyn and said, "Before we decide to pay the bills on this, Jack, I want you to talk to these guys and see if they won't come around. Tell them that what they're doing is bad for our image, and that we don't need no hippies in the department."

"I already spoke to them," the Brooklyn trustee said, "and they want to see this thing through. The three of them are nice, easygoing family men, and I think we should just go ahead and give it to the lawyers. The problem began when

125

a deputy chief who happened to be filling in out there one day stopped into their quarters. He told them to get a haircut, that they looked shaggy and dirty. There were witnesses to this. The men had just returned to quarters from a second-alarm fire, and they got pissed off and told the deputy that if he went into a fire once in a while he would look dirty and shaggy too. The deputy reacted to this and hooked the three of them up. I went out there that day and tried to squash it, but the deputy wouldn't talk to me."

The young man sitting at the end of the table, the trustee from the Bronx, interrupted. "This is something that has got to come up again, so we might as well fight it now as later. The commissioner says the hair regulation has to do with safety, but we all know it has to do with age. The commissioner is sixty, and these men are in their twenties, and the commissioner and maybe even some of us in this room still think that anyone with long hair is a Communist or at the very least a subversive. Long hair has nothing to do with safety. If a man gets so close to a fire that his hair is going to burn, he's in a lot of trouble anyway. A man has a right to wear his hair however he wants, and long hair is in style now. To force them to cut it is an infringement of their civil rights. I met these three men when they came up to talk to Jack, and their hair isn't much longer than mine. We better fight the suspensions."

The financial and recording secretary again looked up from his writing and said, "Maybe we should also give the Bronx trustee three bucks for a haircut."

"That's a lot of crap," the Bronx trustee said dispassionately, "and the financial and recording secretary is out of order. I just want you all to know that our membership is changing, and that the men coming on the job now are from a different culture than John Wayne's."

"Okay," Sorvino said. "It is resolved that the union's attorneys will represent the three men. Is there an objection?"

The vice-president, still twirling a pencil in his fingers,

said, "I want to abstain on this, because I don't think a haircut is too big a price to pay for remaining in the Fire Department."

"I don't think it is either," the treasurer said, "but I agree with the Bronx trustee that the question will certainly arise again, so we should take it on now."

Sorvino looked down the table for additional comments, and when he saw there were none forthcoming he said, "Now we come to the motion of the strike vote that was carried last night. You all know I'm against this. The city is not going to give us a contract until after the elections in November, and all this talk about a strike will cause undue pressure on everybody. I thought the job action would settle the troops for a while, but I was wrong, and there's no point in discussing what I should have done or said last night. The question now is, what are we gonna do about it? And if we have to send out a ballot, I think we should send with it a letter signed by all of us urging that they vote no on the strike."

Sorvino sat back in his chair, waiting for his executive board to respond. He had made it simple enough. They would be either for his idea or against it, either for him or against him.

The vice-president was the first to speak up. He dropped his pencil heavily on the desk, saying, "Why don't we just let the ballot go alone? The majority won't vote for it anyway, probably. And even if they do, what's the harm in it? The proposal is open-ended. It doesn't bind us to a date or anything."

"The harm," Sorvino replied, "has probably already been done, since the story was carried in both newspapers this morning. But the fact remains that it's a dangerous precedent to set. If the vote comes in positive, what have we got? A power, a paper tiger, that means nothing to me, for I am not going to take my men out on the street unless the city really screws us, breaking the parity with the cops or something like that."

127

"Why the hell not?" the Bronx trustee asked angrily, rising from his chair at the far end of the table. He attempted to continue, but Sorvino interrupted.

"I'll tell you why. Because my men are not like other workers who simply become a pain in the ass when they withhold their labor. When my men stop working this city burns, and don't forget it."

"And why the hell shouldn't it burn?" the Bronx trustee, still standing, asked. "It's time we became like other workers. Are we kidding ourselves? What the hell is work, anyway? What's the difference if a man picks up garbage, operates a lathe, or fights fires? It's all the same thing. There is nothing ennobling about work by itself. It's only when you consider work in relation to the future that you can find value in it, when a man can look at something he did and say to himself, 'Yeah, tomorrow is going to be better because of this.' I'm damn tired of people telling me that we're different, that we don't make things, or sell them, or service them, that our job is the protection of life. If this city wants us to act out the responsibilities of doctors, let them pay us like doctors are paid. I want to go on record as saying this. There is nothing that says we have to wait until an election is over to get a contract that is due us. There is nothing that says we have to be a part of the game playing of the politics of this city. When you come right down to it, all they're going to give us after the election is enough to catch up with the inflation. Labor unions are supposed to be for the betterment of workers, but it turns out that all we do is fight to maintain the same buying power we had two years ago. If you want to send a letter out with the ballot it should be an endorsement of it, and then, dammit, we should take the men out of the firehouses and begin to think about our work in relation to the future."

The Bronx trustee sat down and nervously lit a cigarette. The other members of the board, all but Sorvino, were dumbfounded, surprised that the youngest of them would speak so strongly against the president. Sorvino was reminded of the time he was punched away from the micro-

128

phone by his predecessor, and he saw something of himself in the young trustee.

The treasurer spoke next, disregarding completely the Bronx trustee's words. He talked without emphasis, but his speech left no doubt in Sorvino's mind which side he was on. "I feel," he said, "that the tone of the membership at last night's meeting leaves us no choice but to go with them. I'm not about to say to four thousand men that they're wrong."

That was three against, Sorvino thought. There would not be a letter with the ballot. When he first came to office his every suggestion was approved unanimously, but now the executive board was being swayed by the angry voices of the membership, by their votes.

In his mind Sorvino decided then to let the events run free, to play them as they came. "Okay," he said, "the ballot goes out by itself. I'll live with the paper tiger—but, ah, I think it's wrong. We go now to the next item, a report on negotiations in progress."

A knock came from the door behind Sorvino, and when it opened Sorvino's secretary appeared. Sorvino knew that she would not interrupt a board meeting without urgency, so he rose, saying to the board members, "Just give me a few minutes."

In the hall his secretary said, "There's a call from the governor's office."

Sorvino hurried down the hall to his corner office, flipped the switch on the recording device beneath his telephone, and lifted the receiver.

"Hello. This is Angelo Sorvino."

"Angelo, this is Olden Hirschfield, Governor Bennett's secretary. You might remember that we met a few times at labor receptions and things like that."

"Yeah, sure. How are you?"

"I'm fine, thanks. I'm calling about two things. The first is to tell you that we have just received notice of Dr. Gareth's retirement, which will open up the office of state's mediator on the first of the year. The governor, of course, has already

129

begun the search for someone to fill this important and prestigious post, which leads me to item two. The governor has asked if you could possibly meet him here at our Madison Avenue office this evening at six."

"Yeah, sure, of course I'll be there. At six."

"Fine, and thank you. Good afternoon."

"Good-by."

Sorvino replaced the receiver and flipped off the recorder. He sat back in his chair and thought, Jesus, state's mediator. The state's highest labor position—chauffeur, limousine. The governor has begun the search. Not me, Jesus. This couldn't happen to me. Meet the governor. Possibly! Why?

His secretary intruded upon his thoughts. "There was also a call from Hamilton Stein from the Office of Labor Relations. I told him you were at a board meeting, and he asked if you would call him back. Shall I get him for you?"

"Yeah, sure," Sorvino said, still bewildered.

The phone buzzed, and Sorvino flipped the recorder on. "Mr. Stein?"

"Yes, Angelo. Listen, the mayor's office is groaning over this report in the newspapers, and I was asked if I could do anything to calm the flames of passion, so to speak. What is the problem?"

"The problem, Mr. Stein, is that my men have been working without a contract for over three months."

"Well, Angelo, we have been working on it, you know. We did arrange for you to have preliminary meetings with the Bureau of the Budget, and we are currently surveying the cost factors of the demands. It takes time, you know."

"Yes, I know, time until the election. Listen, Mr. Stein, we would like to have a bargaining session as soon as possible on this contract so that we can show some movement forward."

"Certainly, Angelo. Of course. What about a week from today, here at my office, at four o'clock?"

"A week today, okay, but you and I know there is no sense talking unless you have Jefferson there."

"That might not be easy."

"But it's possible, Mr. Stein. See you then."

Sorvino replaced the receiver and switched the recorder to the rewind position. The conversations thus far in the day were not defamatory enough to save.

He sat again at the head of the table in the board room, saying as he gathered together the papers in front of him, "I was getting to a negotiations report, but we'll put that off. I just set up a meeting with Stein, a week from today, at four. The treasurer and sergeant-at-arms will go with me. Put it down for four o'clock. I told them they better have Jefferson there. Now, we'll conclude the meeting unless there's something else."

The trustee from the borough of Manhattan threw a copy of the *Daily News* on the table, saying, "I guess you all saw this picture on the front page. I suggest we send this man Ritter a letter of congratulations or something."

"Yeah," Sorvino said, "that's a good idea. Write it up and I'll sign it. If that's it, we can adjourn."

Sorvino bought a copy of the *New York Post* at the corner newsstand and hailed a cab. Sitting back in the cab, he was startled by the headlines: "MAYOR KENEALLY TO RUN FOR GOVERNOR." He leaned over on his knees to read the story inside.

When he finished, he again leaned back in the seat, thinking to himself, I guess this is why he wants to offer me something, but I wonder what he wants in return?

The cab stopped in front of the glass office building at 48th Street and Madison Avenue, and as Sorvino walked toward the building he noticed the long, low, wax-gleaming Cadillac waiting at the curb, its license plate, NY-1, making the car unmistakably important. The car was running, the chauffeur sitting behind the wheel keenly watching the entrance of the building. It won't be a long meeting, Sorvino assured himself.

The building lobby was strangely empty, except for a uniformed guard standing at the elevators.

"Can I help you?" the guard asked.

131

"The governor's office," Sorvino declared.

"Penthouse suite," the guard said, lifting a wall telephone and pointing to a waiting elevator.

Olden Hirschfield was standing in the small foyer as the elevator door opened. He greeted Sorvino and escorted him to the end of the hall, to a large mahogany door with the state seal implanted in the middle. Hirschfield opened the door for Sorvino but did not enter the room.

The governor was sitting behind a large, ornately carved table that served as a desk. He was dressed in evening clothes. Sorvino had been in the governor's office once before, but it was for a bill-signing ceremony and the room had been filled with people. He didn't notice then how clean, polished, and stately the room was.

The governor rose and shook Sorvino's hand across the table, saying, "You will excuse my dress, but I must rush off in a minute or so to dinner. Please sit."

Sorvino sat in a velvet-covered chair, wishing he could feel natural, as if he were used to sitting alone with a governor, but he was uncomfortable and his hands were sweating.

The governor shuffled a few papers on the table, arranging them in two neat piles. "For tomorrow." He smiled, looking at the two piles.

Sorvino expected to be offered a drink, or the traditional political cigar, but the governor did not have time for the amenities. He sat back in his chair, folding his arms, and said, "Angelo, I think Mr. Hirschfield has told you that Dr. Gareth will be leaving us shortly."

"Yes, sir, he did."

"He is well schooled in labor relations, and he has done an admirable job as state's mediator, but I have decided that the job should next go to someone from labor and not from the academic world. You and I, of course, go back a long way, and I not only remember the significant help you and the firemen have given me in past campaigns, but I have followed closely your own career on the labor scene. If you will permit me to say this, you have always represented yourself and your organization in a very commendable way. I think

132

it would be fair to say that you are a labor statesman . . ."

"Thank you, sir," Sorvino interrupted.

"And," the governor said, nodding in recognition, "I think that you should know that I am carefully considering you to replace Dr. Gareth. I asked you to come here this evening to find out how receptive you were to this position."

Sorvino stirred in his seat and answered, "Well, sir, I'm, uh, honored to be considered and naturally I'd be, uh, glad to serve the state in any way I can. It would be a job I'd like very much, you know, uh, the challenges of it, and the chance to do some good."

The governor stood and walked around the table, saying, "Well, that's good, fine. I'd just like to know where we all stand on these things before we make any decisions."

The governor extended his hand, and Sorvino rose to shake it. "I appreciate," the governor said, "that you took the time to come up to see me, Angelo, and you'll be hearing from us again, perhaps in a month or so, as soon as we make a firm decision."

"It's been my pleasure, sir," Sorvino said, as he was escorted to the door.

"Oh, by the way," the governor said, stopping near the door, "I see in the *Times* that you are coming close to a strike."

Sorvino reacted quickly, saying, "It's just talk now, governor. I don't think you'll ever see the firemen strike in this town, not if I have anything to do with it."

"Oh," the governor said, seemingly disappointed.

Sorvino was puzzled, not knowing what to say. He looked blankly at the governor, his mouth partly opened.

The governor paused, looking at the floor as if searching for the right words written on the rug.

"Angelo," he said, "have you seen this evening's paper?"

"Yes, sir, I have. I read it on the way here."

"Well, then, you will understand that the coming campaign will be a difficult one for us. The mayor of New York will be a strong candidate, and he will get stronger still if he settles harmoniously all the labor contracts that are now

133

due—without obstacle, if you know what I mean."

So that's it, Sorvino thought. He wants me to burn the mayor. He would not have had me come up here, he would not have brought the subject up, if it were any other way. I've got to think. I've got to leave myself an opening.

"Yes, sir," Sorvino said. "I know what you mean, but in any event the people of this state would realize how much more you have to offer in leadership than the mayor." Patronizing. Jesus, patronizing the governor.

The governor extended his hand once again, saying, "Well, thanks for the confidence, and thanks again for coming."

"Thank you, sir." Sorvino grasped his hand.

The governor opened the door, and Olden Hirschfield, who had been sitting in the foyer, started to walk down the hall. "Mr. Hirschfield will escort you to the elevator," the governor said.

Sorvino did not see the governor wink at Olden Hirschfield as he approached.

It began to rain slightly as he walked to the subway at Grand Central Station, but Sorvino hardly noticed it. The governor's words kept echoing through his mind. Labor statesman . . . stronger still . . . labor contracts . . . without obstacle . . . obstacle.

On the subway going to his apartment in Queens, the words hammered through him with the speed of wheels crossing over rail ends. Commendable . . . statesman . . . obstacle . . . state's mediator . . . chauffeur . . . limousine . . . obstacle.

The train pulled out of the Long Island City station and rounded the severe curve that breaks off from the other tracks and heads to Astoria.

The screeching of the wheels was deafening, louder than the screams at Union Hall, Sorvino thought. Then the thought came to him as the filtered voice, that ballbreaking voice, became clearer in his mind. It was Dan Fanilli's voice, full of bitterness, and hatred, and envy, yes, lots of envy, saying, "I just want you to take one goal, just one, and stick

134

with it for once." And what was it he was saying before the walls shook with cheering and applause? Thirty-two hours. Sure, that was it. "We must stick fast to the demand of a thirty-two-hour week." He remembered exactly, word for word, verbatim.

Then Sorvino relaxed confidently into the clickety-clack movement of the train.

6

THE OLD LANDMARK RESTAURANT ON Church Street was crowded with civil servants hurrying through their lunches. Angelo Sorvino was growing impatient with the man sitting across the table from him who was staring at a young waitress scurrying about.

"Listen, dammit," Sorvino said, "and never mind about that girl. Maybe you would've had a chance twenty years ago, but you're dreaming now."

Harry Silverman, president of the Integrity Balloting Company, kept eyeing the square-shouldered woman in the short uniform skirt and said, "Angelo, next time I come to this restaurant I'm going to sit at one of her tables, and then we'll see about that. Dreams, you know, are nothing but goals."

An old waiter came with plates of sausage and sauerbraten, and Harry Silverman turned to his lunch and to Sorvino. He picked up a knife and fork and said, "So we'll get down to business, yes?"

Sorvino stuffed a forkful of food into his mouth and then pulled an envelope from the inside pocket of his jacket. He said, between chews, "This is a copy of a referendum I want to go out as soon as possible. You can rush it to the printer's this afternoon, send it out in the morning."

Silverman opened the envelope and read the typewritten page. "So." He laughed, replacing the envelope. "To strike or not to strike, that is the question, may the bard forgive me. I'll get it out sometime tomorrow."

"Okay," Sorvino said, "you can send your envelopes over to my office this afternoon, and I'll have them run off on the addressograph and returned to you this evening."

"That's fine. I'll send them over as soon as I get back."

"There's only one thing," Sorvino said, putting his knife and fork on the table and leaning toward Silverman.

"What's that?"

"This is not a general election vote where counters and overseers are authorized by our constitution. This is a referendum ordered by me, and it is important for the future of our negotiations that the results of this referendum are known only by you and me. Understand?"

"Angelo," Silverman said, pointing his fork in Sorvino's direction, "so you want a secret vote, so what's the big deal? Me and Mrs. Silverman alone will count the votes, and no one else will see. I can promise you that, because what else does the Integrity Balloting Company have to sell but its integrity?"

Two miles above the Old Landmark Restaurant the fire truck screeched to a stop in front of Mishkey's Parlor, one of the city's many topless restaurants along Broadway. Jerry Ritter ran past a gathered crowd and through the curtain-covered front door, carrying an ax in one hand and a six-foot hook in the other. Behind him were the other men of Ladder Company 7.

The waitresses, their bare breasts tipped with tassles,

137

stood with a few remaining customers at the bar near the entrance, not yet threatened enough to leave the restaurant. There was only a light mist of smoke throughout the Persian-style room.

Jerry ran to the rear of the place, where a white-hatted cook was waving frantically. The cook pointed, and Jerry pushed open one of the large double doors that led to the kitchen. The thick, light colored smoke surged out into the dining area as if under pressure, and Jerry automatically fell to his knees. He crawled through the kitchen, coughing close to the floor, feeling his eyes smart from the smoke glaze. He saw a small red glow at the far corner of the room and felt relieved, yelling, "Hey, Tom. Tom Sullivan. It's a can job."

Sullivan was kneeling just behind Jerry, and he chuckled. "Must be a Greek restaurant." He coughed a little and directed the extinguishing can at the fire, spraying the water until the fire was safely smoldering. It had started in a pile of rags, greasy dishtowels that had been used by the cook as potholders and discarded in a plastic laundry basket. Someone had dropped a cigarette there, Jerry thought, or perhaps a burning match.

In the street the men of Engine 20 repacked their limp, unused hose, and the men of the surrounding companies waited for the chief to complete his inspection and give the order to take up. Jerry Ritter was taking a ribbing from the firemen.

"How's it feel to be a celebrity, Ritter?"

"Did ya get a modeling contract yet?"

"How about an offer from Hollywood?"

"What did you pay the guy from the *News*, Ritter?"

"You know, Ritter, you're on the road to being mayor now."

The chief walked out of Mishkey's Parlor and gave the order to take up, to return to the firehouses. As Ladder 7 went up Broadway, past the other firemen preparing to move out, Jerry yelled from the side step of the ladder truck, "You guys are all jealous."

He then laughed to himself, pleased that the firemen

138

who used to just nod a friendly greeting now knew his name. His picture on the front page of the *Daily News* had made him famous among firemen.

In the firehouse the men talked briefly about the bare-breasted waitresses and then went about passing the rest of the day's tour of duty. Some, like Dan Fanilli, talked about the future of the union. Some read, some watched television.

It was a quiet afternoon. There were no alarms, no visiting chiefs, no complaints of fire hazards to be investigated.

Jerry daydreamed the afternoon away, lying on a cot on the second floor of the firehouse, studying the whites and grays of the ceiling.

He would call for Susan Goldman at seven, go to an inexpensive pub-like place on 48th Street, and then to his apartment, one flight up above a chandelier shop, where he would hold her in a soft ceremony of music, poetry, and harmless words.

For several minutes he dreamed soft images of sexual love. Then he shook his head, as if awakening from a drunken sleep, and chided himself. What was it, he thought, that made him think of her only in relation to the movement of her body? Why didn't he picture her smiling on a ferris wheel, her hair blowing against a backdrop of ocean, or leaning over a railing by the river, watching the gulls fly? He composed the title of a poem, "And Someday You Will Find Her Spirit Too," and left it for another day to fill in the spaces.

He arrived at the gleaming brass entrance of the Park Avenue building at seven, spoke briefly to the doorman, and commented on the calmness of the evening to the starch-collared elevator operator. The elevator opened to a small foyer, where an old, gilded wall table made fresh with flowers stood next to a single door. Jerry had known women whose doors were down rich, carpeted corridors, but he had never known the wealth of an elevator foyer leading to just one door, one apartment, and he was impressed by it.

The door opened as the elevator operator slammed shut his gate, and before Jerry had a chance to ring the doorbell. Susan stood before him wearing an ankle-length dungaree skirt, bordered around the waist by a thick gold-link chain, and a ruffled blouse, of the kind Jerry remembered seeing in a book of Gibson prints. She held her hand out, casually, as if she had greeted him a hundred times before.

"I thought I heard the elevator," she said, holding his hand, guiding him into the apartment. "How are you, Jerry?"

"Better," he said, "now that I've seen you."

"You don't look so bad yourself," she said. Jerry was wearing a blue corduroy sports jacket, black flared pants, and an Italian-knit blue shirt, opened at the collar, so that the hair on his chest showed.

"I'll tell you what," he said, now holding both of her hands. "Why don't you permit me to give you now the kiss that you might feel obliged to give me later? Or don't you kiss on the first date?"

"I'll tell you what," she replied. "Not only can you kiss me now, but I'll still meet the obligation later."

He kissed her gently on the lips.

They sat in a large living room, the rose-patterned draperies coordinated with the couches. A maid entered, looking cheerlessly at Susan.

"Will you have a drink?" Susan asked.

"A coke, please," Jerry said looking toward the maid. Then to Susan he said, "I never drink anything stronger."

"I'll have a coke also, Annie," Susan said, and the maid left the room.

"Now," Susan said, "if you don't have something particular planned I have an invitation to a dinner dance that I'd completely forgotten. It's at the St. Regis Roof, and the food is always good there."

"Whatever you want to do is okay with me."

"The only thing is that most of the people there will be in evening clothes."

"You mean tuxedos."

"Yes, but I don't care about the rituals of propriety, and I can lend you one of Daddy's black ties so that they can't throw us out."

Jerry nodded his head in agreement but said nothing.

"You don't mind, do you? If you do, we can go to another place."

"No," Jerry said. "If you don't mind, why should I? Anyway, the whole purpose of my being here is to make you smile."

"I'm smiling, look. I'll go get the tie."

Susan left, passing the maid, who entered with the drinks on a small silver tray. Jerry thanked her and commented on the calm of the evening. The maid looked at him inquisitively and left the room.

"This will do nicely," Susan said, holding in front of her a black velvet bowtie. "Let's try it on for size."

She sat next to him, fixed his shirt buttons, and placed the tie around his neck. "Perfect," she said, standing, looking down at him. "Now let me introduce you to Daddy, and I'll bet you a thousand to one that he will not recognize his own tie."

They walked down a long, parqueted hall and into a mahogany-walled room. A tall, white-haired man rose from a reading chair as they entered. He held a book in his hand.

"Daddy," Susan said, "this is Jerry Ritter."

"Good evening, young man."

"Hello."

The man sat again, and Jerry stood before him.

"Susan tells me that you are a fireman."

"Yes I am."

"That must be very interesting work."

"Yes it is."

"Well," the father said, pausing a moment, uncomfortably, "enjoy yourselves."

"Thank you, Mr. Goldman. Good evening."

"Good-by, Daddy," Susan said, leaning over to kiss her father. She added, "I won't be late."

There was a row of chauffeur-driven cars waiting for the doorman of the St. Regis Hotel to open their doors. Jerry and Susan did not wait but got out of the cab and walked to the hotel entrance. In the lobby they waited, with men in black tuxedos and gold-buttoned shirts and with women in long

141

dresses and short furs, for the elevator to take them to the roof.

"Who's this for, anyway?" Jerry asked.

"A good friend's sister. Her name is Donna Robertson. It's a coming-out dance. A ritual that very nearly died during the age of relevance, but it's back in vogue now. Au courant, and all that."

"Yeah, I know, like a Knights of Columbus installation dinner. It's a big deal, right?"

The elevator opened at the Roof Restaurant, and they lined up with the others before a long table where two women checked names on a guest list.

"Susan Goldman and guest," Susan said to the woman.

The woman flipped a few pages back, went down the side of the list with her pencil, made a check mark, and said, "Thank you."

The woman looked at Jerry, made a slight grimace, but was polite enough to quickly look away.

Jerry and Susan began to follow those before them who had walked around the table and down a long, carpeted hall, but a man in a pinstriped suit, the restaurant manager, held Jerry gently at the elbow.

"Excuse me, sir," he said. "May I see your invitation?"

Annoyed, Susan said sarcastically, "We've already passed the Gestapo."

The man smiled, a broad professional smile, and said, "The name, please?"

Susan glared at him, saying, "Goldman, comma, Susan, comma, and guest."

The other guests, not wanting to push past Jerry and Susan, who were standing in the middle of the hall, waited while the manager went down the page of his own list. Satisfied, he said, "Thank you, Miss Goldman," and he turned away.

They walked down the hall to a reception line at the entrance to the large dining room. A man in a tuxedo, the first in a line of five people, leaned toward Jerry and said, "Your name please?"

142

Jerry extended his hand in expectation of a handshake, saying, "Jerry Ritter."

The man turned toward the gowned and corsaged woman next to him and whispered in her ear. Jerry dropped his hand to his side.

"And Susan Goldman," Susan said.

The man again whispered into the ear of the woman next to him.

"Hello, Susan. How good to see you."

"Hello, Mrs. Robertson. I'd like you to meet . . ."

"Mr. Ritter."

"Yes, Jerry Ritter."

"Hello, Mrs. Robertson."

"Good evening," Mrs. Robertson said, quickly shifting her eyes to the next guest whose name was being whispered into her ear.

Next Susan introduced Jerry to the guest of honor, a pretty girl with an aristocratic nose. Corsaged and jeweled, the girl stood before a grotto of daisies. "How very nice to meet you and how good of you to come," she said, sincerely, even modestly, and Jerry did not resent her happiness, her exclusiveness. This was a part of New York that was not his, but only a part, he thought, and the rest of it could belong to him.

There were thirty round tables in the big room, each centered with daisies and rimmed with ten velvet-cushioned chairs. They sat at one of the few unoccupied tables. A waiter asked if they wanted something to drink, but they declined.

An older man and woman came to the table and, before sitting, introduced themselves. Jerry felt the man's eyes looking at his corduroy jacket. Friends of Susan's waved from a table across the room and then laughed among themselves.

Other couples came to the table, each introducing themselves. Jerry felt an uneasiness with each introduction. Susan was warm and generous in her conversation, considerate. But still he felt alone and cold, like a dolmen on a plain. He looked about him at the busy tables, seeing teenagers, sheltered and secure in stylish innocence, their parents, chatting

143

and drinking rapidly, content, waiting for the drunken dizziness that would permit them to say things impertinent and seductive for which at other times there would be no excuse, and old doffers and their ladies suffering the last of their evenings—all of them, young, middle-aged, and old, dressed as if members of a wedding. He felt singularly different, out of uniform, and it was a new feeling, anxious and insecure.

He held Susan's hand with both of his and said, "I don't feel comfortable here, a little like a beer can in a collection plate."

He didn't have to say it, for she could sense it.

"Do you want to leave?" she asked.

"I wouldn't mind."

"I don't care one way or another, but perhaps since we're here we ought to stay for the food. I'm famished, and I don't mind pretending that it is just you and I sitting alone in a quiet restaurant. Everything else doesn't exist."

"All right, until the food then."

A man and a woman came to fill the last two chairs at the table. They needed no introduction, but the man introduced himself, saying, "Hello, I'm Kevin Keneally, and this is Mrs. Keneally."

The men at the table rose, the women smiled brightly, pleased that the mayor would sit at their table. Jerry was the last to introduce himself. "I'm Jerry Ritter, and this is Susan Goldman."

Jerry felt the blood surge to his cheeks as the mayor nodded.

Everyone sat, waiting for the mayor to say something.

"Well," the mayor said, "Donna Robertson is just lovely."

"An angel," one of the women said.

"A beautiful young woman," said another.

Mrs. Keneally was sitting next to Jerry, and the mayor leaned across her, saying, "You look very familiar, Mr. Ritter."

"I know that we've never met," Jerry said, "because I'm sure I would've remembered it. I'm one of your firemen."

"Oh, you're a fireman. Yes, now I remember. Was it your picture in the newspaper just yesterday?"

"Yes," Jerry said, "in the *News*."

"That was a great tragedy. You know, David Allen was a good friend."

"We could have saved him if we had gotten there just a little sooner. In our business a minute or two can make all the difference."

"Yes, I'm sure it does make a difference, and you know we're very concerned about this talk of a strike that's going about."

"I can only tell you, Mr. Mayor, that the men don't like working without a contract."

"What about yourself?"

"I'm a single man. I don't have a family to feed."

"Well, I know that the Office of Labor Relations is working on it, and not only on the firemen's contract. There are other city agencies working with expired contracts, but to have the firemen strike in this city where we have the highest fireload in the country would be outrageous."

Jerry squirmed a little in his seat, wondering, what the hell is he telling me this for, *me?* "I think," he said, "that you would have to be a fireman to understand it, in a position where you're not sure if the next week's check is going to meet the next week's bills."

The mayor paused. One of the other men at the table took the opportunity to wish him well in the run for governor, and the mayor thanked him at length. The dinner was served.

During the meal Jerry and Susan remained outside the table conversation, talking between themselves, finding each other's level of humor, concern, and intelligence, holding and squeezing hands intermittently, listening to the low tones of the quartet that played appropriate dinner music.

After dinner a full band replaced the quartet, and they played "The Sidewalks of New York." The mayor and his wife waltzed across the dance floor, the room erupting in polite applause, as other couples joined in the dance. Jerry

145

and Susan walked past the dancers to the elevators, Jerry still feeling the eyes of the crowd on his corduroy jacket.

They took a cab to his apartment on 73rd Street, and there on the floating bed in his living room-dining room-bedroom they laid arm in arm. A single candle lighted the room, flickering, making the shadows move on the walls.

"I never cared much for the rules," she said.

"Maybe I'm naive," he said.

"But it was a good dinner, and something to do," she said, her lips moving up to kiss his neck.

"Why couldn't I just relax and enjoy it?" he asked, stroking her hair.

"I wonder why they keep inviting me," she said, laughing a little.

"I never felt so defenseless before."

"You were marvelous, standing up to the mayor like that."

"It's amazing how the manner of dress can separate you from other human beings."

"There's something to be said for nakedness."

"Is that a suggestion?" he asked.

"An observation," she laughed, kissing his neck again, "but an inviting one."

Anne was watching television, a late movie. Tom had slept only an hour, and the dream came early. Anne heard him, and he was in her arms as he awakened, as he saw the black waiter's face writhing, as he yelled "Watch the floor."

Anne turned on the light, saying, "A glass of warm milk will do you good."

Tom lit a cigarette as Anne left for the kitchen, and he stared inexpressively at a print of Holbein's *St. Thomas More* on the wall before him, the smoke casually lifting before his eyes.

"Here you go," she said, handing him the glass and then snuggling in beside him. "Warm milk and a warm person is all anyone needs to relax."

"Maybe just a warm milky body is enough." He smiled, putting his arm about her.

"Can we talk?" she asked.

"Sure."

"About seeing a doctor."

"There's no point in it, Anne," he said, putting the emptied glass on the night table and wrapping his other arm around her. "A psychiatrist can't help me find out what I already know, and anyway we simply can't afford it."

"There are clinics."

"Sure, for the welfare cases. We're not a welfare case. We're not even a case."

"That's not true, Tom. The majority of people in this country can't afford private doctors, and so there are clinics."

"How much does it mean to you, Anne?"

"Oh, honey," she said, throwing her arm across his chest, squeezing hard, "if it will let you sleep one continuous sleep through the night it means everything. Just look at our lives, good lives, happy. The kids are healthy, thank God, and we have a love that keeps us close. Our lives are almost perfect, except for your dreams and the worry I have for you."

"Not to mention the bills we cannot pay, and the fact that we can't get the money up to go to a movie once in a while." He laughed.

"Come on now. I know you well enough to know that an occasional movie is not the end of the world."

"You were getting just too close to perfection."

"Well, we are perfect, nearly anyway."

"Did I tell you I almost had a love affair with a woman I sat with in a bar the other night, with Jerry and Dominic?"

"You're teasing."

"No, no. I sat down and told her that I was married and asked if that mattered."

"Was she pretty?"

"Gorgeous. Anyway, she thought I was different, because I told her I was married, and then Dominic started that fight and the romance was over."

"Oh, Tom, tell me you're lying."

"I'm not."

"Was she prettier than I am, at least in your eyes?"

"If she had been prettier than you, I would have run away with her and let Dominic fight his own fights."

"You didn't kiss her, did you?"

"God, baby, I wouldn't go that far with any other woman," he said, smiling, holding her face tenderly.

She raised her eyes to meet his and said, "Well, I'm not jealous, not at all."

"If I thought you were jealous, I'd keep secrets."

She sat up, putting both arms around his neck, and said, almost singing, "Oh, God, Tom. I love you so much."

"That's what keeps me alive, sweetheart."

They held each other closely, saying nothing, and the quietness of the room and the heaviness of their breathing became a statement of their love.

Finally Tom spoke, saying, "You can make an appointment at a clinic if that pleases you, because you are right. Our lives are getting closer and closer to being perfect."

She said nothing but snuggled more tightly against him.

"And maybe I'll begin to study for lieutenant," he added. He was good at facts, he knew that. The facts of personnel management, the book of rules and regs, the chemistry of fire, and all the other subjects in the guide for the lieutenant's examination would come easy to him. It would just take a few months before he would know it all cold. Facts. Spinoza he found difficult. "What the laws of the circle are to all circles, God is to the world" he found difficult. But memorizing clear, exact, separate facts would be brief exercise. Yes, he could be a lieutenant easily enough, there was no doubt in his mind about that, and he would have been a lieutenant years ago if he had only hit the books. But the fire came, and he lost all interest in ambition as his life changed. All that mattered was to live again as a fireman, until now. Anne was right. Their lives were good, happy. And the extra two thousand in salary would make them happier, something extra for Anne and the children.

148

"Yes," he said, "I'll do it. I'll study for promotion."

He looked down at his wife, who just smiled and sighed into his chest. He reached over and turned the light off, and then they slept, peacefully and fully through the night.

A few days later Anne was sitting at the kitchen table sewing a zipper onto a pair of pants, and Tom sat across from her sorting the morning's mail. Among the bills and flyers was an envelope from the Integrity Balloting Company. Tom opened it, pulled a return envelope and a piece of paper from it, and then read them again, studying them, looking for an ambiguous word or phrase, one that might change the meaning. The union had been known to phrase a referendum question so that the voter might actually vote for something he was against. Even state legislators write questions to deliberately confuse the public on referendums. But the language on the ballot that Tom held was simple enough:

ARE YOU IN FAVOR OF AUTHORIZING THE EXECU-
TIVE BOARD OF THE UNITED FIREFIGHTERS OF
NEW YORK TO CONDUCT A STRIKE ACTION BY THE
MEMBERSHIP OF THE UNITED FIREFIGHTERS OF
NEW YORK ON A DATE TO BE DETERMINED BY
THE EXECUTIVE BOARD OF THE UNITED FIRE-
FIGHTERS OF NEW YORK?

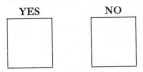

"Jesus Christ," Tom said, shaking his head.

"What is it?" Anne asked, putting the pants down.

"Look at this," he said, sliding the referendum across the table. "I wish I could write all over it, 'You don't have the right to ask this. No one does.'"

Anne read the question and then looked with concern at

149

her husband, saying, "Do you think they'll go through with it?"

Tom shook his head again and said, "I don't know. I hope not. Most of the men at the firehouse are against it, but they also say that the union needs the bargaining power of a strike threat. Then, there are some hotheads too . . ."

"You mean they'll vote for it even if they don't want to really do it?"

"Yeah, it's crazy."

"And what happens if the union really calls it?"

"I don't know. I hope they don't."

"But what will you do if they do?"

"I'll go to work like I'm supposed to—it would be wrong to do anything else."

"Will the other men go to work too?"

"I don't know. I hope so. If it comes to that."

"Haven't you asked them what they would do?"

"No. Honey, it's not something you can ask a working man about, whether or not he would go along with the union."

"Why not?"

"Because a union is all a working man has. It's all taken for granted. But," he continued, reaching over for the ballot, "there are some things more important. I think that."

He paused a moment and added, "At least for firemen."

He pressed down hard on the pen as he crossed lines in the box underneath the word "no."

Jerry Ritter stood on the corner of 72nd Street waiting for the First Avenue bus. He opened the envelope from the Integrity Balloting Company, and as he read the question images of the meeting at Union Hall ran in frames through his mind: A man, his jowls red with anger, yelling, "Do something for us for a change, for *us.*" Another, near crying, chanting hypnotically, "Strike, strike, strike." Still another, his fist clenched in short, shaking jabs, wordless, the swollen veins in his neck saying it all for him.

The bus came. Jerry showed the driver his badge and walked around an old woman leaning on a cane, searching through her purse for the thirty-five-cent fare. He sat on a molded plastic bench opposite the driver and read the question again, thinking, maybe I should vote for it. What the hell? This city never goes out of its way for us. Maybe I should put myself in the position of almost all the guys I work with —wives, kids, mortgage payments. Like I told the mayor, guys who barely get by from week to week. It's easy for me, single, rent-controlled apartment, no mouths to feed but my own. No, this city never goes out of its way for the firemen. The city doesn't care about firemen, guys breaking their horns working a second job to meet the bills. They treat us like everyone else. No different from the clerks, the cops, the teachers, garbagemen, transit workers. The bus driver there, he's a transit worker, same as my father. Is he so different from me and Tom and all the other firemen? Probably got a wife and kids and bills up the ass, just like my father had all those years. God, all those times I could never get a quarter up for a Sunday afternoon movie. But he is different, same as my father and all the other city workers. What the hell do they risk? We get killed doing our job, and people get killed, civilians, even when we give everything we got. Jesus, that poor guy in the theater, just a few minutes earlier. These guys never get killed. Even the cops don't get killed nearly as much as we do. *We are different, dammit.* And all these guys have already struck the city. The cops had a wildcat strike, the teachers go out all the time, the transit workers and garbagemen were out for weeks. Sure, they're different. They can strike and this city won't collapse. It still goes on.

But if we strike. Holy God. Yeah, Christ. If we strike, we'll be just like them. See that's the thing that makes us different. *We can't.* If we do we'll be just like all of them. We wouldn't be different. We could never be different again.

Jerry took a pen from his pocket, marked the "no" box on the ballot, and shoved it into the prepaid envelope. The bus stopped at 81st Street and Jerry got off, dropping the envelope into the postal box on the corner. He felt relieved, convinced of his rightness, as he walked toward Park Avenue and Susan Goldman.

It was four o'clock. Angelo Sorvino walked into the Municipal Building with his treasurer and sergeant-at-arms and took the elevator to the Office of Labor Relations on the twenty-fifth floor. A secretary escorted them down the hall to a plush meeting room, carpeted and centered with a long, oval table made of polished pine. Hamilton Stein, who was seated with two aides, rose to greet the union officials. After shaking hands, Sorvino moved around the table and sat at its center, the treasurer and sergeant-at-arms sitting on either side of him. Stein sat between his associates, directly across from Sorvino.

Sorvino looked unhappy, his face drawn into a snarl, and planned to make his displeasure noticeable.

"I see," Sorvino said crossly, "Mr. Jefferson isn't here. Is he late?"

Hamilton Stein cleared his throat and looked down at the table before answering. "Mr. Jefferson," he said, "asked me to convey his apologies, Angelo. He had a prior commitment of great importance. You know, since the mayor announced his plans, Mr. Jefferson has not had a moment's rest."

Sorvino sat back in his chair and held his briefcase in his lap. "Okay, Mr. Stein," he said, very directly. "Let's not waste each other's time. I came here in good faith to negotiate with Mr. Jefferson, but I guess he didn't think it was important enough to show up. My men are tired of waiting, and they're demanding that I make real movement on this contract. They've demanded that I take a strike vote, and the ballots have now gone out to the membership."

"It is my duty," Stein interrupted, "to tell you that the Taylor Law of the state of New York specifically prohibits strikes or job actions by public employees."

"Don't quote the law to me, Mr. Stein. I've been around longer than you think, maybe."

"I am doing my job, Angelo."

"Your job, Mr. Stein, is to move ahead on our contract, and the only way we're gonna do that is if Edward Jefferson sits at this table as the mayor's representative and signs the approvals. The strike vote is due to be counted in two weeks, and if we have to go right down to the wire, well, we're ready to do that."

"Angelo, please, this office is not intimidating you, and we ask that you not intimidate us. We are fully prepared for the final rounds of bargaining. Here, let me give you a copy of our counterproposals, and now that you are here we can go through them."

Sorvino took the manila-bound counterproposals, put them in his briefcase, and then stood. "I'll read them," he said, "and when I reply to them it will be to Mr. Jefferson."

He walked toward the door, followed by the treasurer and sergeant-at-arms, and then stopped, as if he had suddenly remembered a forgotten hat or umbrella. He turned to Stein and said, "There's one thing you ought to know, though. As in the past, our demands are negotiable, but this time there is one exception. Hours. Our demand for a thirty-two-hour work week is not negotiable. You have two weeks."

When the door closed behind the union men, Stein turned to his associates and said, "He has got to be full of shit."

Sorvino was smiling as he pushed the button for the elevator. It had gone well, he thought. As expected.

When the three men were alone in the elevator, the treasurer said, "Hey, Angelo, what the hell was that all about?"

"What's that?"

"You know, the hours."

"Thirty-two hours a week, like I said. We can do it." He was still smiling.

"The goddam city wouldn't even go for a thirty-seven-hour week, and you're asking for thirty-two? They couldn't do it, you know that. Even our economic advisers told us

153

they'd be fuckin' broke in a year's time if they went for a work-week reduction."

Sorvino's face turned momentarily bitter as he said, "The city is broke now, and don't tell me what the city can or can't do. You're talkin' like that kike bastard we just left."

The elevator door opened at the ground floor, and Sorvino was smiling again as they walked through the Municipal Building lobby, the treasurer pleading in a voice loud enough to turn heads, "But, Angelo, it's gotta be negotiable."

Sorvino did not answer but pushed through the revolving door and walked through City Hall Park to his office on Broadway, smiling all the way.

It was four-twenty. Edward Jefferson was in his apartment bathroom, shaving. He had just enough time to dine with an old friend and then make an early opening of a new Neil Simon play.

Inside City Hall Kevin Keneally threw the report on his desk, pressed the intercom button, and said, "Get me the fire commissioner." Less than a minute passed before his phone buzzed, and on the other end was an apprehensive fire commissioner saying, "Good evening, Mr. Mayor."

"Herb, I have read your report, and I'm frankly not happy with it. I talked to a fireman just the other night, and he didn't seem much against striking, yet you say here you don't think they will strike at all, and even if they do you can handle the situation with the officers' corps and nonstriking firemen. That doesn't seem to me to be a contingency plan at all, but an opinion."

"Well, ah, I'm sorry, your honor, but the contingency plan would operate the same as it would in any other emergency where there is a crucial deployment of manpower. Ah, we would operate the same as if we had a riot situation and use centrally located attack battalions, ah, you know, battalions . . ."

"Listen, Herb, I'm not interested in any of that. I want to know what you would do if you didn't have *any* firemen to work with. Do you understand that, *none?*"

154

"Well, sir, we really don't see any possibility of that happening, but if it did, we, ah, would have no choice but to call in the National Guard and save what we could from the outside, from the exterior, you know . . ."

"Herb, I don't know a damn thing about it. LaGuardia was the fire buff, remember? I want a contingency plan, and I want it tomorrow. Good-by."

The mayor dropped the phone on the receiver, placed the commissioner's report in the file basket, and picked up another manila folder, another report from another commissioner. Things had a way of backlogging now that he was running for governor.

PART TWO

7

NEARLY FOUR WEEKS HAD PASSED SINCE he first met her.

October came and the winds of a declining autumn whistled against Jerry's back as he walked down 73rd Street. He was carrying a brown paper bag from the corner delicatessen, where he had bought a breakfast of milk, coffee, and an Entenmann's cake. He said good morning to the postman, who was red-nosed from walking into the wind. It was a cold Saturday morning, and Jerry ran the rest of the way to his apartment, to the doorway next to the chandelier store.

He took the mail from his mailbox and raced up the one flight of stairs, two by two. His apartment was dark, and after putting the milk in the refrigerator he pulled open the heavy plaid curtains. The day's light flooded the room as in a stage play, bringing it to life. Susan stirred on the floating bed, drew the blanket over her bare shoulder, sighed a little, and turned on her side. Jerry threw his jacket over the back of a chair, propped up a couple of pillows, and lay facing her, watching the easy ins and outs of her sleep. She was very beautiful, he thought, certainly the most beautiful woman he had ever known, but way out of his class, like the real thing might be to a Union Carbide diamond. This was a simple affair to her, a game, another kind of rule breaking, and she would tire of it soon. Just last night she said that she wished all good and happy things were everlasting, but then she laughed and said that she occasionally became unrealistic. Well, that's all right, good things end, and they end. Take life as it comes. But the feeling inside, that's real enough, yes, real enough all right.

He put the back of his hand to her cheek gently, feeling the morning warmth, thinking of the times he had lain with her in the past weeks. How many? Eight, ten, twelve? It didn't matter. They were all segments, seemingly pulled magically from the air and patched into his life, one brighter than the other.

Many times in those past few weeks he had thought of her as a small stream breaking off from a river, a defiant, intense stream coming to rest finally in a quiet, secluded pond, far from the noise and push of the river. But the river was her real self, he was sure of that, and her real self was Parke-Bernet previews, and seminars at the Met, and starch-collared elevator operators. The pond was this efficiency apartment above a store, safe and peaceful. Different but going nowhere. He rubbed his fingers up and down her cheek, and she smiled without opening her eyes. He withdrew his hand, leaving her to slumber.

He turned to his mail. There was a telephone bill, a thin poetry magazine, a couple of grocery store throwaways, and then two envelopes, both from the union, that took his attention from the other mail.

The first was a letter from Angelo Sorvino congratulating him on the fine rescue attempt that resulted in his picture on the front page of the *Daily News*. Jerry crumpled the

160

letter and dropped it to the floor. Christ, he thought, a pat on the back for saving a dead man, and I'll bet he doesn't even know what Tom did.

The second letter was also from Sorvino, but this one was mimeographed. "Dear Brother," it said, "A special meeting of the United Firefighters of New York will be held at Union Hall on Tuesday, October 9, at 7:00 PM, to discuss the future action of this union. It is important that you attend."

"What time is it?" Susan asked. She was on her elbow, her head propped on her hand, looking up at him.

He smiled and put the back of his hand to her cheek again. She kissed it.

"Ten-fifteen," he said in a near whisper.

"Oh, God, no," she yelled, throwing the blanket back. "I have the dentist at ten and my electrolysis lady at eleven."

"Stay," he said, "fuck them both." He put the meeting notice on top of the other mail and dropped the pile to the floor.

"I can't possibly, Jerry," she said, buttoning the side of her slacks. She lifted a thin cotton polo shirt, put her head through its opening, and pulled it over her firm breasts. "I have so much to do . . ."

"I know," he said sarcastically, "after your electrolysis lady there is Elizabeth Arden at noon, then lunch at 21 with an old school friend, and then an afternoon of Pro Musica at Lincoln Center. You told me all that last night, and that's why I let you sleep, it's too much. Stay here with me for the day. You can do all those things next week."

She did not reply.

"Relax a little, Susan. You're too hurried."

She stepped into her shoes and put her arms through the long, fur-collared camel's hair coat. She took her heavy leather bag from the doorknob, opened the door, and then turned to him, saying, "What about tonight? I'm free after seven." She knew she had him.

"I'm working. You know that."

"See, Jerry," she said before closing the door. "You go your way, I go mine."

He listened to her steps travel down one flight of stairs, thinking, I will miss her, a lot, and more than that.

He picked up the small book of poetry from the floor and began to read, trying to take his thoughts from her. He read the words of unpaid poets until the phone rang.

"Jerry?"

"Yes."

"Surprise. It's Olivia Scannel."

"Surprise is right, and a nice one."

"I'll be alone for the next few days. Are you doing anything tonight?"

"I'm working."

"What about brunch, tomorrow?"

"Sure, Olivia, why not?" He dropped the small book of poetry to the floor once again.

Harry Silverman greeted Sorvino at the elevator. Since it was Saturday, the lobby guard had called to announce his arrival.

"Angelo," he said, "it's good to see you, but I don't think you're going to be too happy."

They entered a small suite of offices through a door marked "INTEGRITY BALLOTING COMPANY."

"What do you mean?" Sorvino asked.

Silverman sat behind a glass-topped desk, picked up a piece of paper, and looked at Sorvino, who had taken a chair before the desk. "We went through the ballots twice," he said, "Mildred and I did. Like you asked, we were the only ones to see, to count. We sent out 10,900 ballots, and 8,780 were returned, which is a normal response for your organization. The schoolteachers, for instance, never return more than sixty percent. Of the returns, there were fourteen voided votes, scrawled on and things like that. Voting "YES" on the question were exactly 3,850, and then there were 4,916 ballots marked "NO". Your men evidently don't want to strike."

He pushed the paper across the desk, saying, "Here's the verification."

Sorvino picked the paper up and, without reading it, folded it and put it into his jacket pocket. "Do you have a file copy?"

"Sure," Silverman answered.

"I'd like to have it. There shouldn't be a record of this, you understand."

"I can't do that, Angelo. I have to keep a record of all my balloting results."

"Harry," Sorvino said, "how many times have we engaged you in the years since I became president of my organization? Once a year at least. Twice, sometimes three times a year. That's a lot of business, Harry, and I have a lot of friends in New York labor. You know that because my friends also engage the Integrity Balloting Company for their own elections, their own referendums. Do I make myself clear?"

Silverman went to a filing cabinet for the copy. "Angelo, as far as I'm concerned," he said, shrugging his shoulders, "it's like the priest in the confessional." He gave the copy to Sorvino, adding, "Privileged, professional information."

"Good," Sorvino replied, standing. "Now what about the ballots?"

"They're boxed in the next room. You want I should send them to your office?"

"Yes, first thing Monday."

"It's done. Just one thing more. The billing. We had to raise it from thirty-eight to forty-five hundred dollars for the referendum. It's the inflation. It's killing us."

"Yeah, it's killing us too, but we'll take care of it."

Two days later Edward Jefferson got out of the taxi in front of City Hall and braced into the chilled, Monday morning wind. It was an unusual cold spell for October. He pulled his coat collar up, smiled past the police captain who was closing the taxi door, and bounced briskly up the whitestone steps.

He went directly to the mayor's office and, after greeting him, shed his coat and scarf and sat on the couch beneath a Matisse oil. He went to work, picking up the papers the mayor had left for him on the coffee table. He read first a copy of a letter that Sorvino had sent to the Office of Labor Relations. It was a blanket rejection of all the contract counterproposals. He then read the fire commissioner's most recent contingency report. Kevin Keneally sat at his desk reading and then signing outgoing letters.

When it appeared that Jefferson had finished, the mayor asked, "You have a meeting with them this morning?"

"Yes, in an hour. At the Commodore Hotel. These labor guys think negotiations are not legitimate unless they're held in a hotel meeting room."

"What do you think?"

"Well, we know that Sorvino took a vote to strike—the returns should be in by now—and that he scheduled a meeting of his men for tomorrow night. He's timed it nicely, with the elections less than a month away. We might be able to hold him off for a couple of weeks, make a settlement that appears strong on our productivity demands, and then hold the other unions back until after the elections. One contract won't hurt us too much, providing we can get Sorvino to make some concessions. His demands are ridiculous, particularly the reduction in the work week. Stein tells me he made particular reference to it and is seemingly set on it, but Stein also said he thinks it's an idle threat. I'm not sure. Sorvino just might be stupid enough to be intransigent."

"You know," the mayor said, almost compassionately, "most of organized labor is now working a thirty-five-hour week."

"We realize that, your honor, but the cost projections for a reduction in work week are staggering, particularly for the uniformed forces, the police, fire, and sanitation, and also the housing, transit, and corrections. All of them would have to increase manpower by whatever percentage their hours are reduced to provide service. We can't afford it, and until now I thought the unions would realize the absurdity of such a demand. All they have to do is look around them to see that much of organized labor is now on the unemployment lines. But they have no understanding of governmental and fiscal responsibilities, and if we reduced the firemen by even an hour we would be crushed by the wave of me-tooism from the rest."

"Well, you talk to him. I'm sure he'll be willing to trade it off."

"We'll have to do a lot of talking from now until tomorrow night. He didn't rent Union Hall without reason."

"He's said no to the counterdemands, but he'll come around."

"Yes, that's ritual and expected. He knows where we stand on the issues. We offered five percent across the board on wages and benefits, and we'll go to seven. It's fair. The real problem, evidently, will be the hours."

"And if he refuses to move?"

"We'll have to call him on it."

"He might then go through with it."

"The possibility is real enough. I already have counsel working on a restraining order. But if we can believe the fire commissioner, we won't lose much of the firefighting effectiveness. He thinks it doubtful that twenty-five percent of the firemen will participate and says he can get the job done if even seventy-five percent participate. So we have reason to be optimistic. Something we also have to consider is that this will be the contract all the other unions will study, and in the event of an unsuccessful strike we could ram through one hell of an initial contract. It could turn out to be an advantageous situation for us. On the other hand, if the commissioner is misgauging his men we could be faced with an unprecedented situation. The commissioner's contingency report mentions only one viable protection, the National Guard. The civil defense unit is nothing but a group of fire buffs who would not jeopardize the hangaround status they now enjoy in the firehouses, and the mutual-aid plan with suburban fire departments would depend on other union firemen in unlikely strikebusting. The federal firemen at the military installations are civilians and also unionized. That leaves only the National Guard to provide the essential manpower to successfully meet a crisis, but the political consequences of calling them are too great. Coolidge may have become President by calling the Guard to break a police strike, but we're not going to give Livingston Bennett that card to play with, however much he may welcome it. The only way he'll become presidential material is by running another successful gubernatorial campaign. To call him to ask for the Guard would in effect be announcing the death of your own campaign. We just can't do that."

The mayor, who had listened attentively, rose from his chair and walked around his corner desk, signaling the end of the meeting. "No," he said, "we cannot. It would be ruinous. You'll have to come to agreement with the United Firefighters, at any cost within reason."

Jefferson reached for his coat and scarf and rose from the couch. "Or," he said, sliding his scarf around his neck, "gamble that the fire commissioner is right."

The three boxes from the Integrity Balloting Company arrived at the union offices, and Sorvino carried them, one at a time, to the incinerator room in the hall. He spoke to no one. There he opened the boxes and threw the ballots fistful by fistful into the incinerator shaft.

It was almost ten o'clock. He hurriedly reentered his office and called the treasurer and sergeant-at-arms, telling each that he was ready to leave for the Commodore.

In the taxi Nick Imbroglia, the union treasurer, said, "What are you gonna tell them when we get there?"

Sorvino looked up from the negotiations schedule he was reading and said, "Same as I told all of you this morning. We're going all the way for the hours. I have the support of my men."

"How come you didn't mention what the vote tally was?" Imbroglia asked. The treasurer had been a South Bronx fireman before being elected to office and had been burned many times. An oil burner explosion one night left a burn scar on the side of his face that pulled on his upper lip, so that he seemed to be constantly sneering. Sorvino distrusted him because he could never see the man behind the sneer, and he silently regretted that the executive board had elected him a member of the negotiating committee.

"Because it's in nobody's interest to know what the vote was. It's enough to know that the membership voted approval."

Imbroglia was silent for a while, wondering to himself if there was anything to gain by telling Sorvino that he had seen him carry one of the three cartons from the office, and that he had looked at the labels on the remaining two, the labels that showed they came from the Integrity Balloting Company. No, he thought, there was nothing to gain, for Sorvino had the right to do as he pleased with the ballots. It was enough to know that he shitcanned them.

The taxi had waited through three red lights before Imbroglia spoke again. "Angelo," he said, "how come you changed your mind about supporting a strike? A couple of weeks ago you wanted nothing to do with it."

Sorvino looked up from his papers again, saying, "I got to go with the men if I want to be reelected. We all do, you know."

The three men took the Commodore elevator to the third floor, the ballroom floor, where they were met by Charlie McCarry, the union attorney. McCarry was worried.

After shaking hands with the three men, he said, "I just received word that the corporation counsel has begun work on a restraining order to enjoin you from authorizing any kind of work stoppage at all."

Sorvino said nothing and walked down the hall to one of the smaller rooms adjoining the huge ballroom. There, a long, linen-covered table was set with cups, saucers, and spoons. Sorvino sat on the near side of it, in the middle chair. A waiter was placing sugar bowls and creamers on the table. Imbroglia sat to Sorvino's left, and the attorney and sergeant-at-arms sat to his right.

His group was the first to arrive, and Sorvino was annoyed.

The attorney was offended that Sorvino did not reply to his statement about the restraining order, and he leaned

167

toward Sorvino, saying, "You heard what I said about the corporation counsel?"

"Have you heard," Sorvino replied sarcastically, "of any work stoppage in this city where there wasn't a restraining order? It means nothing."

"It could put you in jail."

"It wouldn't be the first time," Sorvino said, in a tone meant to end the discussion, "that a labor leader went to jail for the good of his men." Then, thinking that the room might be concealing a bug, he added, "But we'll do our best to settle this contract peacefully."

Hamilton Stein, followed by three men carrying briefcases, entered the room. After exchanging greetings, Stein took a seat on the far side of the table, leaving the seat directly opposite Sorvino empty. His aides also sat, emptying their briefcases of papers and reports, as Stein asked, "Do you approve of the negotiations schedule?"

"It's all right," Sorvino answered.

Stein then rose quickly to his feet and rushed toward the door. Edward Jefferson had arrived, and everyone rose to meet him as if he were the Pope's chosen cardinal.

Introductions were made, and as Jefferson and Sorvino clasped hands they glared sternly at each other, knowing that any real argument to be made in the room would be made only by the two of them. They were natural adversaries, Jefferson coming from prep schools and the Ivy League, and Sorvino coming from the High School of Machine and Metal Trades. Even their clothes articulated their differences—Jefferson perfectly pressed and creased in Brooks Brothers, and Sorvino in a baggy Robert Hall suit that his wife had brought home one day.

Jefferson sat, and Sorvino began as a politician. "Mr. Jefferson, when Kevin Keneally came into his office he came with the support of labor, bringing new hope for labor with him. He still has labor support, and I hope it's in the atmosphere of that support that we can wind up a decent contract for the firefighters of this city."

Jefferson nodded his head slightly in acceptance and agreement, but he said nothing. Stein went to the first item on the negotiations schedule, wages.

Each side displayed formulas, graphs, reports, and statistical and cost analyses, and the bargaining went from side to side. Every man at the table said something, a brief observation or rejoinder, but Stein and McCarry did most of the talking, each looking occasionally at either Jefferson or Sorvino for agreement, rebuttal, or acquiescence. The waiter kept the cups filled with coffee, and the room began to hang with the smell of nicotine.

An hour passed, and then an hour and a half. Finally they agreed, as both sides expected to agree, on a seven percent increase in salary. One of Stein's aides wrote the tentative words of the wages clause on an Office of Labor Relations form and duplicate, and Sorvino and Jefferson initialed both copies.

Stein then turned to the second item, benefits. They bargained with little agreement through the morning. Sorvino wanted a two-dollar-a-day increase in each fireman's annuity fund and a change to a better, more expensive medical insurance plan. Jefferson said no to both demands but approved an increase in the line-of-duty-death award. The men adjourned for lunch.

When they returned, Jefferson approved a one-dollar-a-day annuity increase, and Sorvino conceded the medical plan demand. They initialed the tentative benefits clause.

Then Stein smiled, saying, "We go to the third item, hours."

He waited for a response from Sorvino, but Sorvino was silent.

Stein continued, "It is the city's unalterable position that any reduction in hours is unfeasible at this time."

Sorvino lifted his briefcase to his lap and picked out a plastic-covered report. He pushed the report across the linen, saying, "I had this prepared for your information. It's a list of all the locals in New York City who work thirty-five

169

hours a week or less—seventeen pages long, starting with the electricians, who work twenty-five hours a week. It's time for the firefighters to get on this list."

"We also have a report," McCarry added, "that illustrates the health and safety benefits of a reduced work week, the feasibility of such a reduction, and a cost analysis thereof." The attorney pushed that report across the linen.

Stein took the reports and set them aside, saying, "We just can't do it, Angelo. You know, you are bargaining here not only for eleven thousand firemen but for the three hundred thirty-nine thousand other civil servants who will search this contract for an extra equitable penny."

Sorvino grew angry and slammed his opened hand on the table. "Don't give us any horseshit about the other city workers. We're the firemen here that you're talking to, and we're different than those other guys, and that's exactly why no one else counts at this table but the firemen. You understand?"

Stein began, "Angelo, I'm sor . . ."

Jefferson interrupted, saying, "Perhaps, Mr. Sorvino, we ought to go to item four, for the time being. What is it? Yes, I see, job description and definition. Then we can go to working conditions, safety, productivity changes, and so on. Let's agree to as much of the contract language as possible. Then we can come back to this."

Sorvino agreed to go on. It has to be done sometime, he thought.

The talks progressed through the afternoon, as cold and as dogged as the fall wind sweeping against the hotel windows on 42nd Street.

At six o'clock they ordered room-service dinners and talked through the meal. At eight o'clock both sides reached tentative agreement on the last item on the negotiations schedule, a change in the medical-leave procedure, and Sorvino and Jefferson initialed the clause.

The attorney, treasurer, and sergeant-at-arms were relieved. It was a good contract, one that they could present to the membership with enthusiasm and optimism. But they

170

knew it was still incomplete. The hours clause had yet to be written, and the three men became excited by the prospect, knowing that a reduction in work week would make it the best contract ever to be presented before the membership in the history of the United Firefighters of New York. They looked to Sorvino, who had pushed his chair back and was standing before the table.

"All right, Mr. Jefferson, we come back to the hours. Are you ready to talk about a thirty-two-hour work week?"

Jefferson looked up tiredly and spoke matter of factly. "I'm ready to bargain, Mr. Sorvino, and if you'll sit perhaps we can trade off the hours demand in your favor."

"No," Sorvino said mutinously.

"That's hardly in the spirit of negotiations, Mr. Sorvino. The city cannot reduce the work week at this time, but we are willing to talk, to trade."

Sorvino was careful not to smile. It was going as he predicted to himself it would.

"A reduction in hours is our demand, and a reduction in hours is what we'll get. You have until Wednesday morning, Mr. Jefferson. If the city don't come around by then I'm taking my men out of the firehouses."

"It never helps to threaten, Mr. Sorvino."

"I'm tired," Sorvino said, reaching for the coat that he had earlier thrown across a chair. The attorney, treasurer, and sergeant-at-arms also went for their coats.

Sorvino buttoned the herringbone coat from the bottom up, and as he came to the last button he said, "You know where to call me, and maybe the next time we meet you should have the mayor with you. Because I'm not moving until my hours are reduced."

Jefferson wanted to scream, to rise and point his finger at Sorvino and say, "You little punk, reaching out to choke this city with your pudgy little fingers, you and your little group of high school graduates trying to threaten this city, this great and powerful city. Get out. Get out of my sight."

But Jefferson was too smart for that, too experienced, too long in the company of power. He gathered the papers in

171

front of him, shuffled them, and replied casually, "We'll see, Mr. Sorvino."

It was Tuesday afternoon, the second week in October. Jerry was sitting with his legs on the wall of the closet that was used as a public phone booth in the firehouse.

The maid answered the phone, and Jerry said, "This is Jerry Ritter. Can I speak to Susan, please." It was not a question.

"Hold on," the maid said, and left the phone for less than a minute.

She came back on the line and said, "She's not at home, Mr. Ritter."

Jerry took his feet from the wall and stood. "Annie," he said, "is she really not home or did she tell you to say that?"

The maid flustered. She liked Jerry. "I really don't know what to say to you, Mr. Ritter."

"It's okay, Annie, I understand. I want to leave a message for Miss Goldman. You tell her for me that I have a lot of happy memories. You got that, Annie? Happy memories."

"Yes, Mr. Ritter. Happy memories."

"Thanks, Annie, you're terrific."

Jerry hung up the receiver and sighed as he listened to the dime drop into the box, thinking that another segment of his life was ended. He pictured her face, felt again for just a moment the soft heat of her skin, and heard her easy, genuine laughter. Yes, he would miss her.

"Hey, Ritter," a voice rang out. "Department phone."

Jerry, shaken from his thoughts, went to the phone at the housewatchman's desk. Tom Sullivan, on the afternoon watch, handed him the phone, and after listening for a moment to his brother's voice on the other end Jerry said, "Sure, Tom, I'm going. I'll meet you there in the diner next to Union Hall. Only this time no bar fights, all right?"

Tom Sullivan got up suddenly and yelled with the fullness of his voice, "Chief in quarters!"

Jerry turned and then spoke into the phone, "I'm glad Dominic is working tonight, but I have to go. We have a

172

visit." He put the receiver down and made sure his shirt was properly tucked into his pants as the men hustled to the front of the apparatus floor, from the upstairs, the kitchen, and the cellar. They lined up in front of the apparatus in two rows, the men of Ladder Company 7 behind the men of Engine Company 20.

The lieutenants from each company came down the stairs, their ties properly placed at the neck, and saluted the battalion chief.

"Do you want a roll call?" one of the lieutenants asked.

"I expect you to do what the book of regulations tells you to do, lieutenant."

"Yes, sir," the lieutenant said. He faced the men, called them to attention, ordered a dress right dress, and then called for a hand salute. The chief returned the salute, and the men relaxed, thinking the ritual complete.

But Chief Joseph McDermott of Battalion 5 had not come to the firehouse routinely, and even if it were routine he would not permit the slightest informality.

"No one called you at ease," he said harshly. "Stand at attention."

The men responded grudgingly, some forcing an exaggerated stance. Among these was a man in the back row who was wearing a knitted seaman's cap, placed like a large skullcap at the back of his head.

Pointing, the chief called to him, "You, take that thing off your head. What are you, a clown? Where the hell do you think you are?"

The man humbled in a slouch, saying, "Sorry, chief," and took the cap from his head.

The group, rigid at attention, reminded Jerry of students at a military prep school being spoken to as children, and he thought then of the long haul through the heat and smoke with the body of David Allen. He smiled at the incongruity.

Chief McDermott scowled. "Something funny, fireman?"

Jerry stood straighter and said, "A personal thought, chief. It was impolite. I'm sorry."

173

"There's no room in this department for personal thoughts, fireman. This is a semimilitary organization. That's why I have you standing at attention, and don't you forget it. When a chief talks to you, you think only about what he is saying."

Jerry said nothing, felt nothing, except perhaps an understanding of the man before him, and therefore acceptance.

The chief then addressed the group, saying, "You all know the rumor throughout the job that there's going to be a strike called, maybe tomorrow. In that event, according to the commissioner's directive number 143, dated today, I will be assigned to supervise this firehouse. So I'm here now to read the regulations to you."

But the chief did not read, for he had memorized it years before.

"Paragraph one, point three, point twelve reads, 'Any willful failure to respond to a direct order of a superior officer of the department will result in immediate suspension without pay until a full hearing is made by the fire commissioner.' "

The chief lit a cigarette and threw the match, still burning, on the apparatus floor. "That," he continued, "is cut and dry, and I suggest you read it again to yourselves. Now I want to give you a personal message. I've been in this job for thirty years, and I never thought I'd see the day the men in this job would think about a strike. I vow to you that I'll do everything I can to keep my battalion operational under any conditions. This job of ours is vital, the most vital job in the city, and to think of dishonoring it is disgusting. This job doesn't belong to you or to me, but to all the men who served proudly before us, and to the men who will come after us. And it belongs to all the men who gave their lives in the line of duty. The graves of those men will be spit upon if you strike, and I can tell you men that I fully expect you all to follow my orders if that happens. Think about your families, and your futures, and about having some pride in yourselves and in this department, and think about those men who died

174

because they believed in this job. Dismissed."

The chief turned and left the firehouse.

In the kitchen of the firehouse Dan Fanilli said, "That McDermott thinks he's Dana Andrews or Pat O'Brien talking in a goddam foxhole. What he should have said was think about all the inequities in this job, and think about how we've been deluding ourselves for all these years as we put men in their graves, while the city laughs their asses off, screwing us with every contract."

Some of the men sitting around the kitchen table nodded.

Jerry was eating dessert in the diner when Tom arrived.

"Sorry I'm late," Tom said, "but we had a job at five o'clock and didn't get back to the firehouse until after six. We'd better go. It's seven already."

"Yeah, I don't want to miss a minute of this." He left two dollars on the counter.

"It looks like we're going to go all the way," Tom said.

They walked toward the sergeant-at-arms at the door of Union Hall.

"Well, we'll see what Sorvino says," Jerry said. "You got your badge this time?"

Tom laughed. "Yes," he said, drawing it from his pocket, "I remembered."

The hall was already packed with firemen talking quietly among themselves. There were no chants, no jeers, no angry voices. They had all been touched by the rumor of the impending strike, and the hall was sticky with uncertainty and apprehension. The situation was new, there was no precedent to remember, and so the behavior was subdued.

The Ritter brothers walked down the center aisle, searching each side of the hall, but there were no empty seats. They decided against going to the balcony and walked through the space between the front row and the stage, beneath the executive board which had just arrived, and leaned against the side wall.

Sorvino stepped to the podium and, after testing and

175

adjusting the microphone, said, "This is a very important meeting, brothers, and we ask for your complete cooperation." There were no catcalls, no Bronx cheers. The hall was heavy with the seriousness of the moment. "Please rise, and we'll say the Pledge."

The Pledge was reverent, delivered as prayer.

Sorvino then read the words he had written an hour before. "As you know, this is a special meeting. We're here to talk about a strike, and because of the great importance of the things I have to say, and the things you have to understand, I will not open the meeting to a discussion from the floor. Before I go on, I want to make absolutely sure there are no reporters or strangers here, so will you please look at the badge of the man next to you. That's it. Please take your badge out and show it to the man sitting next to you . . ."

The side wall had become buttressed by a line of leaning firemen, and Jerry and Tom extended their badges, looking at the badges held to them.

"Thank you. Now, to fill you in on our negotiations, let me say first that I have met with Edward Jefferson, the mayor's assistant, and we have agreed on many of the items of a new contract. But the city refuses, absolutely refuses, to meet certain demands we have made, or for that matter to even talk about them, especially our demand for a reduction in hours. But I'll tell you this . . ." He paused. "We don't have a fairer demand than the reduction in hours, and dammit we're going to get it, just like every construction trade in this city. But . . ." He paused again. "I'll tell you this also. Either we pack it in right here and now or we go all the way for it, and we're going all the way." There was applause, some applause, but most men waited. "Now, I have the results of the strike vote, and the overwhelming majority of the membership voted an authorization to strike, and that's what we're going to do tomorrow morning at nine o'clock."

An overwhelming majority, Jerry repeated to himself. God Almighty, Tom thought. Most of the men were now applauding, made secure by the phrase going through their minds as through Jerry's. Soon those who did not clap felt guilty among their comrades, different, and fearing isolation within their brotherhood they smacked their hands together, becoming a part of the applause as each fireman was a part, a working part, a contributing part of the group—here in the hall, in the firehouse kitchen, or in fires. Tom leaned against the wall, his hands in his pockets, watching Sorvino smile as he held his palms forward for order.

"Now," Sorvino went on, "I have made arrangements with WYNS radio to inform my membership of any change, any agreement. Listen to that station tomorrow morning, take the kid's portable with you, and continue to listen. Do not be intimidated by outside information, rumors, newspaper reports, or anything. WYNS will put me on the air, live, whenever I call them, so wait for word from me only.

"The delegates will make sure that every man is in front of his firehouse prior to nine o'clock. We will have picket signs delivered to the firehouses. If your company is at a fire at nine o'clock, finish the operation, return the apparatus to the firehouse, and get on the picket line. I talked with the president of the officers' association and he has promised that his men will not perform the work of the fireman rank. They have sworn to protect life only, and not property, and therefore we have given them permission to drive emergency vehicles that firemen would ordinarily drive. But they will not carry hose, and they will not operate the pumps. They won't scab our job. There will be no water on any fire in the city of New York."

The men, hearing of the support from the officers' union, were on their feet applauding. Sorvino put his hands up again and continued.

"I want no destruction of the department's property, no sabotage of equipment. We're gonna have a tough enough time as it is without being accused of destroying property. Just make sure you get your firefighting gear out of the firehouse and picket in an orderly fashion. Remove all Fire Department identification from your cars, and park your cars a good distance from the firehouse. This is for your own protection."

177

Sorvino looked up from his prepared speech at the thousands of men sitting before him. Hardworking men, he thought. Men who work too hard for too little, yet men who love their job. If anything can be said about firemen, it is that they love their job as much as they love anything. Yet they would follow him in this strike, follow the leadership of their union. He loved them for that and silently cursed Keneally, Jefferson, Stein, the whole city, for not caring about them.

"Brothers," he said, "I know that this is going to be hard on each one of you. None of us wants to turn our back in the face of fire, for we are all men here, stand-up guys, proud of ourselves, our families, our flag, our religions. *But this city doesn't give one flat shit about any of us, and we are being forced with our backs against the wall to let this city see what they can do without us.*"

The applause was great and sustained, and Sorvino had to pound the top of the podium to regain order. He continued, in a more moderate voice, "All this information is printed, and please take a copy of it on your way out. The copies will be stacked by the door. Now, the press will probably be outside when you leave. Don't talk to them. And, most of all, don't worry about anything except what you have to do. *No man will be fired. If they fire one, they fire all of us. Our strength is only in our unity. We'll go out together, and we'll come back together.* This meeting is adjourned."

The men filed through the narrow doors of Union Hall to the blaze of camera lights on 34th Street. "No comment," many of them said to the questioning reporters. One, disregarding Sorvino's order, said, "We're all together here, you can see that. We're united."

The reporters surrounded this lone speaker. "Will there be a strike?" one asked. "Are you really going through with it?"

The fireman, knowing they wouldn't put his words on the air, said, "Fuckin' right we are."

Sorvino came to the door, surrounded by his executive board.

178

"Angelo," a television reporter said, microphone in hand, "Is there going to be a strike? Are you really going to leave this city without fire protection?"

Sorvino read from a piece of paper the attorney handed him. "Due to the failure of the city negotiators to meet our contract demands, which are just and fair, and due to the recalcitrance of the city negotiators in refusing to continue discussions, the firemen of New York City will be on strike effective nine o'clock tomorrow morning."

A large, disheveled man in brown checkered pants pushed his way to the front of the crowding reporters. It was Vinnie Grant. "What about the strike vote?" he said, "How did your men vote?"

Sorvino did not look at Grant but stared at the glaring camera lights behind the cameras. "I have called this strike," he said. "The overwhelming majority of my men voted for it."

Tom sat in his car and reached over to pull the lock up for Jerry. They drove across 34th Street toward the East River Drive.

"I'm not going out, Jerry," Tom said.

"It will be hard, Tom, if you don't."

Tom turned onto the drive and headed toward the 61st Street exit.

"I couldn't keep the job if I went against my own feelings."

"Well, I'm not happy about it, but it's what the brothers want."

"The brothers are wrong," Tom said, slapping his hand on the wheel.

"But we have to keep together," Jerry answered.

"That's not high on my list of priorities."

"It's the only thing we have working for us. Look, I voted against this thing because I felt that the right to strike was the one thing that makes us different. Maybe we still don't have that right, but we can't split the job. That's what's important now."

Tom turned off the drive and went uptown on York Avenue.

"We are different, Jerry, because we live in a closed world that no one knows about, or cares about, but it's a world of decency where men care about other human beings and love each other as brothers, as I love you. This strike is going to blow that all up."

The car stopped at the corner of 73rd Street and Jerry opened the door. He put one foot on the street and thought of the many other times Tom had dropped him off, times when he would simply slam the door, saying, "See you around."

But now he just sat on the seat, one foot resting on the street, surveying the man across from him. God, he looked old, more like forty-two than thirty-two, the eyes wrinkled at the sides and puffed at the bottom. And tired. He looked beaten and worn, no fight left.

"Tom," he said, raising his voice just a little, imploringly. "Jesus Christ, Tom, you can't do this. You can't walk into a firehouse everyone else has walked out of and scab this job."

Tom raised his eyes, but Jerry continued. "That's right, scab this job, because that's what they are all going to say and you might as well get used to it."

"Maybe they won't all go," Tom said, a quiver in his voice. The cold air was sweeping into the car.

"Bullshit. You heard them there. Every man there was for it, the goddam clapping and the goddam screams when Sorvino said we'll go out the door together and we'll go back together, every man."

"And every man will be wrong."

"Come on, Tom, don't tell me that eleven thousand men are wrong. We're being pressed by this city, and we can only beat them if we stay together."

"But you're wrong, Jerry. Can't you see?" Tom's voice was growing loud and impatient, as he continued. "What do you think Spinoza and Kant and Spencer would say about it? You know something about ethics, don't you? Do you know what Spinoza would say? He'd say only the informed and

180

mature can judge, Jerry, and you don't know a goddam thing about it. You are not informed, Jerry, and this has nothing to do with staying together."

Tom looked into the disappointment of his brother's eyes and felt pain. He listened to his brother's words and felt more pain.

"Tom," Jerry said quietly, exhaustedly, "none of those guys are going to help you when you have to walk into a fucking firehouse in the morning."

The traffic signal was red, and Tom sat in the car watching his brother walk strongly, determinedly down 73rd Street toward his apartment.

He turned the radio on to the all-news station as he drove up the Bruckner Expressway, and he heard the last part of a message being delivered by the fire commissioner. He turned the volume higher, listening intently. ". . . And every officer of my department will assist and encourage those firemen who will live up to their sworn oath to protect life and property in New York City. Any fireman who might be disinclined to go to his own firehouse for whatever reason may go instead to his division headquarters, or to the division headquarters nearest his home."

The newsman's voice came across, saying, "That was Fire Commissioner Herbert Thomas in a special announcement of advice to the city's firemen. Negotiations in that contract dispute between the United Firefighters of New York and the city have been stymied. Edward Jefferson, the mayor's right-hand man, has just released a statement saying that it is possible for negotiations to resume if the United Firefighters of New York would readjust their demand for a thirty-two-hour work week. . . ."

Tom shut the radio off and thought of the commissioner's words. No, he said to himself, I belong in my own firehouse. Why should I be afraid of what's right?

In his bed, after kissing the children good night, after an hour of coffee and toast with Anne, telling her of the morning's threat, and after the frenzied moments of love sharing, he held her in his arms, his eyes closed, thinking as he

181

thought each night of a long, unbroken sleep.

Anne cut the quiet of the room, saying, "It won't last long. It can't."

"I don't know," he said. "I hope not."

"And when it's over, everything will be all right. Everything. I meant to tell you something earlier, but with the news of the union meeting and everything it slipped my mind. I made an appointment for you with a staff psychologist at the New Rochelle clinic. They normally have a waiting list for weeks, but someone canceled and they put you in. It's for Saturday morning, ten o'clock."

"That's good, Anne," he said pensively. "Maybe it will help."

"Oh, it will, Tom. Everything will be perfect, I know it."

Tom held her tighter, reassured by her enthusiasm, and then thought of the coming strike and of the disappointment in his brother's eyes. Christ, he thought, would sleep ever come this night?

8

JEFFERSON ARRIVED AT GRACIE MAN-
sion at seven o'clock. The cold spell had not moved off as
predicted, and he shivered as he ambled up the porch steps.
It was another early day, he thought, and it would be a
long one. Behind him, the October wind whipped the fallen
leaves on the mansion's lawn, as if in warning.

Breakfast was served, and Kevin Keneally, still in pajamas and bathrobe, listened intently as Jefferson talked, nodding his head in agreement or grimacing in anger. The
negotiations had not gone as he had hoped they would, and
his mind was running with options as his assistant continued.
But there were only two real options, he realized, that would
be effective. He could call Sorvino, or he could not. It was as
simple as that.

"I think it is the best course, sir," Jefferson concluded,

"to see it through. Sorvino is in trouble politically, his reelection is doubtful, and finally it all seems orchestrated. He has his strike vote. He wants to go."

"We cannot move on the hours," the mayor said forcefully.

"No."

"You don't think it would help if I spoke to him?"

"No, it might even prove embarrassing."

"Then we'll stand firm. We cannot be dictated to."

"No, sir."

Angelo Sorvino sat in a room on the third floor of the Hotel Shelton on Lexington Avenue, safe from the pursuit of city marshals and the restraining order issued by the Supreme Court of New York County.

The sounds of the television and radio competed in the small room, and Sorvino went from one to the other, as an engineer might monitor boiler-pressure graphs. The television's network news program made no mention of the impending strike, and the radio announced it just periodically, between other news. There were no special fire prevention appeals, no special emergency instructions. It was just another strike, another hardship to be endured by New Yorkers.

The bed was unmade, and a telephone lay upon it. Sorvino had slept irregularly, waiting for it to ring, expecting to hear Jefferson's last-ditch offer to reduce the work week to thirty-seven and a half hours. He had, in the night hours, memorized a rejection speech, polite but firm.

But it was growing late. And when the phone finally rang at eight-thirty it was only his secretary, who had worked through the night, calling to say there was no word from the mayor's office. There were a few calls from newspaper reporters, but he would not return them.

He was surprised that Jefferson did not call, and he regretted a little that he would not have the small triumph of saying no. But still there were no obstacles now, and it was going as he had hoped it would, as he knew it would.

184

On East 48th Street, the men of Engine 20 and Ladder 7 stood in small groups in front of the firehouse. It was twenty minutes to nine. Jerry was reading the picket signs that had been delivered to Fanilli and stacked against the firehouse wall. They were of two kinds. The first read "FIREFIGHTERS ON STRIKE," and the second, "THE CITY OF NEW YORK UNFAIR TO FIREFIGHTERS."

The small wicket in the bigger apparatus floor door opened, and Tom Sullivan came out of the firehouse smiling. "Hey, guys," he said, "listen to this."

The men walked toward him, expecting some news of the negotiations.

Sullivan went on. "I just called my wife and told her that the strike was coming off, that the picket signs were here, and that everybody was walking off the job. And do you know what she said to me? She said come on home and we'll do some shopping. Don't let the whole day go to waste." The men laughed a little, their breath fogging the cold, but they were not distrac̣ from the coming moment. In just minutes the nine o'clo̱ test signal, eleven bells, would ring through the firehouse, and then it would be a matter of waiting for the alarms to come in.

The thought had occurred to each of them that if a fire broke out across the street, they would run to it and do what they could—a reaction as natural as breathing. But if the fire was around the corner, that would be a different story. They couldn't see it, they couldn't react. They would be picketing as they knew they had to. Let the city handle it.

A squad car with two patrolmen parked near the firehouse, but the men sat in the car as ordered, their trained eyes watching for disorder.

Vinnie Grant pulled to the curb in a gray Checker staff car, the side door emblazoned with a picture of a camera and the words *"Daily News."* He had already talked to other firemen at a firehouse on 41st Street, around the corner from the News Building, and he would go to as many firehouses as possible for the duration of the strike.

185

He looked the men over carefully, and he went directly to one, a husky fireman in a red and black windbreaker who seemed isolated from the group, saying, "I'm from the *News*, and I'd like to ask you just one question."

The man looked closely at Grant, who was in baggy pants draped over spoiled shoes, and decided he looked un-bureaucratic enough to oblige, enough unlike a boss from the fire commissioner's office who might be nosing around.

"Sure," the man said.

"I'd like to know," Grant said, pad and pencil readied, "why you are about to strike for the first time in the firemen's history. Now, I'm not asking about the others, but about you personally."

The man's answer was ready-formed, instantaneous, like the click of a calculator. "I'll tell you this," he said, "I voted against this thing. I didn't want to do it, and I'm still not for it. But the majority of the men want it, and I can't go against them."

It was the same answer Grant had heard on 41st Street, the same answer he would hear again and again.

As the man talked on, Jerry, who had overheard the question, began to form an answer in his own mind. Why? Because we are all firemen here. It's hard to see, to know what we do. To understand. This is not a clean job, not tidy, not mannerly. It's as dark and as dirty as the depths of our own bowels. We give more of ourselves, but maybe because we believe in giving. That's the kind of men we are. I'm not looking for sympathy, understand. The nails on our coffins are not sacred. Not anymore. Not after this. Just give us something in return. Something different. We've had enough sympathy. The brothers want something real, and the giving will stop until they get it. Right or wrong, I'm with them. Either stop us from believing in ourselves or give us what we want.

What do we want?

Is hours good enough?

It's something.

Tom Ritter parked his car two blocks south of the fire-house, on 121st Street and Lenox Avenue. It was eight-forty-five. His head was pounding from lack of sleep as he stepped into the cold air and began the walk toward the firehouse.

Dominic was standing on the outside of a group of men in front of the quarters of Engine 51 and Ladder 22. He held two picket signs loosely bound with string, waiting for the time to come to hang them over his shoulders. Tom stopped some distance away and called to him. Dominic turned upon hearing his name, smiled, and walked to Tom, saying, "Tom, sweetheart."

Tom leaned against a parked car and pressed his fingers against his closed eyes. Dominic put a hand to Tom's shoulder and said, "Hey, you all right?"

Tom turned away, just enough so that the hand dropped.

"Dom," he said, "I don't want to say anything to any of the other men. Just to you. Maybe I owe you something, maybe not, but we've been together for a long time, and I want to tell you to your face that I am not going to strike this job."

Dominic reacted quickly. "That's a lot of crap, Tom," he said, "and I don't believe you're saying it."

"I have reasons, and I hope you'll respect that."

"I don't respect nothin', unless you walk on the street with your brothers."

"I'm sorry," Tom said, and he began to move toward the firehouse.

Before he opened the firehouse door, he heard Dominic's voice behind him, calling, "If you go against us like this, I can't talk to you anymore, Tom."

He pushed the door open, and the voice of his friend continued. "This is our job at stake, Tom. This ain't a goddam party."

He stepped into the firehouse, and as the door closed behind him he heard the last strains of the voice, yelling now, "Don't do it Tom. You gotta be shit to scab your brothers."

187

The nine o'clock signal broke through all the firehouses in the city, a primary series of eleven bells, and then a secondary series of eleven. The strike had begun.

In Jerry's firehouse on 48th Street, as in all 290 firehouses in the city, the men of 288 engine companies and 144 ladder companies walked off the job. Those who had completed the night's tour of duty joined the other firemen on the street without ceremony, and the city that records each year over three hundred thousand fire alarms, one hundred and thirty thousand actual fires, and six hundred major-alarm fires was, for the first time in over a century, without adequate fire protection.

There were no men left in Jerry's firehouse, except the two duty officers, six officers who had been recalled for emergency duty, and Battalion Chief McDermott.

Fanilli, the union delegate, was proud that his firehouse went out a hundred percent.

Jerry lifted a picket sign from the stack against the wall and began to march on the street with the others in a small, elongated circle. Fanilli spoke words of confidence as they marched, using the same tone the firemen used to support one another in fires, a tone that was meant to subdue the fundamental fear of being alone.

"Beautiful," he said, "nice and orderly. This is a model picket line."

Passersby gazed indifferently at the men and walked around the circle, avoiding them as they would a drunk or a blind beggar, continuing in haste to their work.

"A paradigm of discipline," Fanilli said.

Vinnie Grant walked around them, taking pictures from different perspectives.

Suddenly the large red apparatus door opened upward, its clicking gears drowning out all sound but its own. Chief McDermott stood on the shadowed floor of the firehouse, tense and shaken, his eyes flaming in hysterical rage.

He walked to the street, shouting, and the circle stopped moving. Even passersby stopped, frozen in a mixture of in-

188

quisitiveness and alarm. The chief roared, "You men don't know what you are doing, but God will never forgive you. Get back in the firehouse. *Get back.* How can you dishonor all the men who gave their lives for this job?"

He was screaming, and white, foamy spittle began to form at the sides of his mouth. The firemen and passersby looked at him in wonder, as he began to wave his arms erratically, indicating the length of the circle.

"God will never forgive you," he screamed again. "You'll all go straight to hell for this. Get back in the firehouse. Do you hear me? *Get back.*"

"This is a strike, chief," Fanilli called out, "so do your own job and mind your own business."

For a clear, brief moment Joseph McDermott thought of his last fire, the final fire, and of a small cottage in County Sligo, surrounded by the never-ending greens of the Irish hills. Then his mind clouded in gray listless smoke as he ran into the circle of firemen, grabbing one, then another, pushing, shoving them toward the firehouse, his voice cracking at its limit. "Get back in the firehouse, get in there you cowards, damn cowards. *Get back . . ."*

Jerry moved to catch him on the fall, but he was too late. Chief McDermott bounced from the sidewalk and then lay in the middle of the firemen's circle, a thin trickle of blood running over the white foam at his mouth. His heart had stopped.

Tom Ritter went to his locker on the second floor of the firehouse and changed his clothes. The pain in his head increased with each movement—as he bent to tie his shoes, as he reached up for a bottle of aspirin, as he walked to the latrine for water.

In the latrine a bowl flushed, and the stall door opened. Ernie Edwards stood there, zippering his pants. Tom looked at him, expecting to hear him say, "How ya doin', ya gettin' much?"

But Ernie was not smiling. He looked at his watch and said, "It's almost nine."

189

Tom put two aspirin tablets in his mouth and bent to the water tap, forming a cup with his hand. He raised his head to force the aspirin down, and the pain traveled down to his eyes, causing him to grimace.

Ernie waited at the door.

"You're going, huh?" Tom said.

"Got to," Ernie answered.

Tom moved his head slowly, in dejection. "I don't understand it," he said. "The president of the Raven Society walking off the job in a black neighborhood. This is a neighborhood of fire. It's your people who are going to suffer."

"Everyone is going to suffer," Ernie said.

"Then why? Why are you going?"

"Tom, there are six hundred black men in this department, and we have come a long way since the days when there was a special bed in the firehouses for niggers only. If we didn't go out things would go back to where they were forty years ago."

Ernie waited for a reply, but Tom was silent. There was nothing to say.

Finally Ernie said, "You're not coming?"

Tom drew in a heavy breath and stared into the eyes of the man before him. He let the breath out and said, "No. I can't do it."

Ernie walked toward him, holding out his hand, saying, "Well, I'll see ya, huh?"

"Yes, okay," Tom said, shaking his hand.

He followed Ernie Edwards through the bunkroom and down the stairs and watched him walk out of the firehouse as the bells began to peal the nine o'clock signal.

It was two minutes after nine. Edgar Pell and his wife were in the second-floor kitchen of their duplex apartment at 85th Street and Fifth Avenue. The maid had been given the week off, and Mrs. Pell, still in her robe, fussed with an omelette at the stove. They had awakened early and lounged in their bedroom, watching the morning network shows on the television set. They were not rushed, for the plane to

Jamaica, where they owned a holiday bungalow, was scheduled to depart at two. Mrs. Pell had complained several times of the snapping noise the new color television set was making, and her husband made a note to call the appliance store about it, just one of a list of calls he had to make before they left the city.

Edgar was on the kitchen extension talking to his secretary and Mrs. Pell was turning the eggs in the frying pan when the explosion occurred. Edgar dropped the phone to the floor in fright, and Mrs. Pell's eggs hung over the side of the pan. They ran to the bedroom, each remembering that they had neglected to turn the television off, but they were kept from entering it by the rolling fire that had quickly spread from the television to the draperies to the cluttered papers on top of Edgar's desk against the wall.

"Edgar, save the luggage," Mrs. Pell screamed, but Edgar ran to the kitchen and lifted the intercom receiver from its hook.

Speaking calmly, he said to the doorman, "Alert the tenants that we have a fire, and then go to the corner and pull the fire alarm." He then picked up the dangling phone and told his secretary to call the Fire Department, thinking, two alarms are better than one.

"But they're on strike," she said.

"Just do as I say," Edgar said before hanging up, as Mrs. Pell pulled a floor-length mink and her husband's topcoat from the closet in the smoky hallway.

Edgar put his arm around her and escorted her hurriedly through the service door in the kitchen, as the fire in their bedroom curled and jumped with each new object it consumed, burning the desk, the tables, the bed, feeding the heat and forcing new currents until it slid across the ceilings of the bedroom and the hall, finding the pipe recesses, entering them, and rising forcefully upward through the building.

In an old red brick building off the 67th Street transverse that runs crosstown through Central Park, Fire Commissioner Herbert Thomas sat with a phone at his ear, watching

191

the hands of the young dispatcher who sat across the room, waiting for the hands to move as the dispatcher reacted to the first alarm. The commissioner was nearing sixty, and the anxiety of the morning made him look it. His white hair was disheveled from running his hands through it, and the crow's feet at his eyes became puffy bags. The skin of his face seemed a transparency over the masses of small, broken red corpuscles in his cheeks.

It was three minutes after nine.

"Come on," he yelled into the phone. "What the hell is keeping you?"

A deputy assistant chief placed at the commissioner's office was collating the reports he had received from the sixteen fire divisions throughout the city. He had the phone on his shoulder but ignored the commissioner's anger, as he re-counted the numbers before him. Finally he said, "All right, commissioner, I have them now. The total number is 109. Do you want a breakdown?"

The commissioner's mouth dropped in disbelief, and he ran a hand through his hair, saying, "Are you sure? Are you sure there wasn't a mistake made in the divisions?"

"No, sir, it's verified and accurate."

"Christ. Dammit to hell. Give me the breakdown."

"Yes, sir. From the top, 36 in Brooklyn, 34 in Queens, 22 in the Bronx, 13 in Staten Island, and 4 in Manhattan."

The commissioner replaced the phone on the cradle, shaking his head and thinking, less than one percent, how could that be? How could so many firemen dishonor their oath of office? How am I going to tell the mayor that we were wrong by a margin of seventy-four percent?

He crossed the large, cork-walled room of the communications center to a wide table especially set up for emergency command. On the table were five telephones, direct lines to each of the other borough dispatching centers and a line to City Hall; at the back edge of the table were five radio receiver sets, one for each borough. The lines and the radios were threateningly silent. It was four minutes after nine.

The commissioner picked up the phone marked "City

Hall" in shiny red plastic, but he dropped the phone as the dispatcher sitting at the semicircular communications console moved his hands to flip up the connecting voice-alarm switches to the appropriate firehouses. The first alarm of the day shift had been received by telephone.

"Box 769," the dispatcher said into the microphone, "Fifth Avenue and 85th Street. Engine 49, Ladder 13 acknowledge."

The electric alarm clock buzzed in Harley Hughes' Seventh Avenue apartment at eight-thirty. Harley threw an arm over his wife's shoulder and gave her a quick kiss on the neck, but she was dead asleep and did not stir. They had gone to a dinner party the night before and stayed until the early morning. Harley did not want to get out of bed, but he had a meeting with a client at ten o'clock, and Harley never made excuses about meeting clients. He had never canceled a meeting with a client in the four years he had been practicing law. He brought his legs to the side of the bed and lit a cigarette. He walked as if hypnotized to the bureau and picked out a pair of socks, grabbed his pants, which were neatly folded over a chair, and walked through the railroad flat to the living room. He put his pants on before sitting on the couch. It was a new couch, bought only recently since Harley's law practice began to pay off, and he sank deeply into its softness. He began to bend over to put his socks on, but instead he leaned back onto the couch arm, put his feet up, took another drag on the cigarette, and closed his eyes.

It was five minutes after nine when he awakened again, screaming in pain. The couch and his pants were on fire.

Commissioner Thomas was talking to the mayor. Because of all the electrical equipment and circuitry in the communications center the temperature was kept constant at a cool sixty degrees. Yet the commissioner's hands were slipping down the telephone receiver because of his perspiration.

"We will certainly try to meet any situation, your

honor," he said, "but with only 109 firemen and 50 men from the probationary training school it will be difficult. It all depends now, sir, on what the officers do. If they all refuse to do firemen's work they'll be no one to carry the hose, but I guarantee you that they will all be prosecuted under the Taylor Law if that happens."

"Now is not the time to consider future prosecutions, commissioner. Just get your men to do the job."

The commissioner held the phone out in front of him, looked at it, and said to no one in particular, "The bastard's hung up on me."

It was six minutes after nine.

A red light on the dispatcher's console lit up, indicating that the alarm button on the Seventh Avenue circuit of the voice-alarm system was being pressed. The dispatcher flipped a switch and spoke into the microphone. "Where's the fire?" he asked.

A young boy's voice was transmitted through the small loudspeaker on the console. "Hey, man, there's a fire on Seventh Avenue and 124th Street." Like most New Yorkers, the boy still referred to the avenue above 110th Street as Seventh Avenue, although the name had been changed for several years to Adam Clayton Powell Jr. Boulevard.

"What is the address?" the dispatcher asked, but there was no answer. The boy had run to watch the excitement.

"That's Engine 51 and Ladder 22," the assistant dispatcher said, writing the numbers on a small pad. He placed the numbers before the dispatcher, as the switches were thrown and the voice alarm activated: "Attention Engine 51, Ladder 22. Respond to Box 1906, Adam Powell Boulevard and 124th Street. Acknowledge Engine 51."

Edward Jefferson handed the phone to the mayor, saying, "It is the borough president."

"Good morning, Sal," the mayor said.

"Kevin," Dursi said, "can't you do something about this thing before any real damage is done?"

"We've done everything possible, Sal. This man Sorvino

194

is not open to negotiating his demand."

"I read it in the *Times*, but I think you should give him what he wants. If you offer him thirty-seven and a half hours it won't be too bad. He'll have to come around. You know there is more at stake here than a majority in the council. The big-money support in the future will depend on this sports and entertainment center. There are too many influential people interested in this thing to risk it all for two and a half hours a week."

"Sal, we can't afford it. If we give it to the firemen, we have to give it to every civil servant."

"Why? The problem here might be in your Office of Labor Relations. Maybe they should think about the firemen by themselves for a change."

"Sal, they are trying to blackmail us. We cannot permit it."

"I have never burdened you with anything, Kevin, but I hope you will consider this call a burden. Good morning."

In midtown the apparatus of Engine 49 and Ladder 13 passed through the small opening made by the pickets in front of the century-old firehouse on East 88th Street. The captain and three lieutenants manning each fire truck made small, waving gestures to those they knew so well, those with whom they had shared so many times the hazards of fire.

The men let the apparatus pass without incident. But then the chief's car passed, driven by the battalion chief, and one of the men sneered and raised his middle finger in defiance.

The chief ignored the finger. He was a boss and therefore a target for harassment. Captains and lieutenants were a part of individual companies, part of each firehouse family, living and working intimately. But a battalion chief was alone, responsible for three or four firehouses in his battalion, six or seven companies, and over two hundred and fifty men. He was a supervisor, an overseer, and because of that he could not enjoy the confidences of the men, or even the banter and humor of the firehouse kitchens.

195

The chief followed the fire trucks to Fifth Avenue, making a mental note of the man who had gestured with his middle finger. He would remember. The strike would not last forever.

Engine 49 and Ladder 13 turned down Fifth Avenue, and the officers saw a wall of smoke blowing across the avenue and through the trees of Central Park. As they wailed toward 85th Street they saw the fire cracking from the windows on the second and third floors of the stately fifteen-story building, and smoke pushing from the sills of the windows above.

The lieutenant driving the pumper, trained to spot hydrants, drove past the burning building to the corner of 84th Street and pulled to the curb next to a hydrant. The intensity of a fire situation forced his mind to click into a series of preconditioned questions. Location of fire? Size of structure? Kind? Occupied? Water source? Lengths of hose? Exposures? Ordinary hazards? Extraordinary?

"We've got to feed the standpipe," he yelled to the captain over the fading sound of the siren.

"No," the captain answered quickly. "We are just concerned with life. Just search, and assist evacuation."

"Christ," the lieutenant said, "I nearly forgot about the firemen. This is going to be one hell of a job."

The captain did not reply, for along with the other lieutenants he was running to the fire building. They ran past the standpipe connection lodged in marble in the side of the building, past the Pells, huddled together like lost waifs, past other tenants and their servants comforting one another, and past a growing crowd of excited pedestrians looking up at the rising fire.

The doorman was holding a small book in his hands, a list of tenants, and he was checking each name as he saw them coming through the lobby from the fire stairs.

"How many are upstairs?" the captain asked.

"I think they are all out," the doorman replied nervously, "but I'm not sure. How can I be sure?"

The captain's radio, strapped across his chest, blared

196

through the lobby: "BATTALION 16 TO ENGINE 49."

The captain pressed the transmission button, saying, "Go ahead, Battalion 16."

"CAPTAIN," the chief's voice transmitted, "GET YOUR MEN OUT HERE AND STRETCH A LINE TO THE STANDPIPE."

The captain pressed the button again and said, "No good, chief. My men are here to protect life, not to do a fireman's job."

"THIS IS A DIRECT ORDER, CAPTAIN," the radio blasted. "YOU AND YOUR MEN REPORT TO ME IN FRONT OF THE FIRE BUILDING."

The chief transmitted the order again, but the captain did not answer. He and the other officers were racing up the fire stairs to search the building. On the fourteenth floor the captain split the team in two, one group to search the even floors, one the odd. The fire was below them, crackling its way upward, and smoke began to seep into the fire stairway, glazing their eyes. Yet they knew they had to search every room, every closet, under every bed for as many floors as possible until they would have to run down the stairs to save their own lives. Without water it would be just a matter of minutes—ten or twenty—before the fire stairs would become kiln hot.

In Albany, Livingston Bennett escorted three advisers to the door of his state house executive chamber. He put his hand on the back of one man, saying, "I don't see how it can possibly last more than an hour or so, but we will take all the necessary precautions. It's better to play it safe than sorry, don't you think?" The governor smiled.

"Yes, sir, I do," the man replied. Then, with the other two men, he walked through the reception room and down the wide, carpeted hall to the marble stairs. The governor paused at the door of his office and said to his assistant, "Olden, get me Colonel Collins on the phone, please."

Hirschfield pressed a button on his intercom, saying, "Marie, get me Colonel Peter Collins, 42nd Division, National Guard."

197

The governor's phone buzzed and he picked it up, saying, "Hello, Pete. This strike by the firemen concerns me greatly, the problem of public safety. And if it continues the conditions for looting, even rioting, will be present, so as a matter of caution I am signing an executive order mobilizing the state's militia forces. However, I do not want the whole division, just those who live in the New York City area. And those I simply want alerted and readied. How many will that give us?"

"Well, sir," the colonel answered, "between the 69th Regiment, the 71st, the 106th, and the 142nd Armored, that will give us approximately eight thousand men."

"How long will it be before they are ready?"

"It's a little past nine now. I can have them in the armories by noon."

"Good. My state's mediator is on his way to see the mayor now to try and resolve this thing. Olden Hirschfield will get back to you before twelve. Incidentally, have your public information officer convince the press that this is simply a precautionary alert. We don't want the people to be unduly alarmed."

"Yes, sir. Will do."

In the firehouse kitchen Tom Ritter made a cup of tea and sat with the officers at the table. The officers made no reference to Tom's presence, and Tom felt alone. They did not question his reasons for staying, yet he felt alienated from them and sensed a silent disapproval in the room. He sat quietly, watching the second hand revolve on the big wall clock before him, wishing that the hand would move faster.

Battalion Chief Morris Gelman called in his manpower report to the division headquarters and then entered the kitchen. He poured a cup of coffee and sat at the table across from Tom. "You are the only fireman we got in the battalion and in the division," he said to Tom. "Are you a qualified motor pump operator?"

"No," Tom replied.

"It wouldn't matter much anyway," the chief said.

198

"Since we have sixteen pumpers in the division, just one pump operator wouldn't make much difference. You ride with Ladder 22 and carry the can. Two and a half gallons isn't as good as the city's water supply, but it's something. We'll play it by ear, okay?"

Tom nodded in acceptance of the directive and finished his cup of tea. He said nothing but continued to watch the second hand move around the face of the clock, and then the minute hand. At seven minutes after nine the voice alarm announced a fire at 124th Street.

Tom sat in the bucket seat next to the motor casing of Ladder 22, and as the truck passed the striking firemen he made eye contact for just a moment with Dominic Gallo. Dominic, his arms folded on his chest, stared ominously, his lower lip caught between his teeth. Tom looked away.

There was a large crowd huddled in front of the burning tenement on Seventh Avenue, and Tom had to shove people aside to enter. There was another crowd of people in the lobby, standing around a man writhing in pain on the polished linoleum floor. As Tom pushed by them, the heavy extinguishing can in his hand, he saw Harley Hughes shaking in convulsion, barefooted, barechested, scattered remnants of his pants braised to his skin. "Get a sheet and cover him up," Tom shouted as he ran to the stairs.

On his way up the stairs he heard a man call out, "His wife is up there, caught in the fire."

The fire on the fourth floor was shooting out into the public hallway, and Tom directed the nozzle of the extinguishing can at the burning door frame, as the captain of Ladder 22 tried again and again to pull the apartment door closed. Suddenly they heard a high, screeching voice yelling for help. It came from above them, in the public hallway, but they could not get past the fire. The captain put one hand over the side of his face and leaned into the fire, judging the distance to the doorknob. His hair was singed and his ear was burned, but he reached the doorknob and pulled the door shut as the last of Tom's water spurted onto the frame.

Tom dropped the can and ran through the smoking hallway up the stairs, but he was too late. He looked up and saw an old woman in a wheelchair begin to tumble down the stairs, falling out of the chair to the hard angles of the marble stairs. The chair fell on top of her. Tom rushed up the long flight of stairs, diving to stop her fall, but she was upon him before he reached the second step. He put his hand out to stop her rolling body, and the chair crashed into him, knocking the helmet from his head. The captain was behind him, and Tom leaned down low to the woman's breast so the captain could lift the chair out of the way.

Through the lifting smoke Tom could see that her frail, crippled body was laying peculiarly, her head seeming to be fixed to the end of one shoulder. Tom pressed his ear to her chest but heard nothing. He lifted her light, aged body as the captain lifted the fallen helmet, with little effort, and ran past the closed door that was beginning to burn through. He thought of the wife who was said to be inside, and he made a small ejaculation asking God to accept tenderly those who are taken so cruelly.

Completely out of the smoke and walking down the bottom stairs to the crowded lobby, Tom looked down at the old woman in his arms and realized her neck was broken. He sat on the bottom step, closed his eyes, and put his head down onto the woman's stomach. He felt a swell within his chest, but he controlled himself, remaining impassive, resting on the body until the captain lifted her from his arms.

In the South Bronx, a man who had come to be known to the local fireman as Gasoline Gomez climbed up the rear fire escape of a six-story abandoned building on Fox Street. All the windows of the tenement had been broken by neighborhood children, and he entered through an open frame on the second floor. Why won't they tear these buildings down? he asked himself in Spanish, as he placed the brown paper bag he was carrying on the floor. He reached into the bag and took one of three beer bottles filled with gasoline, ran up the stairs to the top floor, and poured the gas over the entry hall floor in the apartment nearest the stairs. He returned to the brown paper bag, took another bottle, and climbed to the fourth floor. Methodical. He had done it so many times before. He returned for the last bottle, brought it to the apartment nearest the stairs, and emptied it, throwing the bottle on the hard tile of the public hall and taking pleasure as it cracked apart. With a package of matches in hand, he opened his zipper and urinated over the stairs the firemen would use. Then he lit the match. It would take time for the fire to build to the fourth floor, and then the sixth. Sometimes the firemen put it out before it extended. Sometimes not. It was a game within a vendetta against the city that did not care about him.

In Brooklyn, two brothers walked out of the small shed they used as an office in a corner of their lumberyard and entered the corridors between the two-by-fours and four-by-sixes that were stacked ten feet high. They had bought the lumber at a good price, expecting a good year, the best year since they had been in business. But sales had suddenly stopped, as if it had become a crime for men to build houses in Brooklyn. Damn economy. Why this year? Why the one year they had gotten a real bargain on their stock, when they had taken a second mortgage on their property to finance the biggest deal they had ever made? When they came to what they thought was the middle of the yard one brother hammered wedges between the lower planks, making air spaces in the lumber stacks; the other pressed the trigger of a large oil can, aiming the nozzle into the air spaces. They did not need a big fire. What the hell? The firemen were on strike. It would spread.

In Woodside, Queens, a teenaged boy sat in a public telephone booth at the rear of a candy store. The boy was talking to his girlfriend, who had stayed out of school because of a head cold. He had lit a cigarette, and as he talked he kept flipping the throwaway butane lighter on and off. Next to the booth was a pile of newspaper returns, old news waiting to be recycled, and the boy casually, insouciantly, reached over

201

and lit one of the paper edges sticking from the pile. It burned, and the boy slapped it out with his hand. Then he relit it and slapped it out again, mindlessly, as he talked. He lit the edge a third time, said good-by to his girlfriend, and slapped at the pile of newspapers. Thinking the sparks had died, he left the telephone booth and walked out of the candy store. The store was located in the middle of a row of attached wooden frame houses. Old wood. Dry. Wood that would burn as quickly as balsa chips in a furnace.

"Where the hell is Golden?" the fire commissioner yelled into the telephone. "He's supposed to be here."

The deputy assistant chief on duty in the commissioner's office answered, "I don't know, commissioner. He left here before nine o'clock and said he was going to make a field check. That's all I know."

The commissioner cradled the phone and turned to the dispatcher at the console, saying, "See if you can raise Car 2, and have him respond here to the communications center."

The dispatcher depressed a red transmit button, saying, "Manhattan dispatcher to Car 2. Car 2, are you ten-eight?"

There was no answer. The dispatcher switched from the Manhattan frequency to the special citywide frequency and said, "Citywide dispatcher to Car 2. Car 2, are you ten-eight?" Again there was no answer, for the chief of department was sitting in his car on the Staten Island Ferry, saying to himself, no, I am not ten-eight, I am not on the air, I am not the fire commissioner. This is his baby, his strike, and he'll have to handle it himself. If they had wanted me to run this department, they would have made me the commissioner. But I am the chief of department, and Car 2 is going to Staten Island to survey the manpower problems, and then to Brooklyn, and Queens, and the Bronx, and finally Manhattan. Legitimate, and explainable.

The dispatcher switched back to the Manhattan frequency and was about to call again for Car 2 when the transmission squawked through the room: "BATTALION 16 TO MANHATTAN."

202

"Manhattan responding, 16."

"I HAVE A MEDIUM FIRE CONDITION AT BOX 769. FIRE ON SECOND AND THIRD FLOORS OF 1030 FIFTH AVENUE, BRICK, FIFTEEN STORIES, SEVENTY-FIVE BY A HUNDRED. TRANSMIT A SECOND ALARM. PERSONNEL ON SCENE WILL NOT STRETCH HOSE, AND FIRE IS EXTENDING."

Christ, the commissioner thought, it had to be in a goddam high-rise building, and close to the bottom at that. Son of a bitch!

"Ten-four, Battalion 16," the dispatcher said.

The commissioner rose and walked to the dispatcher's console, saying, "Transmit the second alarm. Maybe we can get some officers there who will do their duty. And get the probies there too."

The dispatcher announced the second alarm as his assistant turned to the commissioner and said, "We split the probies up between the high-hazard areas, twenty-five in the South Bronx and twenty-five in Bedford-Stuyvesant. Do you want 'em all?"

"No, not yet. Just get them down from the South Bronx."

The commissioner returned to his control desk and sat back in his chair, trying to picture the fire. Why, that's less than twenty blocks from here, he thought, and he walked to the front door of the communications building, opened it, and looked up toward 85th Street. He could see the smoke rising beyond the Metropolitan Museum, but he could not see the fire. A medium fire condition, a three- or four-hose-line job. And no one to stretch the lines. Those goddam officers, I'll have every one of them hooked up for this. It will be a heavy fire condition, more than four lines, before the probies get there. Goddam probies. Kids really. I only swore them in less than three weeks ago. What the hell do they know about pushing into a fire? They'll learn, though. They better. Where the hell is Golden, that goddam Golden? What the hell is he trying to pull off here? He'd be here if he thought he had something to gain.

He went back to his control desk and listened to Chief Gelman's voice on the radio: "BOX 1906, MEDIUM FIRE CON-

DITION, EXTENDING FAST BECAUSE OF HEAVY WINDS. THERE
IS ONE DOA, ANOTHER POSSIBLE DOA, AND ONE CIVILIAN
BADLY BURNED. REQUEST AN AMBULANCE, NO, TWO AMBU-
LANCES, AND A SECOND-ALARM ASSIGNMENT TO ASSIST
EVACUATION. THERE IS NO WATER ON THIS FIRE. WE NEED
MANPOWER TO STRETCH LINES."

The dispatcher turned from his console and yelled across
the room to the commissioner, "Sir, should we reroute some
of the probies to Box 1906? They have two pumpers, and we
could send one to Harlem and the other downtown."

The commissioner thought a moment. What would
Golden do? Two DOAs already, heavy winds. Winds. Christ,
I better get a weather report. What kind of damage would
I have in Harlem? Shit. Tenements.

"No," the commissioner replied, "have them continue
straight to Fifth Avenue. The property risk is greater there."

"Yes, sir."

"And get me a weather report."

"We have it, sir. Temperature is thirty-nine degrees; the
wind from the northeast at twenty-five miles per hour, gusting to thirty-five."

It was twenty minutes after nine.

Fifteen minutes later an old civil defense pumper
manned by twelve young firemen turned off the East River
Drive at 96th Street. Following closely behind was another,
more battered pumper with thirteen men crowded onto its
sides and back. The pumpers turned down Fifth Avenue, and
the probationary firemen, as yet innocent of fire, were
stunned into small, nervous gestures by the sight before
them, scratching their faces, squeezing their hands, or pulling their helmets farther down around their heads. The fire
on 85th Street had taken the full fifteen stories of one building, and in great heaves the flames surged across and down
the avenue, forced by the blasting wind into strange, erratic
shapes, curling, jumping, wave over wave.

There were policemen at every corner, redirecting

204

traffic from the avenue, not knowing that only minutes before the police commissioner, under the direction of Edward Jefferson, had been considering sending an order to the patrolmen to carry hose and assist the Fire Department in any possible way. He had been prevented from doing so by the president of the Police Brotherhood Association, who had threatened a strike by his own men rather than let them be used as strikebreakers.

The probationary firemen went as far as they could on Fifth, to 85th Street. The fire between 85th and 84th made passage impossible. They left the pumpers and ran down to Madison Avenue, went around the corners, and returned to Fifth on 84th. The building on the north corner was now burning, and the probies crossed to the south corner and reported to the frantic battalion chief. The chief was facing the biggest fire of his career, and there was no one to respond to his orders. The officers of the second-alarm companies had begun to evacuate the buildings between 84th and 83rd, but like the officers of the first-alarm companies they had refused to carry hose or operate the pumps.

The fire, which had extended to the corner building, was now shooting into the street, blackening the paint of the Engine 49 pumper parked in front of a hydrant. An officer tried to enter the pumper from the street side, but the heat beat him back, leaving the pumper a small, symbolic token to the intensity of the fire.

"Are any of you MPOs?" the chief asked the probies, now huddled around him as around a quarterback.

"What's that, chief?" one replied.

"Christ," the chief said. "Motor pump operators. Do any of you know how to get water through the pumper?"

The probies looked at him dumbly. It was only their third week of training, an indoctrination period really, familiarization with department rules and regulations, the alarm system and signals, lots of physical training drills, but little experience with actual firefighting.

"Christ," the chief said again, "I'll operate the pumps

myself if need be. I want you to set up stangs right here in the middle of the avenue. We have to stop this fire from jumping the street. You understand?"

The chief expected the probies to jump, to scatter to the pumpers crowding the avenue in search of equipment, but they remained before him impatiently.

"What's a stang?" one asked.

"Christ, *Christ,*" the chief yelled. "It's the pretzle-shaped nozzle that sits on the top of every pumper. Get them, take them down, carry them here, and then feed them."

"You mean with hose?"

"No, with fucking pea soup," the chief said, pushing the men two at a time toward the fire engines on the avenue below. "Go on, get every stang you can find."

The probies ran down the street to the pumpers, stopping in small groups at each pumper, climbing to the top, disconnecting and lifting the ninety-pound stang nozzle. There were six pumpers, and they placed six stang nozzles at the corner of 84th Street.

"Now get the hose," the chief said, "two lines for each stang."

Below them, on the corner of 83rd Street, standing across from the museum, were Mr. and Mrs. Edgar Pell. There were tears sticking to Mrs. Pell's cheeks. Behind the Pells were most of the firemen from the 88th Street firehouse, faces in the crowd, worried faces.

The probies went to the back of one pumper and began to grab hose, their hands pulling indiscriminately at the folded lengths. They had not yet learned the system of hose packing, the simple system of laying the hose on the pumper from left to right and then pulling it off from right to left.

The hose was laying at the probies' feet, entangled in knots of dacron and brass connections. The chief looked in dismay and then ran to the cab of the pumper and lifted the radio phone. He was about to press the transmission button when he looked up the avenue and realized he could no longer see the pumper that was parked near the corner hydrant. The fire had raced through the corner building and had jumped across Fifth Avenue on one side and across 84th Street on the other, the wind whipping it violently.

The chief thought of the hose laying like sphagetti behind him and laughed a small, hopeless laugh. It didn't matter. The probies were too late.

He pressed the transmission button. "Battalion 16 to dispatcher."

"MANHATTAN TO BATTALION 16."

"The fire at Box 769 is of fifth-alarm and greater intensity and has extended across the street to the south side of 84th Street. Even the trees in Central Park are burning. We have lost one pumper and six stang nozzles and will now retreat to 83rd Street and try to set up a holding screen. The situation is desperate and completely out of control."

"HAVE THE PROBATIONARY FIREMEN ARRIVED?"

"Yes, but they won't be of much help unless you get me some more stang nozzles, and personnel to operate the pumps."

"TEN-FOUR, BATTALION 16. WE WILL TRANSMIT A FIFTH-ALARM FOR BOX 769."

"That will give me the stangs, but what about the personnel?"

"WE ARE ALL DOING OUR BEST, BATTALION 16."

It was ten o'clock. The strike was one hour old.

9

In Far Rockaway, Queens, a battalion chief stood alone in the middle of the apparatus floor. The engine company was covering another firehouse, relocated because of the multiple alarm for the fire in Woodside. An alarm came in, and the chief walked out the door, stepping briskly toward Beach Avenue and 36th Street, twelve long blocks away. I'm a chief, he thought. It is below my rank to drive myself, and I'll be damned if I would let some scab drive me—if there were scabs around to drive. The chief had once been a union delegate.

In Woodside, Queens, the candy store, the row of frame houses, and an adjoining row of three-story brick houses were burning freely. Three nonstriking firemen, older men who were about to retire, men with nearly a century of service between them, carried stang nozzles and pulled hose slowly, one step at a time, routinely connecting the hose to the nozzles, safely upwind from the fire, understanding the futility of their action, shaking their heads, attempting to perform as a hundred men.

In Brooklyn, two officers determined to do something. Something. The lumberyard was almost fully ablaze, two acres of naked, tightly stacked wood from which a towering column of smoke and heat bent with the wind, threatening the outer building of the Bush Terminal across the street, once the largest warehouse in the world. The two men began to pull hose from a pumper, intending to connect to the ladder pipe on the top rung of the hook and ladder. They pulled resolutely past the cursing firemen who had come from a nearby firehouse, where the firemen had abandoned their picket signs for the excitement of the fire. Suddenly one officer was struck in the middle of his back, and then the other. They turned and covered their faces as a barrage of stones came hurtling toward them. They abandoned the hose.

Around the corner a television news team was filming an interview with the owners of the lumberyard. "We are going to sue the city," one of the brothers was saying. "Look at our business burning right out from under us as the firemen stand around doing nothing. This is crazy. Absolutely crazy, and we'll sue for a million dollars. At least."

In the South Bronx, a man sat on the cold slate stoop of a building on Fox Street. The stoop was crowded with on-lookers. Suddenly the man burst into laughter, pointing at the fire officers who were standing around with their hands on their hips or in their pockets. He did not know that he had been named by the firemen, and that the faceless name of Gasoline Gomez had become hateful to them. Had he known, he would have laughed even harder as the fire bobbed and bucked through the windows on the top floor of the abandoned building.

Angelo Sorvino sat in his hotel room, listening to WYNS radio. There was no news of the strike on television. He had switched the channels but found only the morning soaps and quiz shows. The radio had little news other than that of the fires in Manhattan, Queens, and Brooklyn. The fire in the abandoned Bronx building was mentioned only once, but news of the deaths of two civilians in Harlem and a battalion chief in midtown was repeated over and over.

Sorvino was troubled. He had not expected fires of such magnitude in such little time. But he had proved a point. The city of New York could not manage without its firefighters. He had said it many times, to his men, to the Office of Labor Relations, to the public. Now it was proved, the test of fire complete. It was, in his mind, over. It could end. If only the mayor would call, or even Jefferson. The hours could be traded now. He could still look good.

The phone rang and Sorvino jumped at it, uttering an optimistic hello. But it was only the treasurer, Nick Imbroglia, and Sorvino winced as he pictured the burn-scarred, sneering face speaking into the telephone.

"Yes, Nick," he said.

"Angelo, I don't think it's worth it," Imbroglia said.

"What do you mean?"

"It's getting out of hand, Angelo. The people of the city will never forget it. We'll never make it up. I'm not speaking only for myself; the board agrees you should call WYNS."

Sorvino's eyes flared. "I am the president of this union," he said, "and I don't give a shit about you, the board, or the people of this city. When I say it's off, it's off. Do you understand that?"

But the treasurer of the union had hung up on him, and Sorvino cursed, slammed the phone, and punched his fist into his palm.

Vinnie Grant had talked to the still-shaking doorman, and he was searching through the crowd for Mr. and Mrs. Pell when the beeper attached to his belt sounded. He went

210

to a telephone booth on the sidewalk near the south end of the museum and called his office. As he talked he watched the fire take hold in the building on the downtown corner of 84th Street.

The operator said she had a man holding, and then she connected.

"Grant here," he said.

"Mr. Grant, this is Nick Imbroglia, the treasurer of the United Firefighters of New York. I got something you might like. In one of your stories you quoted Sorvino as saying he had an overwhelming majority on the strike vote, but I don't think he had the vote at all. I saw him dump the ballots, and he wouldn't have done that if he had it."

Grant wrote two addresses on his pad, and fifteen minutes later he walked into the office of the Integrity Balloting Company. The secretary in the outer office smiled a good morning, but Grant went past her so quickly that she was forced to stifle a scream.

Harry Silverman was listening to the radio news. He looked up as Grant slammed the door and saw the reporter's credentials, which were thrown on the desk before him.

"It says V. X. Grant, of the *Daily News*, Mr. Silverman," Grant said, speaking above the volume of the radio. "I have just one question for you, and if you don't answer it right I'll have you in the Tombs for reckless endangerment. What was the count on the firemen's strike vote?"

"That's, ah, confidential information, Mr., ah, Grant. You have no right to it."

Grant picked up the worn plastic identification card and said, "Don't bullshit me about rights, Silverman. There's fires going on in this city big as you've never seen, and you might be in the middle of one of them yourself. If Sorvino didn't have it, you can bet your ass there will be a criminal indictment, and if you withhold knowledge now you'll be an accessory. I'll see to that."

Silverman nervously fingered a piece of paper on his desk, saying, "Now wait a minute, just one minute. I am not an accessory to anything. I just offer a service, a balloting service. What the unions do with the results is their concern, not mine."

"You can tell that to the grand jury," Grant said. "Tell them you sat on your ass while the city burned. Three people have already died this morning." Grant walked to the side of the desk and turned the radio off, continuing, "Tell me you don't know that."

"Yes, of course I heard," Silverman said, crushing the piece of paper in his hands. "But what am I supposed to do, call the cops? This is a confidential business. I'd never get another contract."

"What was the tally, Silverman?"

Silverman paused a moment to think. Finally he sat back in his chair, saying, "I don't remember, and there is no file copy. But the fireman voted against it—that I remember, I swear to God."

Grant was walking out of the office as Silverman called to him, "Hey, I did you a favor, right? Just remember that, and keep my name out of the newspapers. It won't help business, you know."

Grant did not look back. The secretary was on her feet, saying, "Please don't slam the door."

Grant slammed it, and his huge frame wobbled from side to side as he hustled to the elevator. He looked at the second address on his pad, barely able to read his own scrawl. It read "HOTEL SHELTON."

The buildings on Adam Clayton Powell Jr. Boulevard were one large frame of fire between 124th and 123rd streets, and the wind was pushing the flames across the narrow cross street at 123rd.

Tom Ritter was running through a building near 122nd Street, rapping on the doors, kicking at them, yelling, "This building is being evacuated, you must get out." There was a constant, throbbing pain inside his head, and as he ran and yelled he felt as if sword blades were slicing through it.

But it was the last building on the block. Maybe it would end soon. Maybe the wind would die, and the fire would burn

212

straight up into the sky. Maybe then he could rest. Maybe he could sleep.

He worked from the top floor down, going through all the rooms, calling with the fullness of his voice. The doors had been opened, the occupants safely out in the street. On the second floor a door was closed. Tom jammed a haligan tool into the frame and forced it open. But it was empty. No one to alert. No one stranded. He thought of the woman in the wheelchair, alone and infirm. God, that poor, helpless woman.

There was a policeman stationed at the building entrance, as there was one assigned in front of each vacated building that was not yet burning. "This one's clean," Tom said to the cop. A woman then came, pleading to pass, claiming she had forgotten something, money, but the cop turned her away.

Across the wide boulevard, white faces speckled in a crowd of blacks, stood Dominic Gallo and the other men of Engine 51 and Ladder 22, watching the fire, sharing small verbal comforts with one another. Jesus, Dominic thought, how far is it going to go? The city has got to learn now. Listen to the radio. There's goddam fires everywhere. I don't think they know the size of this one. It's got to be a borough-call fire, eight, maybe ten alarms. Man, why doesn't Sorvino come on?

An assistant chief, four golden trumpets shining on the front of his helmet, had taken command of the fire, and Battalion Chief Morris Gelman was giving orders to idle officers to move the trucks and the engines down the boulevard, just a block or so away, safely south of 122nd Street. Safe, he thought, for the time being.

The fire pushed against the windows of the top two floors of the corner building on the south side of 123rd Street, and the glass shattered, eating a pathway for the flames to travel another block, to take another row of buildings.

Tom walked aimlessly in the street. What should he do now? he wondered. Should he stretch a line? Yes. Get the hose. Pull it. That's something. But for what? There's too

213

much fire. Like pissing in the wind. A David and Goliath romance.

He heard a voice calling, "Hey, Ritter."

It was Chief Gelman.

"Check the rear of the building. See if the fire extends down the avenue or up 123rd Street. See what the wind does back there." That was something, Tom thought, and he said, "Yes. Yes, sir."

He began to walk into one of the evacuated buildings. As he moved, a young woman broke through the police lines, a handsome woman, a bandanna stylishly tied around her head, wearing a long suede skirt and a short fur jacket. Tom stopped as she ran to him, and he saw the fright and the desperation in her eyes.

The woman was screaming, pointing to the fire coming from the top floor of the corner building, "My baby is up there, my baby is up there. Oh, God, God. Get her. Please get her."

Tom thought quickly. Couldn't be. I wasn't in that building, but someone was. Had to be.

"Don't worry, lady," Tom said, "the buildings are all evacuated. We've been through them all, all the apartments."

"But you don't understand," the woman cried. "She's deaf. She's only six years old and she's deaf. And she hides, she hides on me all the time. Please, God. Oh, please, get her for me."

A pumper was retreating slowly down the boulevard, and Tom ran to it and pulled a mask container from a side compartment. As he was throwing the air tank over his back and harnessing it, he heard the woman sobbing uncontrollably, "I never leave her alone. Never. This is the first time. She understood I would be right back. I went to an audition, a goddam small-time audition. It was a job, I needed the goddam job. Please, my baby, my sweet baby."

Tom held the facepiece of the mask in his hand. "What apartment, what floor?" he asked, grabbing the woman's arm, shaking her.

214

The woman threw her head back. "6A," she yelled, "on the top floor, where the smoke is coming. Oh, God, God."

Tom looked at the top floor of the corner building. Fire was spilling from the two windows on the right of the fire escape. It had not yet extended to the windows on the left, though he saw the smoke, thick and black, pushing through the frames. His heart sank when he noticed that the fire escape window on the left, rimmed with smoke, was covered with a full iron gate. A lockbreaker, he thought. I need a lockbreaker. He began to run toward the drop ladder of the fire escape. There isn't time. I can't go looking for a lockbreaker. There isn't time.

He ran up the ladder and then up the stairs of the fire escape. Chief Gelman held a captain by the arm, saying, "Get a truck over here and raise the ladder to the sixth floor fast. Do it fast."

The captain hesitated and said, "That's a fireman's work, chief. I can bring a truck here, but I can't operate the ladder."

Chief Gelman glared at him and said passionately, "If you don't do it, captain, you're a fucking murderer."

Then the chief ran to the drop ladder and began to climb.

It was pointless to picket an empty firehouse, for the officers of Ladder 7 and Engine 20 had responded to the fire on Fifth Avenue. Jerry stood with the other men of his firehouse behind the police barricade placed across Fifth Avenue at 79th Street, four blocks below the fire.

Even at that distance the wind would occasionally sweep the smoke through the crowd of onlookers, warming the chilled air around them. The firemen seemed hypnotized by the largest fire they had ever seen, and they cursed in amazement as they listened to the reports on WYNS.

A battalion chief was operating a pumper that was attached to a hydrant at 81st Street, and as he pulled a lever the limp hose laying on the avenue became full with the first stream of water to attack the fire.

But it was just a gesture.

The probationary firemen had finally arranged hose and four stang nozzles across the avenue, but the heat was so great they could advance only as near as the south side of 82nd Street, a full block from the wildly burning buildings, all fifteen stories high, now completely involved from 85th to 83rd streets. The water that poured from the nozzle tip with deadly force became a small sprinkle as it neared its target, broken by the wind and distance into mere droplets.

The fire commissioner sat at his command desk and listened to the field reports on the radios before him. Assistant chiefs had arrived at and taken command of the separate fires. Where the hell is Golden? the commissioner kept thinking, although he knew the chief of department was cooped up somewhere, dogging it for the duration. The lumberyard fire in Brooklyn had extended to the Bush Terminal warehouse, the fire in Queens was taking a full block, the fire in Harlem had jumped across a side street just as it had on Fifth Avenue. The fire in the Bronx was his only break, he thought, and God knows we need breaks here. The interior of the building fell through, leaving the fire to smolder in a great pile of plaster and brick.

The Manhattan-frequency radio began to blast with the words of the assistant chief: "THE FIRE IS EXTENDING TO THE NORTH WALL OF THE METROPOLITAN MUSEUM OF ART. I HAVE ORDERED THE PROBATIONARY FIREMEN TO ABANDON THE STANG NOZZLES AND TO ADVANCE HAND LINES INTO THE MUSEUM."

"Jesus S. Christ," the commissioner uttered, as he picked up the direct phone to the mayor's office. "That's all we need now. Why didn't they put the museum farther into the goddam park? Hello, hello? Mr. Jefferson? I'd like to talk to the mayor, ah, sir."

It occurred to the commissioner that Jefferson might resent the tone of his request, and he regretted that he did not say "please."

"Yes," the mayor's voice said.

216

"Hello, **Mr.** Mayor," the commissioner said. "I'm afraid we can't do it, sir, not with fifty probies and a handful of men. We have three fires out of control, one of them threatening the Metropolitan Museum of Art, and if we don't get multiple large-caliber streams on them soon they'll be beyond any kind of control. Perhaps, sir, that is, if you concur, we should call in the National Guard."

"How will you work it if they come in?" the mayor asked.

"Well, sir, we have an old national emergency coordination plan, part of the civil defense plan worked out years ago, but we can still use it."

"I'll get back to you, commissioner," the mayor said. He hung up the phone and faced Jefferson, who was sitting on the couch.

"Ed," he said, "when the city was first chartered in 1686 it was a law that every citizen had to provide water buckets and contribute their service in defense against fire. Now the city has three hundred and fifty thousand municipal employees, and we can't get anyone to pull a fucking hose."

"It's a problem, your honor," Jefferson said.

"It is not like you to be given to understatements. We have the fire commissioner's report, the police commissioner's report; it seems all twenty-four city councilmen have called, and Salvatore Dursi, not to mention the other borough presidents and the Citizens' Union. We've got to stop these fires before we lose another life, before we lose all of Fifth Avenue, before we lose the museum. I don't know why they didn't build it farther into the park—the thing is such a sacred symbol in this city. Get me the governor on the line, and you better cancel that B'nai B'rith luncheon out in Forest Hills."

"If you call the governor," Jefferson replied furtively, standing now in front of the mayor's desk, "you might as well cancel every luncheon for the duration of the campaign. I'd like to suggest that we wait awhile. Let me call Sorvino first. Perhaps he won't be so intransigent in the face of disaster. We have to consider the political aspects of this."

The mayor brought his full palm hard against the desk

top, saying, "Don't speak to me of politics when my city is burning."

It was ten-forty-five.

In Albany, Olden Hirschfield held the phone in his hand and said, "It is the mayor of New York."

Livingston Bennett's face expanded into a broad grin, and as he reached for the phone on his desk he said, "Front paws up, I assume."

The fire smacked against three of the six windows on the north wall of the museum, like storm waves against a sea wall, enormous pulsations fed by the gusting wind. The windows were designed as Romanesque triptychs, twenty feet high, and the panes were originally of wired-reinforced glass. But the windows gave little light to the storeroom area on the first floor at the north end of the building, just beyond the Egyptian wing, the area that would soon be part of an expanded Egyptian exhibition, so the middle panels, the larger ones, had been replaced with clear, double-paned storm glass.

The fire reached only halfway across the width of the building, painting the white sandstone in an irregular pattern of black, but it would have been as impending had it reached just one window.

Inside the storeroom area men worked feverishly, loading crates and statues and pieces of large Mesopotamian metopes onto dollies and delivering them to the relative safety of the main promenade. The museum's four fire marshals pulled hose from a wall rack and turned the valve that connected the hose to the city's water supply system. There wasn't much pressure in the system, they knew—fifteen or twenty pounds—but it was something.

The probationary firemen dragged the hose past four heavy granite sphinxs and a large Nefertiti-like head and into the building-wide storeroom area. Through the already blackened glass they watched the fire shifting, and then they heard the cracking. First the outer panes of the storm glass shattered, and moments later the inner panes. The middle panels of the three windows seemed to collapse at once, the glass falling on ruined monuments, and the fire seemed to shoot into the room in three giant tongues. Then, just as quickly, it disappeared as a gust subsided. After a moment it lashed back with even greater force, activating the alarm system in the ceiling. The probationary firemen and the museum marshals pulled the nozzle handles back and aimed the water at the window openings, five streams gushing through the fire as though through air, hitting nothing but super-heated atoms and falling to the ground like rain. The fire kept coming, curling around to the plasterboard walls, up to the hanging asbestos-tiled ceiling, between the wall and the ceiling, and up to the second floor.

An assistant chief stood with the museum's director of operations, behind the hose-burdened men, watching the volume of the fire float past the water streams.

"What's above us?" the chief asked above the ringing alarm.

"Why?" the director asked. "Do you think it's jeopardized? There are no windows up there."

"Just look at the ceiling, where it meets the wall," the chief answered.

"My God," the director gasped, "the Leutze."

"What lutes?" the chief asked, confused. "You mean musical instruments?"

"*Washington Crossing the Delaware,*" the director said. "The American wing is right above us."

The chief ordered four probationary firemen, who were holding against the back pressure of the hose, to follow, and he and the director ran through the skylit Egyptian gallery to the stairs.

"How will we ever get it out?" the director was yelling. "The damned thing is the biggest canvas we have."

They kept running, up the stairs, past the marble balcony, down the corridor between the plaster wall that hid

219

the skylight above the Egyptian gallery and the standpipe hose on the opposite wall, and into the wide room of American oils directly above the storeroom.

They were too late. Not that it would have mattered, the chief thought.

On the middle of the north wall, set between a Cole landscape and a Stewart portrait, was Frederick Church's *Cotopaxi, Ecuador 1862*, a vague oil painting of a bright sun setting beyond a steaming waterfall. Below the painting the fire burned through the wall and rose up, stabbing at the gilded frame and lacquer-covered canvas.

On the opposite wall, next to the chief and the director, was the huge Emanuel Leutze painting, hanging prominently alone. The chief was surprised. It was much bigger than life, bigger than he had imagined the famous painting to be. And, curiously, it was much bigger than the corridor door leading to the room.

The chief turned to the probationary firemen, who were standing directionless, and ordered them to stretch the standpipe hose. The amount of fire was yet small, but he knew it would keep coming. He looked again at the Leutze and asked the director, "Can you get it out of the frame?"

"Unfortunately, no," the director answered sullenly. "It's adhered to a specially made wooden backing."

The chief pressed his radio transmitter and spoke to a deputy assistant chief in the street.

"Herb," he said, "get me as many battalion chiefs and deputy chiefs as you can find. Tell them to bring axes and saws and to be prepared to operate them. If we don't cut a wall down soon, General Washington and his troops are going to burn up in the Delaware River."

Dominic Gallo saw the figure on the fire escape and said, "Hey, that's Ritter. What the hell is he doing? What's going on?"

"The scabbing bastard," somebody said. "He should fall off the fire escape."

Dominic said nothing but watched intensely as Tom

220

pulled on the iron gate, a symbol of New York crime and a deathtrap in fires. He watched as Tom pulled once, and once again.

The hinges were planted firmly in the frame, and Tom gave up. He went to the fire escape railing, put his facepiece on, attached it to the air regulator, and climbed over the railing. While holding with one hand, he leaned out, a distance of thirty inches, and smashed the window on the left of the fire escape with the metal tip of his helmet. The smoke poured past the jagged edges of broken glass.

"Shit," Dominic said, "there must be somebody in there."

Tom grabbed the crossbeam of the window frame and pulled himself to the sill, almost losing his balance because of the thirty-pound air cylinder on his back. There was no place to fall except sixty feet to the pavement below. But he held and pulled with his full might, and in one fast, graceful movement he slid himself into the circling smoke.

The apartment was dark, and Tom was nightblind. He groped through the room, feeling before him, instinctually yelling through the mask's facepiece, "Hello, hello," even though he knew the girl could not hear him if she were there.

He went first to the gated window, bent low, the mask heavy on his back, his head pounding relentlessly. He searched around the floor. "Hello, hello," he kept yelling. He came to a bed, felt on it and under it. Suddenly he began to feel a tingle on his ears, like small needles pricking gently, and he went to what he knew to be the wall between the two top-floor apartments. He took a glove off, yelling "Hello, hello," and placed his palm against the wall. He pulled back quickly, feeling the hot melted paint like burning glue on his hand.

In the street Dominic watched increduously as Chief Gelman climbed to the top of the fire escape, ducking past the fire that was coming forcefully from the end window. He went to the gate, pulled on it, and moved to the railing. "Christ," Dominic said, in a nervous, quivering voice, "they don't have much time."

Tom put his glove on, moving rapidly to the next room of the railroad flat. He dropped to the floor and began to crawl, searching the corners, under another bed, on it, opening the doors of a large metal wardrobe closet, drawing his hand across its interior, moving forward, little by little, but quickly. He stopped yelling, and he felt the sides of his mouth tightening inside the facepiece, pulling his jaws together like a vise, fighting the scream within him. *She's dead. If she's here, she's dead. The paint's melted.* He thought of the body, and he thought of his own children. He could see now to the end of the apartment and watched the fire rushing across the ceiling, lapping in a strange, fearful design; he saw Anne's lips, briefly, moving, forming the *p* in perfect. His head swelled with the pain as he moved into the next room, feeling, swimming, kicking. His ears began to feel as if acid was pouring from the needles. Where is the body? he thought. Oh, God, *Where is it?* Then he heard his own voice in his mind, yelling, *"Watch the floor,"* but he was looking at the ceiling and at the rushing fire. He crouched up and began to run toward the window two rooms away. He made it to the next room and began a defiant sprint to the window, just one room away now, but he banged the door of the metal closet, and the doorknob caught in the harness of his mask, stopping the sprint in one powerful jerk, pulling him to the floor, pulling the closet on top of him. He tried to turn. He tried to crawl backward, then forward, the fire now menacingly above him, but he was inextricably attached to the metal mass on top of him. He thought of Anne again, just as he always expected he would, in the picture with the English pram and their newborn son, her brown hair flowing, her face radiating in the brightness of innocence, all pain momentarily past and forgotten. And in the facepiece of the mask that had given him life and was now taking it, he thought of God and called out the names of his two dead brothers as the fire engulfed him.

In the modern, concrete armory of the 42nd Division on 14th Street, Colonel Peter Collins and his staff officers were

222

standing around a table-top map of the city. In his hands the colonel held the civil defense coordination plan, and he was assigning locations to his staff. There was no time to wait for full readiness, and they would go directly to the fires with whatever troops had arrived at the armories. Although the National Guard had the legal authority of control, the colonel instructed his men to work under the direct supervision of the fire officers. It was ten-fifty.

Dominic watched Chief Gelman bring one leg over the railing and then the other. He saw the chief straddle from the railing to the sill and place his hand around the window crossbeam, through the gushing smoke. "Jesus," Dominic said, "what's he going to do up there without a mask?"

The chief thought he heard a muffled voice, broken up as if coming through a facepiece. He called, "Ritter, Ritter," but he heard only the crackling sounds of the fire as he began to pull himself to the open window frame. Then the apartment lit up in a small fireball that came charging to the window, covering the chief's hand on the crossbeam, crisping the skin. The chief yelled as he pushed away and dove for the fire escape. His shifting weight caused his foot, propped on the outside edge of the fire escape platform, to slip away, and the chief began to fall. But he reached out in sudden hope and felt the round, vertical bar of the fire escape fencing. His hand slipped down the bar until it lodged against the platform, and the chief began to swing like a pendulum, suspended six stories above the street, his burned, swollen hand hanging limply at his side.

Dominic ran. He saw the fire coming from the window, and he yelled, automatically, naturally, "We've got to get in there." Then he ran. The other firemen moved also, quickly, spontaneously, as if a wall had been lifted from in front of them, releasing the trapped fury of their dilemma, resolving their anxiety, transforming it to action. They would do something. Something.

There were forty men from Engine 51 and Ladder 22, running now behind Dominic, across the wide Adam Clayton

Powell Jr. Boulevard. Other men from other Harlem fire-houses, standing in family groups behind the police barricades, pushed through the crowds and followed.

Tom. Oh, Christ, Tom. With each leap forward the words repeated in Dominic's mind.

He ran to the assistant chief, who was watching two officers lift Chief Gelman down to the next fire escape level, and saluted him, saying, "Fireman Gallo."

The assistant chief saw the other men running toward the pumpers on 122nd Street, and he heard Dominic's voice trailing off as he continued to run, "We'll get lines up there. We've got to get lines up there."

The chief watched as the firemen, in the strange, seemingly unnatural colors of their civilian dress, pulled the hose in fast, refined lines toward the fire.

The crowd of onlookers cheered and clapped as radio reporters spoke into tape recorders, as television news crews directed their cameras, as newspaper reporters wrote notes on small pocket pads.

On Fifth Avenue, the fire began to jump another cross street, igniting the wooden window frames of the corner building on the south side of 83rd Street. It was another fifteen-story building.

Across the street, inside the museum, four battalion chiefs were hacking at the corridor door on the second floor. They were older men, and they resented the axes they held in their hands, tools they had not used in many years. They resented the ignominy of doing a fireman's work, resented the assistant chief who ordered it. They tired easily.

Two deputy chiefs and another battalion chief were searching around the Leutze painting for the bolts that secured the painting to the wall. "It's been there for so long," the director was saying, "I forget how they did it. We box it in if we have a special showing in this room. We would never move it. It's hopeless, hopeless."

The fire had burned through the whole of the north wall, but the museum workmen saved all the paintings but the

224

Church and a West and Trumbull landscape. They had begun to dismantle the lower supports for the Leutze, but the smoke had become so thick that they could not control their coughing.

There was no ventilation in the American wing, and the room became dangerously hot as the fire crept across the ceiling. In the corridor the assistant chief spoke worriedly to the director. "I'm afraid we'll have to give it up soon. I don't want to chance a flashback with my men in there."

"A flashback?" the director said, puzzled.

"When the heat builds up like that there is a possibility that the superheated molecules will make contact with fresh oxygen, say from here in the corridor, draw it in, and then explode. If the conditions are right, it's a kind of spontaneous combustion."

As the chief was talking, the battalion and deputy chiefs ran from the room. They were experienced men. They felt the heat banking down, and they bent their bodies low as they ran. Then the fire flashed, for a short instant, like a flashbulb popping, and it surged, pulling the fresh air in, eating it, filling the room like a small sun. Then it died, leaving the blackened, cracked, peeling Leutze as evidence of its brief intensity.

On 79th Street, Dan Fanilli saw a deputy chief carry a power saw from a hook and ladder truck. "I'll stop that scab," he said, as he ran past the police line, hoping that a television camera or a newspaper photographer would see him confront the fire officer.

Jerry, standing with the group of firemen from Ladder 7 and Engine 20, was distracted from the news on WYNS as he watched the delegate approach the deputy chief.

"Hey, chief," Fanilli called.

The chief turned, the heavy power saw hanging on a strap from his shoulder. "What?" he asked.

"I am the company delegate of Engine 20," Fanilli said, "and I want to ask you to stop carrying that saw, to stop doing a fireman's work."

225

The chief looked Fanilli up and down and watched him pull a badge from his pocket and pin it to his jacket. Cracking his mouth open at its side, the chief said, "Get lost," and continued toward the museum.

"Now wait a minute, chief," Fanilli said, grabbing the chief by the sleeve of his fire coat. The chief turned again, and Fanilli continued, "I don't want to get pugnacious, so don't press me."

The chief, a much bigger man than Fanilli, erupted in pent-up anger, grabbing Fanilli by the collar, lifting him to his toes, and screaming, "Get this straight, fireman, company delegate of Engine 20. I know who you are, and tomorrow is going to be another day in this Fire Department. You'll bounce around this city so much you won't remember what the inside of any one firehouse looks like."

He pushed Fanilli hard, and the delegate fell to the avenue tar. A few of the onlooking firemen ran toward Fanilli. Jerry was about to follow, but then he heard something on the pocket radio held by the man next to him.

The chief looked down at Fanilli and said before walking away, "You shouldn't have told me who you were."

Jerry grabbed the radio from the man's hands and listened to the broadcast. He heard the word "Harlem," and he turned up the volume. "We go now to a special on-the-scene report from Dan Meahan. Are you there, Dan?"

"Yes, I am in a public phone booth on 122nd Street and Seventh Avenue."

At that moment Vinnie Grant walked into the third-floor room at the Hotel Shelton. Sorvino turned off the radio and offered him a seat, wondering how Grant had learned of his whereabouts.

"Something spectacular and tragic has happened here," the radio continued. Jerry held it closer to his ear. "Something truly dramatic. One of the nonstriking firemen has been caught in one of the burning buildings. He was last seen going into a window and only moments later the window was

226

filled with the roaring flames that seem pervasive here. The fireman is trapped, evidently, inside a burning room behind that window, and most dramatically the striking firemen are now in the street, in their civilian clothes, pulling hose, setting up ladders, carrying equipment, doing everything possible to control the fire so they can reach the trapped fireman. The striking firemen here have returned to work, but how long it will last I don't know."

Jerry dropped the radio to the ground. A cab, he thought. I'll get a cab. My God, Tom. Is it you? No, Tom. God, say it's no. There had to be other firemen who stayed. It's not you Tom, no. *It can't be.*

He ran toward Madison Avenue, toward the traffic, and then stopped. He saw, double-parked on 79th Street, motor running, pointed toward Madison, a gray station wagon, the letters NBC emblazoned on the door panel. The back door of the wagon was lowered, and a television news crew was standing around it unloading cameras and sound equipment. What if there isn't a cab? Jerry ran past them, opened the door, and jumped into the driver's seat, startling the busy crew. He revved the engine loudly and threw the gearshift down as the crew began to yell, "Hey, stop!" The wagon bolted forward, the wheels screeching and leaving tire rubber in black lines on the street. It skidded at Madison Avenue and turned uptown, boxes of lights and wires falling out of the back. The wagon careened, smashing sideways against a parked car. Jerry almost lost control but straightened the wagon in time. He pressed the accelerator to the floorboard to 80th Street, going through the red light, honking the horn, sending pedestrians running and screaming. At 81st Street he swerved around a crossing car, thinking, Tom, Tom, God almighty, *Tom.* In and out, break, gas, break, gas, up Madison, the horn blasting all the way, to 123rd Street, then west to Fifth, to Lenox, almost to Seventh. He veered around the first fire engine and slid to a stop just behind the second, which was in the middle of the street. He ran to the avenue, Adam Clayton Powell Jr. Boulevard, and saw stang nozzles storming the block of buildings with water. Across the side

227

street he saw the hoselines, eight or ten of them, going into the corner building and up the fire escape. Running past a line of police officers, he showed his badge and looked up at the charcoal-rimmed windows of the top floor, seeing only small wisps of smoke floating lightly into the wind. Tom, he thought. Tom, are you all right?

He saw the assistant chief, radio in hand, controlling operations, and ran to him. "Chief," he said, pausing, out of breath, "the fireman. Did the fireman get out?"

The chief, looking stern and preoccupied, asked, "Who are you?"

Jerry hurriedly showed his badge.

"No," the chief said, looking up the boulevard at the windswept water of the stang nozzles bouncing from the buildings. "He was caught," he added, "roasted." Only a fireman would use the term, and only a fireman could accept it.

Jerry felt his pulse beating faster. "What was his name, chief?" he pleaded, already feeling the answer.

"Ritter," the chief said, and Jerry's shoulders began to shake as the sobs sounded. "Oh, Christ," he cried, tears welling at the corners of his eyes.

"Did you know him?" the chief asked, gently placing his hand on Jerry's back.

"He was my brother," Jerry said, walking toward the corner building, "the only brother left."

Still sobbing, he went to the stoop of the building, put a foot on the first step and a hand on the railing. Did he want to go in? Did he want to see? He put his head down on his hand on the railing. To see, and to grieve his brother's body, a charred ruin of life? No, he thought, his mind a whirl of images. I will not grieve that, but a young man, proud, a father of loving children, a fireman. Oh, Christ. Tom. *Is it all like the fucking Phoenix? Either brightness or ash? Tom?*

The entrance doors were lodged open by the heavy hose, and Jerry heard a commotion in the hallway. "Easy now, watch it," the firemen were saying as they struggled down the stairs. Jerry looked up and into the dark tenement,

228

tears now drying on his cheeks, and he saw four men carrying a long, brown canvas bag, stitched closed on two sides by hemp rope. A body bag. Tom's body bag, held on the front end by Dominic Gallo, his face soot-stained, his clothes drenched and smoke-beaten, his eyes red and watered.

"All right," Dominic said as they reached the vestibule, "put him down here, easy, gently." There was no point in carrying the body any farther until an ambulance arrived, and they placed the body bag on top of the three lines of hard hose that ran through the hall.

Dominic looked to the street, holding his hand up to the sudden burst of daylight framed in the doorway, blinking his dirt-covered eyes. The figure on the stoop became clearer, and recognizing Tom's brother he walked to him.

He spoke gently through the wind. "Jesus, Jerry," he said, "I'm sorry." He put one hand on Jerry's arm and the other just above on the shoulder, leaning on him, the words unsure, slow, mumbled. "That means something, doesn't it, Jerry? Tom knows, God knows, I'm sorry."

"Yeah," Jerry said, closing his eyes. "Yeah."

In the background the radio reporter gave a young boy a dollar to stand in the public phone booth and hold the line open, and along with a television crew he pushed through the crowd and ran to the corner building.

He held the microphone of the tape recorder up to Dominic and, as a strobe light lit and a cameraman focused, asked, "Fireman, would you tell us what it was like up there?"

Dominic stood straight, but Jerry did not turn, continuing to lean against the railing, his back to the reporters, staring at the lifeless bulk of canvas in the vestibule.

"A man died," Dominic said, directly, emphasizing the word "man."

"Who was he?" the reporter asked. "Tell us about him. Was he one of the nonstriking firemen?"

"Fireman Thomas Ritter," Dominic said, trying to control the swell within him. "He was a . . ."

Dominic held his breath. "He was. . . ." he began again

229

but quickly turned his back and reentered the building. He went past the body bag to the back of the hallway, sat against a urine-stained wall, and dropped his face into his open hands. "He was a sweetheart," he cried. "He was a sweetheart."

"What can you tell us, fireman?" the reporter asked, quietly, respectfully. "Did you know Fireman Ritter?"

Jerry turned to the voice, and to the camera, and he spoke calmly as he drew the backs of his hands across his eyes.

"He was my brother," he began, staring unblinkingly at the camera but through it, in a trance of remembrance. "He always loved firemen. He loved this job. He belived in it. Not just some of the time, when it suited him, but all the time. When we were kids, that's all he talked about, the firemen and the Fire Department. His heart was always in this job. Even then. That's why he came to work this morning. This cold and tragic morning. This is where his heart was, and he couldn't, like the rest of us, turn his back on it. He had a wife he loved, four kind and gentle children, a good life. One of decency. He loved to read, he loved to play with his children, he loved his job, and he put his heart and his life into every-thing he loved. That was it. Where else could he have gone this morning but to work? It was wrong to do otherwise, it was wrong to strike. He told me that last night. But I did not listen. To either my brother's conscience or to my own. *Dam-mit, why don't we listen to the voices within us?* My brother did, and he came to work and suffered, doing his job, doing what he believed in. And now—now he lies in a department body bag as the fire is being fought where he left off. The firemen have gone to work again, as I am going to work. If we made a mistake, Tom has paid more than he should have for it, and fighting the fire, doing our job, is the only way we can make it up to him, God rest his soul. No strike can be worth a human life."

Jerry turned away and walked into the shadow of the doorway. He crouched by the brown canvas bag, placing a hand on top of it. There he stayed until an ambulance came, and he and Dominic and the other firemen grabbed at the hemp-rope stitching and carried it to the street.

Eugene Golden, the chief of department, arrived at the fire, finally ready to take command of working firemen, as the radio reporter pressed the rewind switch of the tape recorder and pushed through the crowd to the telephone booth. There in the crowd, looking up at the dying fire and still weeping, the young mother held her deaf and smiling daughter tightly in her arms. A neighbor had looked after the child during the evacuation.

Vinnie Grant plopped into the small hotel-room chair, his thighs pushing against its arms. "I want you to call this strike off, Mr. Sorvino," he said.

Sorvino sat on the bed and crushed a cigarette in an ashtray. "I'm sure," he said, "you're not the only one in this city who wants that."

"But you will do it, Mr. Sorvino."

"When I get what I want, I will."

"No," Grant said, "you'll do it now, because you see I have the evidence that you never had a strike vote from your men."

"You don't have anything. What the hell are you trying to pull?"

"I have a statement from Mr. Silverman. That's evidence enough."

"Well," Sorvino reacted quickly, "I don't care what you have, Grant. If you'll look at the constitution of my union you'll find that I don't need a vote to strike. That vote was made for information purposes only."

"All I know, Mr. Sorvino, is that the vote was mandated by your men and you told them, as you told me, that an overwhelming majority of them voted for a strike. That is coercion, Mr. Sorvino, and it is reckless endangerment of the public. In any case, I think you better call it off. Now."

Sorvino lit another cigarette and silently concentrated a few moments, never taking his eyes from Grant's triumphant and determined grin. Finally he lifted the phone and dialed

231

the number of WYNS. He said, as he dialed, "You might not believe this, Mr. Grant, but I was going to call it off anyway, on account of the hazardous wind condition."

"You're right," Grant said. "I might not believe it."

Distracted, Sorvino spoke into the phone to the station manager. "This is Angelo Sorvino," he said, "and as we agreed I'd like to speak to my men now."

"I'll give you all the time you need," the station manager said, "but you'll have to hold on until we air this special report from Harlem. By the way, I'm sorry about that fireman."

"What fireman?" Sorvino asked.

"Haven't you been listening to the goddam radio, Mr. Sorvino?"

Sorvino jumped for the radio and switched it on. He and Vinnie Grant listened to the playback of Jerry Ritter's words.

Elsewhere, the mayor, the fire commissioner, and almost all of New York listened.

Anne Ritter listened, in the small frame house in New Rochelle, and she collapsed across the kitchen table, propelling a hot cup of coffee and a sugar bowl to the floor. The glass shattered.

And the firemen listened. In all five boroughs, clustered around portable radios, the firemen listened in moribund silence, each word registering painfully in their minds. When the words stopped they breathed again more freely, some of them saying what was in their thoughts, but most of them saying nothing, protectively quiet. And they moved, all of them, in every city neighborhood, as if of one mind, one body, some into their firehouses to await orders, the rest to the fire engines rimming the fires.

The strike was over.

In Harlem, Jerry Ritter and Dominic Gallo stood together, watching the ambulance, its siren screaming needlessly, its wheels jerking over the solid lines of hose on the boulevard, until it went past the police lines and out of sight. Then they looked vacantly at each other and turned resolutely into the wind of the fire. It was eleven o'clock.

EPILOGUE

THE WINDS HAD STOPPED.

It was Saturday morning, three days later, a warm, balmy, Indian summer day.

Angelo Sorvino was in the Prince Street stationhouse, leaving his fingerprints on a square, white card, charged with the felony of reckless endangerment. He was smiling. The district attorney was running for a second term and was anxious for the support of the city's Central Labor Committee. It would be an easy offering to reduce the charge to a simple misdemeanor, an easy trade, the endorsement of labor in exchange for copping a plea. Sorvino's thoughts wandered to the idea of a limousine, the idea of signing "Honorable" before his name as would be his right as a government official. He wondered when the governor would call.

Kevin Keneally sat down to breakfast in Gracie Mansion. Facing him were Edward Jefferson, Salvatore Dursi, and Bill Donnelly. "It will be all right," Dursi was saying. "The indications show the public approves of your actions. You were courageous in the face of crisis, and you stood to your word. Sorvino's lie pulled it all around. The public won't forget. The campaign will go our way."

In the News Building on 42nd Street, Vinnie Grant went to a file cabinet and removed a large cardboard envelope. He carried the envelope to his desk, poured the contents out, and began to sort the pile of clippings—the *Times* clippings on one side, the *Post* clippings on the other, and those from the *News* in the middle. He was breathing hard, almost snorting. When all the printed information about the firemen's strike was in three orderly piles, he sat heavily in his chair, lifted his worn and scuffed shoes to the corner of the desk, and began to read. I have to get all the surface facts in my head, he thought, before I can swim to the bottom of this shit.

St. Raymond's Church in Throgg's Neck was filled with music. The four children were kneeling and fidgeting in the front pew, unsure of the ceremony, not yet truly convinced their father was dead. They looked around, puzzled by the wave of blue uniforms all around them, like Uncle Jerry's, they thought, like Daddy's.

Behind them, Jerry knelt on the sharp creases of his uniform pants, his body rigid from knees to shoulders. Anne was kneeling to his left, holding up, a fireman's wife as strong and courageous as any woman. His father knelt to his right, crumpled over the pew seat before him, crying loudly. Jerry's mother was next to her husband, sitting, staring without concern. She knew only that she was moved from one place to another.

It was pointless to think of poetry, and Jerry tried to pray, but the words would not come. There was something bothering him, something different about this funeral, some-

238

thing unlike the others he remembered. What was it? The Latin was gone, of course, but there was something different still. The colors. Yes. There is no black. *No black!* The casket is covered with white silk. White! The vestments—the maniple, the stole, the chasuble—are white, the priest a rejoiceful celebrant. Rejoiceful? *Where is the black?* Where is the black of mourning, dark and foreboding, the black of death's voyage? Are they mad? Is it no longer tragic, this journey? Sorrowful? What have they done, taking our grief from us? Ourselves the grievers. We are the grievers. I don't understand. White is for alleluias, for purity, for happiness. There is nothing pure here, nothing happy. It is all sadness. Sadness and ash.

God, the world has changed.

God!

Tom!